THE LIBRARIAN'S GARGOYLE

Evelyn Shine

SUNSET HILL PRESS

DIVE INTO SAPPHIC ROMANCE

Copyright © November 2024 by Sunset Wave Press
All rights reserved.
No part of this book may be reproduced in any form or by any electronic or mechanical means, including information storage and retrieval systems, without written permission from the author, except for the use of brief quotations in a book review.
For further information contact Evelyn@evelynshine.com
Cover Art by Madison Brake
Typography by Karen Dimmick Arcane Covers
Editing by Red Adept

ISBN: 978-0-9987538-3-6

For everyone's childhood memories that needed more cozy gay stories.

Prologue

CRADLED IN STONE

This isn't the first time Viola has come to me, seeking comfort. My wings cup above us, blocking the worst of the silvery streaks of rain as her small hands grasp my fingers. The child hauls herself into my arms and settles her damp cheek against my unmoving breast. My stone torso isn't wet with rain, but her tears soak it.

"I couldn't b-bring a b-book tonight, Iggy. The storm would've ruined the pages." She fusses, tears still streaming down her face. "My family promised to take me to the festival but then went without me. I'd been looking forward to it forever. I'd understand if it was just for adults, but then Mother said they didn't go."

Lightning flashes as the little girl pushes her bedraggled locks of dark-blonde hair from her face. Thunder roars, and she wriggles even closer, twisting an emerald band around her tiny finger. She seems upset tonight. Many times, I've thought of moving, of showing her I'm alive—a creature made of the magic she seeks in the world. But it's against the rules to interact with humans, and to do so would put her in danger. Immortals made the Covenant long ago to protect humans from creatures that might prey on them, because once humans know of us, they're fair game. I wish the Covenant didn't forbid me from interacting with Viola, but if I ever did respond to her, it would put us both in danger.

Viola sniffles loudly, wiping her nose on her sleeve, then

snuggles into me. All freckled pale skin and red-rimmed eyes, she barely fills the crook of my arm. I want to offer her more comfort than this. At least it's a warm night.

She stares out over the lights of Paris, which glimmer in the rain. "I saw my parents leave with my older brothers. I'm sure they went to the festival without me. They're always lying to me. I hate liars and pretenders."

Tears run down her cheeks, and witnessing her sorrow, I ache. Most nights, I patrol this rooftop, protecting the tower, the task I was created for. I was in this position, head bowed and arms out, the first time she came to me. Ever since that serendipitous meeting, when I hear the scuffle of her feet on stone, I've assumed this familiar position. I wouldn't want to frighten her, and at least like this, I can watch her in my arms.

Her little hand splays open on my chest. "I guess I could tell you a story. Would you like that?"

I adore her stories—I always have. They fire my imagination as her words magically transform to pictures in my mind. Almost every night, she springs along the rooftops in those gossamer slippers to settle in my lap like a stray cat. I don't know if it's Viola's sweet voice or the fact that she treats me like a treasured friend that entrances me—maybe it's both. Sometimes she sleeps here until dawn. Her clothing is far too fine for her to be an orphan or a street rat. Tendrils of magic drift from her shoes and her gloves. It's a mystery how an ungifted human would possess such things. Regardless, she's too young to wander alone so late at night. Surely, she must have parents who wonder where she's gotten to.

"The little red fox? Oh, you always ask for that one, but I suppose I can tell it one more time." The child toys with her loose braid then tugs its crimson ribbon free. She loops the wet silk around my wrist and ties it in a neat bow before gazing up at me. The stunning blue-violet of her eyes reminds me of forget-me-nots and the warmth of the summer sky. Delicate fingers run along the sharp line of my jaw then tap my chin thoughtfully. Her chest rises. "Once upon a time…"

1

VIOLA
FIFTEEN YEARS LATER...

*D*ust motes float in the rays of light shining from the windows high above. For a moment, I wish to be as insignificant as one of those sparkling specks instead of listening to the excuses pouring from the master librarian's craggy lips.

"I'm sorry, Viola. There just isn't room in the budget to continue the after-school program or retain you as a librarian. Surely, you understand. Besides, the public schools do well enough educating the children of Paris."

I shove my spectacles up the bridge of my nose. Oh, I understand. My face freezes into a polite smile as a rampage of emotion pounds my gut. *How dare they!* This reeks of sexism. First, my family sidelined me as the last of far too many children, and now this. There are kids who need my tutoring or they'll fall behind. Twisting my skirt into a wrinkled mess I hold my breath as he continues a litany of limp excuses.

I fought my way from volunteer to paid librarian, creating many beneficial programs for the public along the way, and I'll hold onto this position with tooth and nail. Dammit. I thought maybe here I could be worth something—important to society as a whole. But it seems, once again, I'm insignificant in the larger scale of things. The antiquities section is huge and full of promising material. It could take me a decade to get through every book. If I lose access to this knowledge, I'll be back to ground zero on my research.

I possess slippers that prove magic exists, but in all my

research, I haven't found hard evidence of magical items beyond them. This is the only establishment where I've ever found books that even hint at the existence of magic—not flakey fake grimoires and superstitious folk remedies, of course, but something odd is going on with the building. Entire shelves of books appear and disappear as needed. Some of the books even seem to refuse to be organized—I thought a person was rearranging them at first, but over the last five years, I've memorized the location of every book in the main collection. I'm convinced the misbehaving tomes somehow move themselves.

"Master Frederick, I'm the best librarian in your employ, and you know it. I can find any book in moments, and I single-handedly organized the first room of the antiquities section. And what about the tangible progress the students have made in the tutoring program I started?" I gulp on an awkward breath. "Those kids depend on me. Surely, there's some way my services can be retained."

Like an ungainly pelican, Master Frederick bobs his balding head in agreement. Light glimmers off his shining dome, and hope bangs against my ribs. But his next words, layered with a dowdy dash of patriarchy, crush that feeling.

"You're very helpful, my dear girl, but isn't it time for you to seek out a husband and look toward marriage and family? Besides, the Archambeau family name is highly regarded in Paris. You have no need for this job."

Sickly-sweet vomit coats the back of my throat as I twist my emerald ring around my finger so hard my skin will likely tear. This job is my sanity. The last thing I want is to be tending to a husband and squalling babes when I could be using my time to raise up other young people who need help with their education.

"Look, you can halve my pay if needed, but please don't let

me go. I love my work here. I've been dedicated to the well-being and improvement of this library for over five years."

He pats my satin-covered knee consolingly. "I can keep you on until the end of this month, but after that, we'll have to close down your after-school and tutoring programs and let you go. I'm afraid we simply don't have the funds. There's been talk that we may have to make the library private again. Lord Kensington from London has generously offered to buy the entire building and collection."

"Kensington? He'll close the doors to the public and likely sell the books off piecemeal to bolster his coffers."

Ugh. I've butted heads with His Lordship more than once. He's awful, and I hate that he still insists on using that noble title even after moving here years ago. It's too bad England didn't handle their nobility the way France did. I fume.

That man will never allow my community programs to continue. He still has the antiquated idea that knowledge should be reserved for the wealthy and privileged, while I've argued information should be available to all who seek it. It's 1912, not the dark ages, for heaven's sake. How can he be so backward? The man has more money than half the noble families in Europe, though, so it's not surprising he's throwing wealth around to get what he wants again.

A lock of hair falls in front of my eyes, and frustrated, I tuck it behind my ear. "What if I find a way to support the library through a fundraiser or benefactors so it could remain open to the public? Maybe we could have a sliding scale of membership fees to help bolster our coffers. If I raised enough money for this establishment, would you keep me on and let the literacy program continue?"

"And who would scrutinize prospective members' finances to determine what they contribute? That would be a herculean task, my dear. I don't think any of us have the time for such an undertaking."

I snarl at his patronizing tone. "This is my life's work. Why wouldn't I have time for it?"

"I believe you will be presented with other opportunities soon." Master Frederick shifts his bony posterior to rise from the scruffy office chair. He offers me a wrinkled indigo-veined hand.

Ignoring it, I gather my long skirt and rise. "Well, if Hercules succeeded, then I certainly will. Do I have your permission to seek out benefactors and create an event to support the library remaining open to the public? And would you promise to keep me on when I succeed?"

Owlish blue eyes widen through the thick lenses of his glasses. The master librarian shakes his head with a small chuckle. "Even if I refused, you would push on, dear girl. Of course I would continue your employment and the children's education programs if we had the funds. Do what your heart wills, but you'll soon be too busy for such pastimes."

"Why do you believe my life would suddenly be too busy to do the work I'm passionate about?" This whole conversation is suspect. What does he know that he isn't sharing?

Master Frederick doesn't answer as he opens the office door with a low creak. Visible beyond it is the sweeping golden oak curve of the front desk and a line of waiting patrons. Chantal tucks a pencil into her wiry black hair before accepting another stack of books. She glances at us—well, me—a harried expression marring her pretty features. Without another word, I hurry to the desk and breezily step up to help the next person. The stamp presses into their card with a little more force than necessary as I think about how disappointed my students will be. There has to be a way around this. I glide my fingers over the rich leather-bound books, hand them back, and move to the next patron.

The library needs to remain free for use, not private. There are enough private collections in Paris. There's got to be a way to keep this one out of the clutches of greedy men like Lord Kensington. Why on earth would he want to buy a library, anyway? I've been to extravagant balls at his chateau. His collection of books is impressive.

"I need a tome on animal husbandry, particularly peacocks," a patron to my left says.

Chantal clears her throat as her pale-brown eyes land on mine. After shoving a stack across the counter to a man in dark clerical robes, I turn to the patron.

"Second floor, twenty-seventh section, third shelf from the top, blue cloth binding. *Understanding Decorative Feathered Fowl*." I wipe my hands off on my gray skirt. I learned long ago this is the best color to wear while working the stacks as it shows no dirt. It's amazing how much dust a pile of old books generates.

The man wanders off as Chantal shakes her head. "I swear, I'll never know this place like you do."

"It's been four months." I give her a lopsided grin as I check in the next stack. "You'll get there."

My heart sinks at the thought of all the tutoring work I've done for the community. The underprivileged girls I teach could grow into young women who make a real difference in the world. How can it all be gone in a morning? I dread telling my students that the program isn't funded. While all children in Paris are required to go to school, the public education in some parts of the city isn't great, and my program really supported those students who needed a little extra attention.

"There are eighty-year-old scholars withering away to bone dust on the tables before us who don't know half of what you do. Face it—you're impressive."

"I wish the master librarian thought so, but it seems I'm

not worth keeping," I mutter softly enough for Chantal to take it as a sigh.

This morning's whole conversation with Master Frederick seemed odd. He has praised me before for my innovation. It's unfair he cut funding to my program and my job with such short notice. We labor in silence for another thirty minutes behind the golden-wood expanse of the main desk, checking books in and out of the library and recording the names of the borrowers. Finally, the rush quiets down.

Chantal groans, dabbing at the sweat beading her tawny forehead with an embroidered kerchief, then she tucks it into the front of her lavender gown. "I may never have the time to know this place like you do. You've heard about the cuts? The entire cleaning staff is gone, along with two of the guards. Honestly, will they be expecting us to sweep and dust next? I'm a scholar. Maid work isn't what I signed up for."

My hair falls in front of my eyes again. Frustrated, I shove it back. "I'd take maid work if it kept me here. Master Frederick informed me this morning I'm being sacked."

"You?" Chantal blinks, her full lips pursing. "Why on earth would they remove you over me? He hasn't spoken to me yet. Old Piney said they weren't cutting essential staff."

My fingers curl into the meat of my palms, nails digging in until the pain equals the stabbing in my chest. Apparently I'm not essential, since I'm out a job while the newest librarian retains hers. Unclenching my fists, I shove the jealousy down and grab a stack of books to shelve. This isn't Chantal's fault.

"I'm going to take care of this stack and the cart I saw on aisle seven. Ring the bell if you need help."

"Do you want me to shadow you?" she asks.

I shake my head and turn. "I'd like some time alone, thanks."

She starts to say something but bites back the words, and I stride away. Today wasn't supposed to go like this. It's a lovely warm spring morning. Flowers are blooming, birds are singing, Paris is falling in love, and I'm getting sacked. A grunt escapes me as I lift the tomes onto the cart and then push it to the end of the row. Taking the first one, a thin book bound in soft green cloth, I read the title, then I slide it back into its proper alphabetical place on the light-colored shelves.

I want to storm back into Master Frederick's office and demand to know if I'm the only staff member being cut. I'm essential—the essentialist. He should know that.

I almost slam a book into its spot but gently set it on the shelf at the last instant. No point in taking my rage out on the books. Determined to go plead my case, I speed through the returns then whip the cart around the corner on my way back to the desk.

"Viola! Goodness, you gave me a start." A plump woman with pretty dark-brown curls fans herself as my cart pushes into her voluminous burgundy skirts. "Chantal said I'd find you over here. That book you recommended on the herbs of Ireland was positively delightful, and I was hoping you'd have something similar about the Scandinavian region."

She adjusts her old-fashioned bodice as if it weren't displaying her assets well enough. I tear my eyes from her cleavage long enough to squint over my round-rimmed glasses at her knowing grin. Mirabelle Griffiths is possibly the most cheerful person in the universe, with her cheeks like ripe fall apples and smile that could melt a glacier. She curves her rouged lips into a sweet simper and bats her long, thick lashes. I'm in no mood for Mirabelle's flirting, but my spirits lift. Her antics affect everyone around her.

"Why Scandinavia?" I push the cart a little faster, half hoping she's too short to keep up the stride for long. I wanted time to stew then burst into that old codger's office and really tell him off, but like a ray through the clouds, Mira is breaking up the storm of my foul mood.

"Oh, reasons. That flush looks particularly lovely on you. Even in all that drab gray. Honestly, nuns dress flashier than you. If you ever want to have a ladies' day out, I'd be happy to suggest—"

"Third floor, second alcove to the right of the centaur statue." I swat at a cloud of dust in front of me. Great. They fire the cleaners, and the place is already going to pot.

Mirabelle sighs as she places one hand on the railing of the ascending staircase. "Well, as always, thank you for your amazing help. You have untapped potential if you're brave enough to access it."

I look away as tears press against my eyelids. "Tell that to my family or Master Frederick."

She untucks a tiny boutonniere of lavender and some unidentifiable greenery from her bodice and, before I can protest, slides it into mine. "I hope your day improves."

I gape, but she beams as if all is right in the world then climbs the steep staircase. Stiff skirts rustle against the wood, and calm blankets me as she disappears around the corner. There's no reason for me to contest Master Frederick's decision now. I'll simply work hard to show him I'm essential and pull this library away from the clutches of His Lordship.

When I glance toward the front desk, the unwelcome sight of Maria, my maid, greets me. That's never a good sign. I abandon the cart in an attempt to disappear to the upper floors before she sees me.

"Viola!" Maria exclaims, followed by a hissing shush from the scholars lining the tables between us.

With a violent sneeze, she bustles toward me. I groan. This day is rapidly becoming the worst I've ever had. Maria would rather saw off her left arm than enter this building—Mother had to have sent her. The short-lived calm evaporates from me as I move toward her to avoid any noise disgruntling the scholars further.

"Maria, what a surprise. My shift is done in two hours. I'll be—"

"Your mother demands that you attend breakfast with the family. The carriage waits outside," she says, her face crinkled as if to suppress another sneeze.

"I ate this morning." It's not a lie. I grabbed an apple from the larder when I left the house just before dawn.

Maria gives me that *this is not negotiable* look, and I sigh. Spotting Master Frederick, I move toward him with my maid in tow.

"Master Frederick, I've been called home. I'll be by later this afternoon to attend to my students."

"That's unnecessary. I'll see if Chantal can cover for you." He gives me the kindly smile of a doting grandfather. "Congratulations. Go spend time with your family."

Congratulations? I frown as he brushes me off and hands my duties to another. My lips part to ask what he's on about, but Maria sneezes again, prompting another round of shushes from the gallery. She tugs my arm insistently.

"Let me grab my things, and I'll meet you outside." It's doubtful my sacking and Mother's summons aren't connected. This positively reeks of my parents' meddling. They never wanted me to take a job in the first place. And now...

I take a deep breath as I grab my overcoat and reticule. My whole family will be present at this breakfast meeting. This hellish day keeps getting better and better.

2

VIOLA

My fork clatters against the plate, spraying bits of strawberry jam across the starched white lace tablecloth. A maid hurries across the dining room, past the morning-sunlit windows, to attend to the mess. Heat flushes through me as I huff and flap a napkin ineffectively at the stain, but she ignores my efforts to wave her away.

Attempting to compose myself, I watch my father carefully. Surely, I misheard him. I glance up at my mother, but her poached egg is suddenly the most fascinating thing in the world to her. Across the finely set table, my older brother, Charles, stuffs more toast into his already full mouth. Of my five siblings, he's the only one present.

Clutching at my pendant, I clear my throat. "Could you repeat that, please, because I could have sworn you just said I'm betrothed."

"Viola, you're twenty-two years old." Father meticulously folds his linen napkin before laying it on the table. "You can't spend the rest of your life buried in the Mazarine Library. Do you want to be labeled a spinster?"

"It's unseemly for a lady of your standing to surround herself with books instead of suitors." Mother wipes her mouth as if it would erase her displeased moue.

Master Frederick's weird congratulations suddenly make sense. "Are you the reason I got sacked this morning?"

"As our youngest, we indulged you far too much. Something I deeply regret now. Your father has made you a fine match with an Austrian duke's son."

"Austria?" I blink. "There's no way I'm leaving Paris. I don't want to live in Austria."

"He's third in line for the throne. You could be a princess one day or perhaps even a queen," Mother says, as if the idea that not every woman aspires to be royalty is unthinkable.

Furrowing my brow, I twist the emerald ring on my right hand. "Only if a bunch of people die."

Charles snorts. I shoot him a glare, and he rolls his shoulders. He pushes back from the table, readjusting the lace cuffs flowing from his crisp brocade suit coat. "Vi, you know they won't let up on this. Angelique was married and had three children by your age. Flora has two and—"

Seriously? "I didn't realize this was a baby-making competition. Can't we declare one of my older sisters the winner and move on? At least they were interested in being mothers." I glare at my father. "You have four daughters married off and two sons. Exactly how many more alliances do you need? I'm content doing research in the library. Let me be the family eccentric. We don't have one of those yet."

My mother makes a noise somewhere between a goose honk and a fainting-goat bleat. "We never should have agreed to let her manage her affairs on her own."

"You've squeezed out so many babies you completely forgot I existed until I was of an age to be used for an alliance. Like a ripe piece of fruit, I'm suddenly worthy of notice." Slapping my palm on the table for emphasis, I stand. "Well, I refuse to disturb my life for some duke's son. I'm doing very respectable research!"

My mother's eyes roll back, and a servant rushes forward to fan her.

I smooth my skirt to cover my agitation. "I refuse this proposal! You promised me a love match. Father, you said that you'd allow me the time to fall in love like you and Mother did."

"That was six years ago, and you haven't considered a single arranged suit." Father rakes a hand through his hair, a gesture he does so much it's a wonder he isn't bald.

"Likely because she was tits deep in Anne, the baker's daughter," Charles mutters behind his hand.

I narrow my eyes and peer over the rim of my spectacles at Charles. "All the suitors you chose for me were undereducated, egotistical bores. You can't possibly expect me to marry some half-witted, inbred—"

Charles coughs. "Point made."

"At least meet the duke's son. He'll arrive tomorrow and be our guest for a fortnight. That should give you plenty of time to get to know him." Father nods, not waiting for my agreement.

Exasperated, I throw up my hands. "Does he even have a name?"

Father's brow knits, and he looks at my mother, who still fakes a swoon in her chair. "Enry? Ethan? I'll review his letter of introduction. At any rate, you'll be available tomorrow to make his acquaintance."

I frown. "Fine." It's not fine. It's about the furthest from *fine* one could possibly get. "May I be excused?"

"The dressmaker will be here at two. Be certain you're not late." Mother, one hand still pressed dramatically to her powdered forehead, doesn't even bother looking at me.

A dressmaker—like this wedding is already a done deal.

"You may go." Father waves with a sigh.

Dismissed, I dart out the arched double doors before my family can add anything else to this pile of horrors. Blindly, I run down the hall as tears of fury bite at my closed eyelids. This isn't fair—none of it. Dammit. I should have known this was coming. They've been making noises about it for the last year, but I was so blissfully buried in my research I ignored it.

I don't want to marry some oaf only to have him put his grubby paws all over me so I can pump out his squalling brats. It doesn't matter that he's royalty. I'd rather be a librarian with my freedom than a duchess trapped in an Austrian castle.

Once I have the tears under control, I open my eyes. I close a hand over the familiar cool brass of my chamber doorknob and yank it open. I need to get out of here. The lacings on my dress are too tight, and the skirt tangles around my legs as I slam the door shut. A plea for freedom screams from my soul, and I hastily strip, leaving clothing strewn around the room.

A few deep, unrestricted breaths calm me as I hurry into my dressing room and roll up the rug. The floorboards here are loose, holding my most precious possessions. After tugging out the worn box, I lay my hand against the engraved golden seal of three winged creatures with long entwined tails. A click echoes in the sudden hush.

"I won't marry," I whisper, grabbing a pair of trousers hidden under the floorboards. I pull them on over my stockings then lift the lid of the box.

Inside, on a bed of dark velvet, rests a set of slippers and gloves made of gossamer silver threads. Reverently, I slide them on. My mysterious grandmother gave these to me years ago, along with a labradorite pendant and a thin-banded emerald ring I always wear. Somehow, the shoes have adjusted to fit me over the years, as has the ring. Of all the secrets I've discovered in this house, these are the most precious. It's proof there's magic in this world. A world I want to belong to.

I pull a vest over my chemise and belt it tight. Daylight isn't the best time to do this, but they've left me no choice. After rolling the rug back into place, I cross my room and step out onto the balcony.

The scent of boxwoods and a variety of flowers almost

cover the grittier smell of the city beyond. The houses here are so close, a blessing that gives me my freedom. I launch myself forward.

Wind whips past me, bringing heightened exhilaration. My hands make contact with the stone wall first, sticking fast. My feet quickly follow. Like a spider, I climb the wall, using the magic of the gloves and slippers to hold fast to the vertical surface. Soon I'm on the rooftops, running as fast as I can. I leap from house to house, across alleyways and narrow streets. I'm not sure where I'm going yet, only that I need to run until my lungs burn and my heart is fit to burst.

When the old tower comes into view, nestled like a gem in the green parkway, I race over the slippery angled roofs toward it. The soft breezes that always blow around the place cool my sweat-damp skin as I admire the large gargoyles carved at intervals on the building. They're the most beautiful I've ever seen. Unlike the grotesques in some parts of the city, these statues look almost human, sculpted from glossy obsidian, ruddy granite, and creamy-looking marble. Their bat-like wings arch as if to worship the sky. With an exuberant squeal, I slide down a slick metal roof on my rump and then jump into the air.

This part is always a little dangerous, but the thrill is worth it. The old tower sits far apart from the other buildings, and while I continue to plummet, the air current will boost me just enough to land me halfway up the rocky spire. I stretch my fingers out, preparing to stick them to the stone bricks and start my ascent.

As the ground looms closer, panic that the current won't be there to buoy me sings through my veins. Suddenly, wisps of wind tease the loose bits of my clothing. The air cushions and raises me to soar like a bird. Those two seconds of lift make me grin like a damned fool before the wind smooshes me against the stone. Muscle memory has me scurrying upward. I have no idea who lives here. I've been scaling the tower walls for over fifteen years, though, and have never heard a complaint or seen a person. Pulling myself up over the crenulations, I pant then beam at the familiar view of my gargoyle.

She's a magnificent warrior, rounded muscles bunched and flexed under a stone toga so masterfully carved it almost looks transparent. Slightly larger than the others, she crouches, one knee on the ground, the other bent in the air over a three-toed foot with wicked-looking claws. Her arms curl before her as if cradling something. I've often wondered if there's a piece of the sculpture missing. With a confident step forward, I rest my palm on her cheek.

"Hello, Iggy, my old friend." I smile as I gaze into her unseeing eyes.

Those eyes look kind. I imagine they'd be a pretty gem tone, maybe blue or garnet, if she were real. I sweep my thumb over her prominent cheekbone and trace the three sharp spikes on the back of her jaw. She's more handsome than beautiful. I've always thought so. Her rough-cut features are fierce, and four thick horns spiral from her wild mane of hair. Using her bent knee as leverage, I haul myself up into her arms and rest my cheek against the cool rounded smoothness of her chest. As a child, I curled against one biceps. Now, as an adult, I fill her stony embrace, but she's still a comfortable perch. Plucking at the faded ribbon I tied to her wrist ages ago, I relax. Iggy is someone I can tell all my worries to without fear of judgment.

"What am I going to do? This has been the worst day ever. I lost my position at the library. Then I find out my parents arranged a marriage for me. Apparently, it's been in the works for a while, because Master Frederick was aware. Cripes, I'm sure half of the upper crust knows by now, the way Mother gossips. They said I could choose, but obviously, it was a lie if they're forcing this on me now. I'm happy with my books and stories and have zero desire to be a wife or mother. There's magic in this world if I just look hard enough." I tug at the crimson ties securing the gloves to my wrists. "Maybe I can speak to the scholars that frequent the library. One of them must need an assistant. I doubt they'd take a woman, though. It was hard enough to get accepted when I started as a volunteer librarian."

I stretch, swinging my legs over the crook of her brawny arm as I continue to spill details and feelings about my day. "Maybe I could write stories of my own—penny novels to get by—and then I could have my own little apartment and not have to worry about my parents marrying me off to some jerk. I don't really care if he's a duke's son."

I tip my head back. From this angle, it almost looks like Iggy is smiling. The very tip of a pointy tooth presses into her finely sculpted lip. I reach up and touch it, letting my finger glide along the black stone. The carving really is quite amazing and so lifelike. I've searched for the name of the artist within the library, but there doesn't seem to be any information on this old tower or its beautiful gargoyles. The architecture of the structure is so different from the surrounding buildings. It's odd there's no history written about it.

My eyes move to the sweep of her wings. That's strange. There's a small tear in the bat-like structure of Iggy's left wing. I don't recall seeing that before. Standing on her arm, I stretch as far as I can, but still can't reach the gargoyle's wing. With a thought, I engage the gloves and slippers, clambering up Iggy's broad shoulder to stand precariously against the curving arch of her wing. It's not chipped. Her wing was carved that way.

Sitting on her shoulder, I drape my arms around her head. Iggy's long coils of mane aren't very comfortable to lean against, though, and soon, I slide back into the cradle of her arms. Closing my eyes, I sigh.

"Ugh, who am I kidding? My fate was always to marry for

some lucrative alliance and birth heirs like some broodmare. I guess I'm lucky my parents delayed it this long." I reach up to place my hands along the gargoyle's cheeks. "Maybe I could marry you, and then they'd leave me alone. That would make quite a story, right? The librarian and the stone lady. What's that? I'm too squishy for you? Well, it might take some getting used to, sure. You'd make a pretty amiable spouse. At least you wouldn't expect me to tend to my 'womanly duties' and push out babies. My sisters make it all sound so gross." I snort. "I was up hours before dawn, and today has been absolutely exhausting. Watch over me, Iggy. Maybe if I nap in your arms, when I wake, I'll find this has all been a bad dream."

3

BOUDICCA

I hold Viola while she sleeps. With great effort I slowly tilt my wing so the sun doesn't burn her fair freckled skin. Her hair spills over my arm to pool in a swirl of gold on my thigh. She's a woman now, filling my embrace in a way I relish. Viola is wrong. She's not too soft for me.

Gentle as a breeze, I run my thumb along her hand. She's perfect, and I delight in every story she's ever shared with me. I'm uncertain where Austria is, but I don't want her to leave Paris. I would deeply miss her nightly visits and the way she sprawls over my stone form telling animated tales.

With great effort, I tilt my head to gaze upon Viola. Moving during the day, when my stone shell covers my flesh, is always painfully slow. In slumber, her brow furrows, making little lines on her forehead. Gold-rimmed spectacles sit askew on her face. To pass the time, I count the constellation of freckles smattering her upturned nose and rounded cheeks. She's still small compared to me—as small as any human—and lithe, like a cat, with only a hint of womanly curves. Her lips move, but no words pass, then she snuggles her face to my chest. She's so beautiful, sunshine and blue skies swirled together with starlight and secrets. My heart presses against its stone prison. If I were a real living creature, I'm certain it would beat faster for her. But I'm pure magic of an old kind, a guardian of this tower, not made of softness and daylight. I don't have a soul like she does.

She stirs, and I raise my head back to its usual position,

leaving my wing arched. She noticed the tear in it from my fight last night, but hopefully, she won't see the slight angle change I made to keep her shaded. It's in my nature to protect, even if only to guard her fair skin from sunlight.

A door creaks, and my maker's heeled boots tap against the flagstone as they approach. My maker stops before us, tsk-tsking, and combs one ring-bejeweled hand through their flaming-red beard. After they mutter a few words, golden magic glitters from their fingertips to alight on Viola's skin, keeping her snoozing peacefully. They brush a hand against my arm, and magic dances along my stone shell, releasing me from the prison daylight brings.

Xander's flamboyantly bright clothing flutters in the breeze. A scarlet velvet waistcoat with a long-tailed bright-purple jacket graces my maker's slim form today, along with a pair of burnt-orange velvet trousers. Xander rubs the patch covering their left eye then lifts it to look at both of us. Maker's farseeing eye is such a pale blue it's almost white. With it, they gaze into my possible future, or perhaps Viola's. Maker Xander says visions of the future can be jumbled and unreliable, but I want to know what they see—to know if she'll leave with this duke's son to live in a foreign land. I don't want to lose her. My tale spinner. My weaver of stories. Viola has looked for magic all her life, not realizing she creates her own with words.

Xander replaces their eye patch, clearing their throat. "Boudicca, that bit of comfort you've kept is about to become a complication."

"She's harmless," I rumble, my voice rough with disuse.

Aided by magic, Viola continues her nap, uninterrupted by my voice. Xander hums, stroking the many necklaces gracing their chest before cupping a pendant nestled above their abdomen. It's large and gold with swooping lines. The stone within is gray but flashes blue in the light. Labradorite.

It calls to me, a low, enticing song of earth and stone. I flick my tongue over my lips.

"Come see me in the catacombs when she leaves. We'll talk then." With that, they cross the flat roof to a red-painted door in a squat cylindrical structure of fitted stone. Maker opens it then pauses, one foot on the step leading downward. A sad look tugs at their lips. "You know you can't tell her."

I give Xander the barest of nods. I'm only a creature, after all, one created from magic to guard and protect. What would telling Viola I'm conscious of her company accomplish?

ORBS OF GLOWING violet illuminate the long descent into the catacombs under the tower. I dislike coming here—it smells of sadness and loss. When I reach the bottom of the stairs, I turn into the large chamber beyond.

The entire room is immaculate, unlike Xander's cluttered study. On a black marble slab lies a gargoyle carved completely from quartz. He's beautiful in his silence, lying in repose as if sleeping, but we all know his story. It's Lysander—Xander's greatest triumph and greatest regret.

"Come." Xander gestures me forward to stand before my eldest brother's final resting place. "I want you to know how much I love you all. You're my children, but you aren't as immortal as I am."

A tear runs down their cheek, but I remain silent, as still as the stone I'm made from. I've always thought Lysander was prettier than the rest of us, or maybe it's that he looks almost human. His body is clear in some places, and tinged with pinks and violets where other minerals mingle with the quartz. He doesn't have the animalistic touches the rest of us have. Maybe Xander felt more whimsical when they carved my dragon-like features. Or perhaps by making us less human looking, my maker reminded themself that we have no souls.

Xander strokes Lysander's cheek. "I miss him so much—my first son. Maybe it will be different this time."

I clear my throat. "What can I do for you, Maker Xander?"

Always in motion, Xander drums their fingers along the edge of the slab. "Have you grown to care for the human?"

Their words tumble through my thoughts. Of course I care for Viola. She's the only human who's ever treated me as an equal. The memories of the nightly stories she tells me resonate in my mind, conjuring images of heroines, lovers, dreamers. In her tales, I live beyond these walls—have tasted the salt of a seafaring pirate and traversed deserts as unending as time itself.

"Well, Boudicca?"

My reply comes slowly, each word dragged from my mind and formed with intent. "I am stone."

"Yes, yes, you're made of stone. But I breathed life into you long ago, as I have all the creations in my tower. Are you fond of her? She's been scampering around my walls for more than a decade, although where she found such a marvelous set of climbing slippers is beyond me. I'd love to have a look at them to see who their maker was and study how they crafted their magic." Xander holds up a heavy gold band with a gleaming yellow stone set in the center. "I have something for you."

"Viola is my friend. I enjoy her stories."

The wind mage quirks a smile as they turn away from the crypt platform to face me. "We're all made of stories, but hers tend to spill all over, don't they? The breeze whispers Viola's tales to me when she's here, and they are delightfully entertaining. Let's see your hand."

Obediently, I raise my hand from where it rests against my thigh. It looks grotesque next to Xander's—huge and clawed with thorny spikes over my knuckles. I flex, flattening the spikes so they don't scrape my maker's skin. Xander touches the citrine ring to my index finger, and the band glows briefly before growing larger.

"You were the last gargoyle I created after I built the Tower of Wind. My youngest daughter, as it were." They pat my hand with parental fondness. "You've always been far more sensitive than the others. Maybe interacting with a companion could broaden your horizons."

My thoughts jumble. The only real beings I've ever met are ones who come to the tower. Xander and the other gargoyles here are my family, but they've never allowed us to mix with people off the property. "Interacting?"

Xander drops the ring into my palm with a careless sort of grace then folds my fingers over it. "I need you to run an errand in the city for me."

Confusion settles like a thick cloud. There's no way I can blithely wander through the city. I'm close to seven feet tall with webbed wings and a long reptilian tail. I look up into their startling green eye.

The words come quicker this time as if earlier use paved the way for them to flow. "I don't understand."

"The ring will make you appear human and allow you to move freely in daylight. You can't tell an uninitiated human about the magical world, per the ancient covenant, but if it would please you to interact with Viola, that ring will allow it. Here's a list of the books I need from the library and some money to treat yourself. Leave the ring and the books on my desk when you return. When you mention me to the nonmagical world, you're to refer to me as Monsieur Xander Albright."

Having flown over the city for decades, I know the layout and buildings intimately. Pensively, I thumb the smooth band. "Who will guard your roof?"

"The twins can handle it in your absence." Xander's gaze drifts to my damaged wing, which aches faintly but should heal by morning. "You likely intimidated the shades enough that they won't be back for a while."

Staring into the ring's golden depths, I pinch it between my thick fingers. Wonder spirals through me. Finally, I'll be able to speak to the woman who's treated me like her dearest friend for years. "What do I say to her?"

Xander pats my shoulder. "'Hello' would be a good start."

4

VIOLA

I wave to the last of the children as they leave the library classroom. I didn't have it in me to mention that the days of these lessons might be numbered—not when their smiling faces look up at me with such hope. I'm going to hate explaining to them that the library is closing.

Seeking sanctuary, I walk past oaken light-colored shelves to the back room of the library. My skin still itches where the pins scraped my flesh during the dress fitting. The seamstress brought over a dozen mostly finished gowns just waiting to be adjusted to my size, and the three hours of standing there while my mother and sisters poked and prodded me like a human pincushion were unbearable.

It's not that I don't like dresses. I do, and the ones the seamstress brought were undeniably lovely. What I don't like is the meaning behind them. I'm being trussed up like a present for some man I've never met. It's gross.

Visions of soft skin and hours making love above the bakery in a bed made of flour sacks fill my mind. I thought Anne and I had something special—that I meant something to her. We met in secret for nearly a year. She never told her family I was her partner, but I never expected her to acquiesce so easily to marrying a man. She even slept with me one last time before telling me of her engagement, like she was savoring the loss but still accepting of it. If I'd meant anything to Anne, she would have fought harder. I squeeze my eyes shut. Feeling this way is ridiculous. I'm used to people discarding me as superfluous—this is nothing new. My parents did it for years, so why should a lover be any different?

Maybe falling in line and marrying this man will make my life easier. If my father picked him, he's wealthy. Perhaps I can still do my research in Austria somehow—the libraries there could have their own magical secrets for me to discover. My freedom always seems to come down to money. I have no income that isn't tied to my library position or my family.

Deep within the secret back rooms of the library, I run a gloved finger along the leather spines of the books then slide one out that looks promising, *A Treatise of Impossible Things* by Durant Lemaitre. The dark emerald embedded in the center of the cover is surrounded by copious amounts of gold leaf scroll work. The book is a work of art, and I can't wait to dive in. I add it to the pile already weighing down my left arm, fully intending to spend the rest of the evening ensconced in the library instead of enduring dinner with my family. I'd rather be inconvenienced by hunger and surrounded by books than have to wade through the shark-infested waters of discussing my impending engagement.

Opening the first page, I admire the painted-silk interior as I walk past polished wooden bookcases to my favorite nook. Images of cherry blossoms grace the fabric endpaper, painted in elegant brushstrokes that evoke fantasies of exotic lands. I turn the corner. Perhaps there's a Japanese influ—

I crash into an unexpected wall. All the air rushes from my lungs as my precious hoard of books tumbles from my arms. A little screech of dismay announces my inelegant bum landing.

"Oh no! Mademoiselle, I'm so sorry." An exceedingly tall lady in a fashionable charcoal suit stoops to gather up my books before offering her hand.

I stare at the proffered hand with its perfectly manicured square nails. Like a sculpture come to life, beautiful strong fingers flex toward me. The glint of a gold band shines against swarthy skin. My gaze travels past the white lace cuffs to the luxurious fabric straining against a delectably defined forearm. I swallow then remember to breathe.

"The fault was mine. I was distracted by..." I'm ensnared by the most unusual eyes I've ever seen, deep gray like labradorite streaked with blue. They're so striking that my words falter.

What was I even doing? And who has eyes like that? Framing her angular square face are a broad forehead and sweeping cheekbones. I haven't seen anyone with such dark skin before, and I'm completely mesmerized by the way the light is both absorbed into and gleaming off her stunning features. Perhaps she's Moorish. That would be exciting. I've read about secondhand encounters but have never met anyone from the southern continent. Tall—so attractively tall. The woman looms so large her shoulders block the light from the chandelier overhead. Dammit—I'm gaping like a land-stranded fish.

"Mademoiselle?" She offers her hand again. Her hair is unfashionably loose. A tumble of deep-russet-streaked black curls cascades over her shoulders to her chest. The top is braided into a double plait, pulling it taut from her forehead.

I like it. Placing my hand in hers, I enjoy the firm smoothness of her palm. "Hello."

The woman's smile is a shy beast, curling her lip with a slow uncertainty. "Hello."

We pause, my hand dwarfed by hers. Speechlessly, she stares at me until I clear my throat. "You were going to help me up."

"Yes, of course." She gives the gentlest of tugs, and I'm standing beside her.

Strength with admirable control. How enticing. I lick my lips, trying to string some intelligent words together as I crane my head back. Goodness, she must be well over six feet.

Smoothing my skirt and then my hair, I hope I don't seem like a besotted fool. "I'm Viola Archambeau, a Mazarine librarian. I haven't seen you here before."

"My name is Boudicca. I'm here to retrieve some books for my... employer." She holds up a rumpled curl of parchment. "Maybe you could help me."

"After the Celtic warrior queen? What a magnificent name." I pluck the paper from her hand. A quick scan of the list shows that most of the books are in the older part of the library. "I'd be happy to help. Huh. There are a few titles I don't recognize, but I'm pretty good at finding things. Let me get my stack settled, and we'll head to the antiquities wing." I look pointedly at the books she's holding then at my hand still clasped in hers.

Boudicca clears her throat as she reluctantly releases my hand. "Where should I put these?" She nods to my stack of books in the curve of her well-muscled arm.

I swallow hard again. Why is she so damned attractive standing there with an armful of books? A froth of white lace sits under her square chin, contrasting sharply with the deep shade of her flawless skin. The soft-gray jacket Boudicca wears is perfectly tailored to the width of her muscled shoulders. My eyes dare to sweep lower, taking in the snug fit of her trousers over powerful thighs, and my tongue darts again over my suddenly dry lips.

Boudicca clears her throat. "Mademoiselle Archambeau?"

Guiltily, I jump. My eyes jerk back to her sly smile. "Oh. Books. Yes. Follow me, please."

I sway my hips as I walk before her then stumble as I realize what I'm doing. Goodness, it took me two seconds to go from busy researcher to panting hussy. Sneaking a glance back, I can't help but admire how stunning Boudicca is. The usual library occupants are crusty old men. She's certainly improving the scenery.

"Do you like to read?" I gesture for her to set the books on a polished wooden table near a velvet wingback chair, praying she'll say yes. There's nothing worse than a pretty face with an empty head.

"I like stories." Her smoky voice stirs me as she sets the stack down gently then straightens the top book. Boudicca traces a thick, blunt finger over the gem embedded in the cover.

Holding my long skirt to one side, I push open the door that leads to the antiquities room. "What type of stories?"

Looking around, Boudicca rubs the back of her neck before admitting shyly, "Heroines and magic."

"Ah, fairy tales! I like those too. Which one is your favorite?"

I turn from her to study the list then walk down the row, plucking the desired tomes from dark wooden shelves. The books are leather covered and dusty with age. After the third one, I pause to set them down.

Boudicca gnaws her lip as she watches me then inhales so deeply that her shoulders swell even wider. "I like the one where the girl is born with a red string around her little finger, and at night, she turns into a fox to follow the long ribbon of it, leading to all sorts of adventures." Thoughtfully, she rubs the frilled cuff of her sleeve.

I grin. "The little red fox! I love that one. Do you know it changes from region to region, but the end is always the same? After years of journeys, she finds a wolf with the string tied to his paw."

"I like the adventure part, but the ending is sad." Boudicca shifts from one foot to the other then flexes her shoulders as she looks away.

I glance at the list then duck down another row to find the book. "They were destined for each other. Why do you think it's sad?"

"Because they aren't the same type of creature, so they can only ever be friends."

I grab the last two books on the list before returning to her. Boudicca watches me with mournful blue-gray eyes. Canting my head, I study her for a long moment. "Just because they're different doesn't mean they can't love each other. They were destined to be together as soulmates, bound together before birth."

"But it's a girl who can change into a fox... and a wolf." Her face screws up in thought.

"Maybe it's a fox that changes into a girl." I tap her nose playfully, hoping to erase that confused expression. A flush creeps up my neck at how easy it is to be with this woman I just met. "Besides, the wolf can take a person's shape too. So they have something in common. It's just a fairy tale, anyway. Things like that aren't real." I rest my hand on the stack of books.

Boudicca seems to mull over what I said. Finally, she nods to herself. "I still like the story. The idea that there is someone for everyone."

"I do too. Well, here are your books. I'll enter your list with the registrar. What's the name of the borrower?"

"Monsieur Xander Albright—it's there on the bottom." Boudicca taps the paper then looks up at me again. "Viola—I mean, Mademoiselle Archambeau..."

"Please call me Viola. The other sounds so formal."

"Would you like to join me for dinner?" The words tumble from her mouth as if she'll lose her nerve if they aren't out in the world. It's adorable.

"Right now?" I rummage through a drawer and find a woven satchel to pile the books into.

"If you aren't too busy. I've already taken up so much of your time." Her fingers drum nervously on the books, and her large citrine ring glitters in the light.

My stomach lets out a roar that would shame a lion, and I give Boudicca a lopsided grin. "My shift just ended. I'd love to. Let me register the books you're borrowing, and we'll be off."

A little thrill courses through me that this fascinating woman is interested enough in me to share a meal. A wash of despair chases the thrill. What if this is the last time I get to be with a charming woman? Why aren't men this intriguing? I can't imagine being stuck with a husband and having to conform to societal rules. My sisters seem happy enough with their marriages, but it's just not for me.

I glance under my lashes once again at Boudicca's beautiful features. She's definitely a bright spot in my day. I might as well treasure our time together.

5

BOUDICCA

"And then my brother purchased this ridiculously hideous carriage because Father wouldn't let him buy one of those new automobiles. Despite Charles being married, I think half the women in Paris have been in that carriage in the last two months since the monstrosity started gracing our side drive." Viola chokes out a little laugh. "Charles is so ungenuine. It's hard to love a brother who's so dishonest."

I pause with the cup halfway to my mouth. I'm being dishonest with her now, wearing this fake body. Would she be angry to find out I'm not who I say I am?

Pushing that thought away, I try to immerse myself in her presence. I've only ever dined with my siblings and Xander, but as Viola chatters cheerfully over chocolate cream pie, I'm utterly enchanted. It's freeing to be close to her and able to respond. She smiles at me again while licking some errant whipped cream from her lips, and I want to kiss the cream from that tempting pink expanse. My hand hovers over my crushed linen napkin on the table, longing to hold hers. What are these feelings?

Maybe the more romantic tales she's whispered to me as a gargoyle have fired up my imagination. I glance down at my wrist, where the loose red ribbon is secreted away beneath these human clothes. I've always considered her a dear friend and can't bear to remove the gift, even though wearing it could give me away.

My gaze drops to her lips again as she licks off a bit of chocolate. What would a kiss feel like? She's so warm and soft—to feel her melt against me would be divine. Words escape me as the impossibility of my desire weighs down my tongue.

Viola has carried the conversation throughout dinner, and now, as the stars sparkle in the sky, I'm reluctant to see our time together end. She doesn't seem in a hurry to leave, so I hail the waitress and order another latte to keep Viola here just a little longer. It's a bit greedy of me to want to prolong this moment.

One thing she said earlier still bothers me: "It's just a fairy tale, anyway. Things like that aren't real." The words press so hard against me I might break.

How can Viola not see the magic in this world? She has slippers that scale any wall, and unlike other ungifted humans, the tower is visible to her. Her stories create vivid images that last in my mind years later. How is that not magic? I want to tell her animal shifters are real, mages exist, and creatures of stone can come to life—but I can't. The inability to mention the magic world wraps around me until I'm trapped by the omissions and half-truths.

Eventually, Viola sips the last drop of coffee, and her fork chimes against an empty plate. I pay for our meal, thankful that Xander had the forethought to give me currency. The mage has always taken care of my siblings and me and been grateful for our service. However, this is the first time Xander has ever asked one of us to leave the estate for an errand. I've left the tower before to fly above Paris, observing the lives of real people, but only at night when no one could see me.

"It's getting late. I'll walk you home." I stand and offer her my hand.

The feel of Viola enchanted me when we touched earlier, feeling somehow different from when I'm stone. This ring isn't just an illusion, like I initially thought. My flesh is soft and warm like a human's, and any excuse for her hand to be in mine is a good one. I catch the way her golden hair tugs free of its coif to sway in the light breeze. Unlike the stone family I'm accustomed to, she's always in motion—a wave of her hand, the beat of her heart. She's so full of life it's intoxicating.

Viola stutters then flushes, bunching the layers of her dress in her fists as she stands. "I appreciate the offer, but I'll be fine. It's not that far a walk, and I'm familiar with it. Thank you for dinner and your company, Boudicca. I had a pleasant evening."

My hand falls to my side, clenching at the loss of her touch. I wanted one more moment. We might never have time together like this again. As the denial tears through me, I step to the side so she can move past. "Thank you again for looking up the books."

"Of course!" Viola beams. Her cheeks turn bright pink, and then she looks away. "Good night."

Hoisting my sack of books, I watch her leave. A sliver of moon peeks between the tall, close-set buildings like a shy lover, and Viola tips her head toward it with a carefree smile. At least I gave her a moment of peace and lifted her worries. Nervously, I adjust the weight of the canvas sack. Paris can be dangerous for a lone traveler at night. I could follow Viola to make sure she gets home safely. That's not too intrusive. She'll never know I'm nearby.

Ducking into an alley, I remove the ring. The shockingly painful change rips through me. My body expands, and the skin tears as I grow larger, harder. I grit my fangs against my lips as horns sprout from my skull and wings unfurl from my back, aching as if they'd been bound too long. My muscles strain as they lengthen and bulge.

I rub the red ribbon tied to my wrist, expecting to see a bloody husk of a human body on the ground, but the only thing before me is shredded clothing. Making a mental note to disrobe next time—if Xander allows me a next time—I sling the satchel of books across my shoulder before launching myself into the night sky. The breeze caresses the cool stone of my body. The chiton I normally wear is back in Xander's study, but I don't mind being naked. There's certainly no shame in it for one made of stone.

Fluffy clouds obscure the stars, and I dip a little lower to watch Viola walking along the street below. Seeing her safe, I exhale. There was no reason to worry. After all, this is the same woman who has climbed all over Paris since she was knee-high. Viola cuts across a public garden then ducks into an alleyway, and I bank on the wind to follow.

Shadows clinging to the buildings above her stir ominously then separate from the surrounding dark to ooze after Viola. A cold lump forms in my throat. Shades. Why would shades be following a human? As conjured creatures, they typically only harass magical beings.

Oblivious to her stalkers, including me, Viola hums a merry little tune as she spins in a circle. Normally, I would enjoy seeing her happy, especially if I caused it, but right now, I want her safely indoors. The inky shadows creep down the building, slinking behind her. Soundlessly, I glide closer. She turns onto another street, out of view, and I strike.

The first shade hisses in surprise as my claws sink into its body. It takes a magical creature like me to even grasp one of these evil things. I shred the shadowy substance in my claws, and it dissipates back to whoever summoned it as the others swarm me.

Icy fingers of panic seize my chest. How many of these damned shades are there? I've never encountered so many at once. The creatures swirl around me, plucking at the satchel and sweeping chilly hands against the stonelike flesh of my body. Snarling, I claw at them, trying to do enough damage to send the conjured beings back to where they came from.

Several rush me, and we tumble sideways through the air and slam into the limestone wall of a nearby building with a crunching thud. I explode in a flurry of blows. One by one, the shadowy beings evaporate into oblivion.

Ribs aching and tears in my skin burning, I gather myself. Why would they be after her? In my peripheral vision, I see a shade slip around the corner after Viola. A host of them darken the sky like a flock of malevolent crows.

No! Growling, I spin through the air, catching the remaining creatures on my wing spikes. The shades shred into smoke, disappearing into the evening breeze. One clawed foot touches a spire, and I spring up over the building, only to see my worst nightmare.

A shade has Viola pinned on her back against the deserted cobblestone street. It shouldn't be able to touch her. Her frantic eyes widen, gleaming in the yellow light cast by the nearby gas lamp. The high, lacy neckline of her dress lies in tatters around her chest. The shade yanks at the silver necklace around her throat, and the glint of a labradorite pendant catches my attention.

I know that stone well. It's Xander's pendant of the earth that breathed life into me. How Viola possesses it is a mystery that needs to be solved now.

6

VIOLA

The shadows are alive. How?

I shove against the thing tearing my dress to ribbons, but my hands pass through the chilly specter. A claw rakes down my shoulder, catching on the chain around my neck with a sharp tug. Forcing a breath down my constricting throat, I still. How can they touch me but I can't touch them? There's no way out of this if I can't affect it. My necklace digs into my skin, pulling even tighter. Frantically, I try to wedge my fingers between the chain and my throat as stars dance before my vision.

I'm going to die. Hysterical laughter scrapes its way out of my rapidly collapsing windpipe. I've been searching for magic all my life, and now some paranormal being is going to murder me. In vain, I lash out with desperate kicks that toss my skirt up to obscure my vision. This was not the night to wear pretty but mundane shoes instead of my slippers.

Wind rushes past in a gale, shoving hair into my eyes. The attack stops, and I struggle to stand, clutching my tattered dress to my chest. My heart hammers as I glimpse something large rolling into the Seine.

A splash echoes against the walkway. I exhale in relief as I brush down my skirt. What was that? Unwittingly, my feet move toward the sound before my brain takes over. *Run, run, run!* This is no time for curiosity.

I take off down the street, smooth-soled shoes skidding on

the slippery stone. For all the world, I wish I had my magical slippers and gloves on me.

Lights. I pant, trying to organize my thoughts into something that doesn't feel like a bunch of chaotic squirrels. Shadows don't like light—I'll stay in the light. My breath huffs out in great panting sobs as I pass the Louvre. My scrapes burn. I glance down briefly, relieved to see nothing is bleeding. I'll be fine. My teeth sink into my lip. Why are the streets so damn empty? It's still early.

I resist cutting through the usual alleys and private gardens, keeping to the pools of gold cast by the street lamps. No carriages or automobiles thrum down the streets, and the absence of other people out for the evening is eerie. Has everyone been wiped from the world? Did I somehow magically cross over to somewhere dangerous? This doesn't make sense.

The familiar curling bronze of the gate to my home comes into view, and I rush past it, taking only a moment to latch it behind me, as if that could ward off ghostly invaders. Relief floods through me at the sight of light from the tall windows gracing the front lawn in elegant stripes. I lean against the wall, breathless. The remains of my dress cling to my skin, damp with sweat. The house. I need to get inside. It might not be safe out here.

Damp grass sticks to my shoes and ankles as I race across the lawn to the side servant entrance. Annoyingly, Charles's bulbous carriage blocks the side door. Why did he park so close to it? I can barely get past. The thing is actually worse than I described it to Boudicca. I squeeze past its sickly-green onion shape topped with orange gilt. The vehicle color reminds me of vomit baked on an alley wall.

I can't resist a glance over my shoulder as I shimmy past the horses attached to the monstrosity, but there's nothing amiss. Shadows haven't detached themselves to murder me.

Inside the manor, the familiar sound of the kitchen staff sets my mind at ease. Tonight's events were beyond insane. I've always felt safe running on the city's rooftops after dark, but now the very thought of encountering those creatures again sends a tremble of fear through me.

I slip through the door and quickly pass the entrance to the large kitchen. The scent of soap mingled with roasted meat wafts in the air. Just my luck—my family is lingering over dinner. My mother's voice comes from the nearby dining hall, and instead of walking past the open double doors, I cut down the narrow hall toward the staff wing and take the side staircase up to the second floor.

All my movements are too loud against the bare wood of the uncarpeted stairs and echo off the unadorned walls. My neck burns as I clutch the tattered remains of my dress close to it. I don't want anyone seeing me like this. The last thing I need is further restriction of my freedom. A peek down the main corridor shows it's empty. I step onto the thick royal blue rug that runs the length of the corridor and dart toward my room at the end of the hall.

Just as I reach it, Charles steps out of the room across from mine. A brunette, who is certainly not his wife, giggles drunkenly as he unsuccessfully tries to fumble his cloak over her head—like I won't notice she's there.

We stare at each other for a long moment. Charles taking in my disheveled state, and I'm trying not to gag on the smell of sex and cheap perfume. He waves a half-full wine bottle at me, staggering to one side.

"You didn't see me," my brother slurs.

I nod. "Likewise." Then I tug my chamber door open and throw myself inside.

A fire burns low in the hearth despite the warm evening, and it appears Maria tidied up my room. I cross quickly, throw the glass doors to the balcony open, and let the chilly night air rush in to replace the stifling heat. The cool metal lever rests in my palm, and a trickle of apprehension wends through me. I pull the door closed and kick off my dew-wet shoes then pace while stripping off my destroyed dress.

My pleasant evening with a new acquaintance ended in disaster. What if those shadows come back? Can they pass through a door? My mind spins with the implications. There has to be some documentation on such creatures.

I catch my disheveled reflection in the mirror. The rims of my glasses are bent to near uselessness, and with a sob, I take them off and toss them onto the dresser. Long red scratches cover my shoulders and chest. Who knows what infective agents could be in those wounds? I tip a nearby pitcher of water into a wash basin then dab delicately at the angry marks. It's too bad I didn't take Boudicca up on her offer to escort me home. As powerfully built as she appears to be, I bet she could have handled those things. Except I couldn't touch them, so maybe her strength wouldn't be much of an asset. Still, the company would have been comforting.

I allow myself to linger a mere moment on the flex of her hand on mine, the heat from her skin, and the way I had to tip my head up to gaze into those intriguingly colored eyes. I hope I'm at the desk when Boudicca returns those books.

Ridiculous, being moon-eyed over some woman. Didn't I learn that lesson when I had a year-long affair with Anne only to have it end in her marriage to the butcher's son? Her parents made the match, but she seemed eager to agree to it. What a waste of time. Anne barely gave me a backward glance before she was married and pregnant. After crossing to the books shelved along the wall, I peruse them, looking for something to shed light on this evening's attack. Each bound tome was scrounged from traveling booksellers or estate sales, and they all hold one thing in common—the mention of the supernatural.

Were those creatures ghosts? The memory of the chilly claws makes me shiver even in the stifling heat of the chamber. I've only seen a ghost once before—well, I thought she was real at the time. These things had no distinct humanoid form, though. It was more like darkness with a razor's edge. After scanning the meager lineup of books describing specters, I select a worn leather-bound journal. Someone else has to have seen these things.

As I walk toward my bed, I leave a trail of sullied clothing behind me then grab the robe from where it's draped on the plush duvet. The heavy embroidered satin slips over my skin, catching on the jagged scratches. Flinching, I ignore the irritation, letting the book draw me in.

The journal is a particular treasure. Unlike other fake grimoires and books on weird folk remedies, this book has valid medicinal recipes, as verified by Mirabelle. Written by Inessa, a witch who lived in the fourteen hundreds, it not only describes a variety of herbal remedies but also speaks of the natural spirits she communed with around her cottage in northern Germany. Of course, that comes with the nuisance of being written in German, not French. I pick up my spare set of spectacles and flip toward the middle of the book, recalling her documenting something about conjured spirits, then puzzle over an unfamiliar word. Lips pulled tight, I rise from my bed and check the lower bookshelf containing worn dictionaries of various languages.

Thick with a ragged-edged cover, the German dictionary has seen better days. The pages crinkle in protest as I turn them. The word is one of those overlong amalgamations the Germans are notorious for. "Creeping darkness of service" is about the closest I come to a translation. I frown, realizing I need a more extensive library.

A vague childhood memory tugs at my addled mind. My grandmother had a secret workshop with shelves of books here in the manor. She showed it to me once when I was young, but I never was able to track the room down again. Charles said it was all a dream and our grandmother died shortly after I was born. But the memory is so vivid, and that was when she gave me the jewelry and climbing shoes. There's no way it was a dream—not that I was going to show Charles the treasures she gave me.

Restlessness stirs me to my feet. I belt my robe tighter as I head toward my chamber door. I've searched for my grandmother's study hundreds of times over the last decade—I don't know what makes me think I'll find it this time. Hope? Maybe determination? A stubborn streak as wide as the city? All of the above? I trail my hand along the smooth plaster wall of the hallway. Calm and steady.

The abrasions on my skin burn and throb, and I clutch the satin robe, brutally wadding it in my fists so it doesn't touch the wounds. I start as I always have, in the family great room, surrounded by gilt-framed oil paintings of my ancestors. Closing my eyes, I recall my grandmother, ancient but with an unlined face. She had hair the color of fresh snow and a peony-pink complexion. Her smile was one of patience and love, nothing like the disappointed moue my mother always presents me with.

I still remember seeing her carriage arrive that day, drawn by dapple-gray horses with bouncing blue plumes of feathers on their heads. Grandmother took my hand... no, she reached for my hand, but we never touched. I was so small that she was always just out of reach. We walked down the east hall.

I step through puddles of moonlight cast through the glass windows to my left. The image of her seems stronger when my eyes are closed, so I clench them tight again, focusing on that night. Down the hall, I take a right turn. I trail one hand along the wall, feeling two door frames, first one then the other. Both closed.

I imagine a large room with white sheets over furniture—the room I can never find. This is pointless. I always just end up in the hall near the servants' quarters on the east wing. I open my eyes.

Dust motes dance in the moonlight in a room so pristine white it glows. Sheets cover furniture, the shapes like humped creatures scattered in a haphazard maze. This is it. My ribs swell with an excited breath. Nearly tripping on my long robe, I run to the wall where the switch to the secret door to grandmother's study was. A pattern of gold wooden embossing covers the white wallpaper. It's here. I know the lever is here. It was the tail of a fantastical beast.

But there's no beast to be found, just vaguely floral curls. Grunting in frustration, I close my eyes. Magic. I know magic is real. It's here. The latch must be hidden. I sweep my fingers blindly over the wall, desperate to find the lever, but the surface is unbroken.

Confused, I open my eyes. I'm in the hall by the entrance to the kitchen. *What the...?*

"Viola?"

I spin in place, only to see my father standing before me, a concerned look on his face. "You've been staring at that wall for over ten minutes. Are you sleepwalking, child?" He pats my cheek.

"No, I..." This isn't where I was. Am I the victim of some tricky spell?

"Come, my dear. I'll make you some warm milk and walk you back to your chamber. I think we even have a bit of cinnamon for it, just the way you like."

Was I dreaming and then woke? That must be it. I nod, allowing my father to lead me back to the safety of reality. But the silky fabric of my robe drags against my still fresh wounds, reminding me that the nightmare was all too real.

7

BOUDICCA

The acrid scent of ozone burns on the air as more shades burst into existence. I never expected this when I offered to walk Viola home. Another swarm of damned creatures spirals down from the sky toward her manor. Tucking my wings tight to my body, I plunge through wispy clouds. Wind screams past my ears, and I flick them down to stifle the noise. The mage conjuring these things has to be powerful. It takes a lot of magic to summon so many shades, but why focus them on an uninitiated human?

I twist in the air, pulling the sack of sodden books to my chest with one arm, and sweep my claws out to rake the shades into oblivion with the other. Water from my earlier dunk in the Seine runs down my torso. Tiny fang-filled mouths howl in silent protest before evaporating into mist. These apparitions are smaller and weaker than the ones that stalked Viola earlier. Maybe the being summoning them is running out of power. I slice into another shadow creature, sending it back to its home realm. At least Viola is safe within the manor house. The shades shouldn't enter a human dwelling. It's against the Covenant. No one in their right mind would dare to breach the Immortal council's laws. The leader is an ancient vampire and brutally efficient—and his wife's swift justice isn't something to dismiss.

What if the mage is operating outside the law? I kick at a shade, raking it with my spurs. The puff of smoke from the creature's disappearance quickly blends with the night sky. A dark shiver runs down my spine. Would someone defy the Covenant? I swat another annoying shade, sending it to splat in an inky blot against the garden wall. Going up against magic-wielding vampires seems like a shortcut to a violent death.

Weight smacks against my back, followed by another solid thump against my wing and yet another on the back of my head. The air buzzes with power as the universe tears to let these beasts through. The creatures rip at my skin, tugging my mane and pulling the heavy membrane of my wings. My body burns, growing heavier as it seeks to turn to stone to avoid more damage. Focusing hard against the change, I twist in the air as their claws dig into my tough skin. Affecting magic requires magic, and these things are starting to seriously savage my hide. If they manage to rip up my wings, I won't be able to fly. With too many wounds, I'll revert to stone, rendering me utterly useless.

Icy veins of panic surge through me. Xander warned me I'm not entirely immortal—that too much damage could turn me back to lifeless stone. I never thought it could happen, not with my battle prowess and thick hide. Most creatures can't even scratch me.

Teeth sink deep into my thigh, sending a shock of flaming pain down my leg. Another shade sticks to me, then another. I'm losing this damn fight to a bunch of minions I didn't take seriously.

I give my leg a hard shake, but the things cling tenaciously as the ground spirals toward us. One crumples my left wing, half pinning it to my shoulder. I twirl recklessly through the air, my mind racing as my body stiffens and the hard lifelessness of stone creeps into my mangled limbs. I've never crashed from such a height. Will I shatter into lifeless rubble if I do?

There's no choice. In a last-ditch effort to scrape them off, I relinquish myself to stone.

Instantaneous relief washes over me as the shades slide off my rock-hard hide. But it doesn't stop the ground from looming ever closer. I plummet, unable to control my descent in this frozen state. Without movement or breath, I wait an eternity until the last shade leaves me.

Straining, I force a shift to my softer mortal form, and snap my wings to climb high into the sky. My chest muscles quake, and something in my shoulder pops with the effort to rise on the air currents. The deeper wounds burn in the bracing night wind, but the smaller ones closed during my shift. Still, my strength wanes. Breath eases out of my abused lungs.

That was close, and I'm not sure how much more damage I can take before my stone form forces a change to heal. Below, hulking shades lumber across the garden toward the main house, obviously intent on Viola. Nine hells—these little ones were just distractions. Ignoring my stiffening body, I bank over the garden, leading the smaller shades on before twisting in the air and shredding them to oblivion.

Scanning the grounds below, I look for anyone who could be directing these things. The mage must be close to be able to open so many portals to bring these damned shades through. Another whiff of ozone precedes a soundless rip in the air before me. I roll my tightened shoulders. I'll never let anything hurt my tale spinner.

Five shades. The breath I take expands my lungs like a hurricane. My roar of challenge cracks against the sky, and the blacker-than-night creatures turn to face me, each with eerie yellow flames marking eyes above a jagged hole resembling a mouth. I rally my strength. *Yes, fight me. Forget her.*

I dive, flexing my claws wide to do optimal damage. I've

never seen shades this gigantic before, but surely a solid hit should—

The largest one backhands me like I'm nothing more than an annoying gnat. I slam into the garden wall. Agonizing pain lightning strikes my spine with a sickening crunch. With my wings outspread, like I'm some entomologist's speared captive, I breathe through the urge to sink into my stone form. The world tilts as I try to regain my footing on limbs that cease to obey. Above me, the stars bleed into a myriad of rainbows before swirling in a slow dance. Stone creeps over my skin, freezing me in place.

That... was new. Nothing has ever flung me like a toy before.

With a grinding slide, I land on the thickest part of my tail then slump to one side. The sack of books falls with a wet plop into a clump of flowers. Bright glittering lights still cloud my vision. Paralyzed, I watch helplessly as the shades turn from me and shamble in a hulking, shadowy mass toward the manor. I reach toward them but only achieve the slight quiver of spikes on my outstretched hand before the skin along my arm gleams, shiny and polished. Hopelessness grips me. I can't save Viola.

A sharp flare of magic, blindingly silver, ignites in a bubble around the house. The lumbering shades burn off, turning to ash on the evening breeze. Afterimages of the light seer my eyes. Someone—or something—protected the manor house. The cream lines of the stone building fade back to shadows, and a comforting golden glow shines through the windows. Insects and frogs begin their nightly serenade again, their absence only apparent upon their return.

Slowly, before I lose all control, I roll into a low crouch behind some topiary and let my stone form take over. I'll heal and watch over Viola through the night. It's all I can do—it's what a creature like me is made for.

As the predawn light seeps over the horizon, I land with a clumsy thump on the balcony of Xander's study. I'm too heavy, and aches from a multitude of burning wounds cover my body. My stone form only healed so much in the scant hours when I could take the shape. Exhaustion pulls at my limbs, stiffening them, as I stumble through the arched door into the workshop.

Xander takes the still-drenched books from me and sighs. "Boudicca, there had better be a good explanation for this. Where were you all night?" Their gaze softens as they spot my wounded wing and the crisscrossing wounds on my hide. "Shades again? So soon?"

Tiredly, I shuffle on clawed feet as Xander examines me, tutting. The mage rubs salve into the partially healed membrane of my wing as I try to hold still. The balm warms with magic, knitting my stonelike flesh back together.

"They attacked Viola." I flinch as Xander massages a particularly tender area near the bone.

Xander raises one chestnut eyebrow. "Shades went after a human? Were they able to touch her?" They drape a cloth on top of the ruined books and carefully tuck it around the warped edges.

"Yes. The creatures ripped her dress. She wore a pendant like yours." I tap the labradorite pendant on Xander's chest. The magical piece has something to do with how I'm alive, but in the decades I've been conscious, I've never seen my maker use it for anything.

Xander rubs their thumb over the smooth surface. "I traded an elemental earth mage for my pendant a few centuries ago. I suppose that mage could have made more than one, but how would an item like this fall into Viola's hands?"

I roll my shoulders as I murmur, "Magic is drawn to her. Maybe the pendant liked her stories too."

Xander chuckles quietly, removing the cloth from the now pristine, dry books. An appreciative hum rumbles in their chest. "Viola can access that part of the library. Fascinating." They glance back at me, green eye gleaming. "You watched over her last night? Is that why you were gone so long?"

I nod and examine my nearly healed wing. A faint crescent-shaped indent is all that is left of the bite mark. When I rest, that will be whole again. "Large shades attacked her house, but someone protected it, and they all burned away."

"Hmm. If she doesn't come to you tonight, you should continue to watch her. But, Boudicca, she mustn't see you in your true form." Xander takes the ring from me and sets it on the cluttered desk. "I'll find you some more human clothes. You're too big to wear mine."

My maker huffs a laugh and picks up the flowing dark dress they carved when they made me. "Please wear your chiton when you use the ring next time." Xander tosses the garment into my lap. "The last thing the poor girl needs to see is her beloved gargoyle with her tits out."

I peer at them questioningly, but Xander gestures at my general nakedness. *Oh.* A warmth travels over my neck, stinging the points of my ears.

"Yes, Maker—"

"Goodness, for the last time, Boudicca, please call me Xander. You know I hate that whole 'maker' thing. It's a title I'm expected to use in formal magical meetings, like I have to use Monsieur in the mundane world. What are labels, anyway?"

I duck my head, covering my face with my wingtip. It's better not to rile Xander up over societal conventions they despise.

"Go up to the roof, and get some sleep. I'm sure Baraq will appreciate the company."

Tucking my wings tight to my body, I climb up the stairs. Xander never did answer why shades would be after Viola. Her house flared so bright last night I'm positive there is magic afoot. A protection spell of that magnitude takes an accomplished magic user. Maybe Viola's family is more part of my world than I originally thought.

8

Viola

*C*rimson light pours through the stained-glass window of Father's study, haloing the stranger as he turns to greet me. I tug at the stiff lace hiding the scratches and bruising around my neck. It's an effort not to rub the meticulously applied makeup from my eyes. I couldn't sleep last night. Every time I tried, shadowy creatures chased me through my dreams, shrieking hellishly. They tore at me with their long claws and sharp teeth.

"Mademoiselle Archambeau, it's a pleasure to meet you." A man takes my gloved hand from my side, snapping me out of my musings, then kisses it politely. "You are far lovelier than your portrait."

Yanking my hand away, I spin in place to face Father, nearly tripping on the voluminous skirts of my new dress. "He got to see a portrait? How long have you been planning this?"

My nose twitches at the amount of dust in the air. Is it from this awful stiff fabric? Today is already a nightmare, and it's barely past ten.

Father stifles a groan. "Viola, please welcome Elias Christian Maximillian Leopold of Austria."

What a mouthful. I peer up at the man over the curved rim of my spectacles. He's much older than I expected, ten years or more my senior. His dark-brown hair is parted neatly to the left and clipped in a tight military fashion to the nape of his neck. His unadorned black suit shows a body that's likely more accustomed to being outside than in, and tanned skin confirms that. I move past his ridiculously full mustache to his dirt-brown eyes. There's nothing in them—not kindness or affection, not cruelty or disregard. Nothing. I'm leaning in closer, curious about such a dead, blank stare, when my mother jabs my ribs.

"Welcome to Paris, monsieur." I curtsy, as ladies must, managing to be the graceful daughter my parents wish me to be despite this hot, cumbersome gown. "I'd be happy to show you around." *Not really.* I've got a date with a book at the library, and the last thing I want to do today is have some upper-crust noble shadowing me.

"I'm told you're a scholar, my lady. I'm new to Paris. Perhaps you'd like to give me a tour of the Bibliothèque Mazarine." He smiles warmly at me, and it reaches his eyes, giving them a soft, almost golden glow.

My heart does a weird little skitter. He's interested in the library? This could be less awkward than I thought. I run my eyes over the cut of his clothes again. They're plain but well made, using quality material. He must be wealthy for Father to even consider the match—perhaps wealthy enough to fund the public aspect of the library.

His eyes slide away from mine. Maybe he's nervous, like me, and that blank expression was him covering it. He's well-mannered, if a bit stiff. I suppose I could get to know him and give him a chance at friendship. It's not his fault our families are throwing us together. Elias obviously bothered to find out some background on me beyond my portrait. That's more than most of Father's foreign suitors have done.

"I'd be delighted." I shove a pleasant look onto my face but can't seem to manage the simper I've seen my sisters do.

"Excellent." My mother claps her hands. "Your father and I need the family carriage this afternoon, but you can use Charles's carriage."

"The onion of doom? No, thanks. I'll walk." I'd be afraid

to sit on something gross or catch a disease from riding in his *cove of love*.

Ignoring my comment, Mother continues. "I'll have the carriage brought around immediately. Maria will attend to you."

"Maria? Why would she have to come to the library?" I gesture to my maid. Maria absolutely loathes the library, saying all those old books make her sneeze.

"A young lady needs a chaperone." Father claps Elias-of-the-too-many-names on the shoulder. "Dinner is at seven. Have her back by then."

Seven? I swallow hard. I'm expected to spend my entire day with this stranger?

Longingly, I think of the stack of books I left in the alcove last night. The Mazarine is huge. Maybe I can ditch Elias somewhere and hide with my books. Ugh, then there's Maria. She already has her face scrunched up as if she's thinking about sneezing her way through the tour.

Elias offers his arm. "Shall we?"

I swallow a sigh over his predictable mannerisms. Like I have a choice. Stealing myself, I rest my hand on his arm, with the lightest contact possible. There has to be a way out of this engagement. We walk down the plush blue carpet woven with my family's golden crest, past the oak arched buttress, and into the grand foyer. I watch Elias from the corner of my eye. Is there any chance he doesn't want this either? Perhaps I could break wind or belch loudly to show him how completely unsuitable I am as a wife.

In awkward silence, the three of us wait on the stone porch for the carriage to come around. I stare up at the early-summer sky that reminds me of the deep-blue flashes in Boudicca's unusual eyes.

"What do you enjoy, Monsieur Elias?" I ask, attempting to

break the ice as I drop my hand from his arm. Maria stands off to the side, giving us an illusion of privacy.

"I've been in the military most of my life." He nods as the orange-trimmed olive carriage turns the corner, drawn by two bay mares. Silence falls between us like a granite wall. This day is going to be an absolute bore.

After opening the door, he offers me his hand to help me into the carriage. A waft of tobacco, cheap perfume, and old sex exits the carriage, and I want to gag. I place my hand politely in Elias's. Even through my thin gloves, the rough calluses of his palms rub my skin. His hands are icy—nothing like the enticing smooth warmth Boudicca offered.

Boudicca. I bite my lip. Our meeting happened by chance, but the feel of her still lingers in my thoughts. She was comfortingly familiar. I try to find the least disgusting place to sit then study Elias, who settles himself opposite Maria and me. That blank look is back in his eyes as he stares out the window.

I should make an attempt at polite conversation. "I can't help noticing that you enjoy the outdoors."

For a moment, I don't think he'll answer. Then his eyes swing toward me and light up. The change in his demeanor is so jarring it feels artificial.

"My apologies. I was never one for cities, mademoiselle. I do prefer the countryside. The area around my ancestral home in eastern Austria is wooded and breathtaking. I'm sure you'll grow to love it as I do."

Not likely I can continue my research, then. Grinding my teeth, I turn my eyes to the window. It's smudged with two huge greasy boob marks. Ugh. This carriage needs to be burned.

"Viola, have I said something wrong?" Elias leans forward, boldly taking my hand.

I'm glad I wore gloves today. I don't want this stranger's

touch on me. As politely as I can, I pull away. "My parents announced this arrangement to me yesterday. Forgive me, but I've had little time to settle into the idea of marriage."

Elias gives me a smile so fake it appears to be carved from marzipan. "But you're of courting age. Don't you want this? I thought all ladies dreamed of their wedding day and having babies and a family of their own."

"Not me," I mumble.

The carriage jolts over the cobblestone street as an uneasy silence settles between us. Maria draws away from me in the close confines, looking as if this is the most uncomfortable she's ever been. She's not the one being forced to wed some stranger.

"I didn't know," Elias murmurs. "Perhaps we can simply spend some time together and see if we are compatible."

My lips part as my eyes dart back to his in surprise. "And if we're not...?"

"Then I'll give your father some respectable excuse and bow out. But, Viola..." He takes my hand in both of his. "I'd very much like it if you'd give us a chance to get to know each other."

He leans in close, crowding my space, and I press my lips together, squishing back into the plush leather seats. Elias's offer is far more than I expected and completely reasonable, but I still can't help but hate this whole awkward situation. He asked for a tour of the library, though. It's not like he parroted some trite nonsense about books rotting a lady's mind.

Maria clears her throat. Elias has the decency to release my hands and move back to his proper seat. I guess the whole chaperone thing isn't that terrible. At least it keeps this person from touching me. Through my lashes, I watch Elias's expression go blank again. His body stills as if carved of stone. How surpassingly odd.

Thoughtfully, I rub the pendant that sits under the lace of my chemise. My skin is still chafed from where those creatures tried to yank it from my neck. Though I found the pendant in the same box as the gloves and slippers I use for climbing, I never discovered anything magical about it. The slippers were easy to figure out. I put them on and was instantly stuck to the floor. The gloves had a similar effect. Through trial and error, I figured out how to use them well.

The pendant is a lovely piece of jewelry. Golden swirls frame an oval labradorite stone of deep gray streaked with luminescent blues and hints of green. But I don't even know its origin.

The carriage rolls to a halt, and the door swings open. With polished grace, Elias rises and exits the vehicle then turns to assist me. I force a smile because ladies are expected to do so. My shoe sticks to something on the floor, and with a grimace, I tug it free. It's going to be a long day.

9

VIOLA

Sweat trickles down my spine as we move through the stacks to the sound of Maria's unending sneezes. Elias has asked all the questions any tourist to the city ever has, and while it's not his fault, the conversation is less than mentally stimulating. The desperation to be alone with my books leaves my speech waspish. I'm unaccustomed to wearing so many layers when I work, and this fancy dress is more annoying than comfortable. Beside me, Maria pulls out her lace kerchief as her red face screws up tight. Another sneeze rips through the room, and several elderly men look up from the long tables in a collection of annoyed expressions.

As I turn the corner toward the main desk, a flap of coattails catches my eye. Through the arch of a side alcove, Master Frederick, like a mottled crow, gestures to a tall red-haired man. My heart sinks as the man's profile comes into view. The thickness of his overly styled mustache twirled into horns above his pursed lips is regrettably recognizable. Elias looks over my shoulder curiously as I try to herd this motley crew past the open passage without being noticed.

"Viola, I didn't expect you back so soon. Come meet Lord Kensington, dear. He just stopped by to discuss the acquisition." Master Frederick gestures us in. "Who's your guest?"

He eyes Elias in speculation. I'm certain he knows damn well who he is or at least what. That tea seems to be spilled. I clear my throat, gesturing to the man beside me.

Elias pushes past me, extending his hand to Master Frederick. "I'm Lord Leopold. It's a pleasure to see such a well-maintained collection."

I glare at Lord Kensington. "Yes, the public is indeed blessed to have such a well-catalogued collection to peruse in addition to educational programs. It's fortunate that, through the grace of society, this library will always be available to them."

Kensington gives me a patronizing smile. "Mademoiselle Archambeau, I heard you're finally taking your rightful place in society. Congratulations on your engagement. It must be such a relief to stop passing your time playing at scholarly pursuits."

Master Frederick's forehead creases, pulling his brows together like two fat caterpillars. Through thick lenses, he gazes at Elias then at me. "You brought your fiancé to the library?"

Enraged, I draw a breath. "I am *not* engaged. And just how do you know about this arrangement? Did my mother demand you sack me? It certainly isn't because my service to this establishment is anything less than stellar." The words and all my pent-up fury escape my traitorous mouth before I can stop them.

My boss—soon to be ex-boss—splutters out some gibberish then takes a breath, running his hands over his waistcoat. I can't wait to hear this load of rubbish. Kensington examines his drink, a smirk creeping under his ridiculous facial hair.

I draw myself up to my full height with a sharp intake of breath. "Actually, I came by to let you know I have several patrons willing to front the money to throw a charity masked ball here at the library to raise the funds to keep it public."

"Really? Who?" Kensington looms curiously. His red suit coat gleams like dark wine.

Dammit—no one's agreed yet. "They wish to remain

anonymous, but it's more than enough seed money to get the ball rolling."

"A ball. What a fabulous idea. I'd be happy to contribute to your efforts." Elias smiles warmly at me then looks with slyly hooded eyes toward Lord Kensington. "With your influential reach, I'm certain you could aid the cause as well."

The two men study each other a long moment before Kensington lets out a low laugh. "Of course I could. Knowledge should be open to all. Isn't that what you always say, Viola?"

It's a struggle to keep my face neutral when he purposefully drops my title. When did he start standing on my side of the argument? He must have an angle.

"I do say that. Your financial assistance would be appreciated."

"Excellent. And if you can't raise the funds, the books will remain safe in my hands." Lord Kensington turns his back on me dismissingly, leading Master Frederick back to the office.

Maria sneezes, and I frown. There has to be a way to raise enough funds to block that English lord from buying out the collection.

Chantal appears and rests one hand on my arm. "Viola. Oh, I'm so happy you're here. There's a bit of a mess on floor three. Monsieur Hammond was in today, and I really could use help putting it back to rights." My anger deflates in light of this small escape.

"Perhaps we should break for lunch," Elias suggests with a pointed smile at my sniffling maid.

Perfect. I turn my back toward the office lest I march in there and make another social blunder. "Why don't you and Maria take the carriage back to the house, and I'll rejoin you later?" This has been far more socialization than I ever do in a day, and right now, all I desire is to be curled up in my nook with that Lemaitre tome I found yesterday.

A frown tugs Elias's mouth downward as he glances at Chantal then back to me. "As you will. Should I send the carriage back to pick you up?"

I hesitate. What if those creatures attack me again? Nonsense, it's daylight. "No. It's a pleasant day. I'll walk home when I'm done."

He gives me a curt nod, turns, and makes his way to the front of the building, with Maria scurrying behind him. I breathe a sigh of relief, loosening my collar and opening a few buttons at my throat. Chantal still hovers by my side as I start toward the stairs in the nearby alcove.

"It was just a ruse. Who was that man with you?" she hisses through her teeth once we are far enough away from Master Frederick.

"My parents have apparently set me up with matrimony."

She gasps. "Not with him?"

I stop and turn toward her. "Do you know him?"

Chantal tucks a curl behind her ear. Her eyes dart away from me. "N-No. He just doesn't seem like your type."

"And what is my type?" I stare at her pointedly over my lenses.

"Tits, honestly. I thought you were still with Anne."

I roll my eyes. Is my entire life an open book? "She married a man last month and announced her pregnancy a week ago."

"That does explain the lack of morning pastries in the break room." Chantal's wistful tone makes me grin. "Anyway, that man looks like he's bad news. You should break the engagement—feign cholera or something."

"I'll take that under advisement." I raise a dramatic hand to my forehead. "I can't possibly marry, Mother. I'm dying and will be deceased by next week. Please let my last moments be with my beloved books."

Chantal's eyes glitter with mirth, and her giggle brings

shushes from nearby scholars. "Anyway, I need to get back to filing. Want to help?"

"Pass. I'm not actually on duty right now, and I have a date with a new book." I wink, and before she can say anything else, I head back to the antiquities section.

10
Viola

*E*ntering this area always feels like coming home, and peace settles over me. Elias isn't the worst person to be around—it's just overwhelming to have to entertain him after the terror of last night. Pretending everything is normal isn't my forte.

My shoes plop into the plush carpet, and after another bead of sweat slides down my back, I shimmy out of my heavy satin overskirt and leave it in a pile on the floor. Cooler air flows to my skin through my long chemise and lace underskirt. My bodice is pretty enough to be seen through my open partlet, even if that is scandalous. With relish, I practically fall into the overstuffed chair next to my abandoned stack of books, grabbing the top one on my way down. No one ever comes to the older part of the library, and this hidden side room has always been private. Except that I brought Boudicca here last night without a second thought.

I close my eyes as she seeps back into my thoughts. Why is she so comfortably familiar? Even during our conversation at dinner, I felt like I'd known her for years. We laughed together, and her smile was so inviting.

I shake my head and open the book, excited to finally peruse it. My fingers once again caress the silken endpapers in admiration. As I skim through the table of contents, my eyebrows sweep upward. The author, Lemaitre, is discussing imbuing gems with magical properties. Excitedly, I flip to the first chapter. Dark-blue script fills the margins of the page, and a squeal of delight leaves me. *Personal notes.* Is this a sort of journal? But it's printed, so there must be more than this one copy.

This is proof beyond my slippers. Beyond my word that I saw those awful shades. There's magic in the world.

Hungrily, I devour the information as if it's the only sustenance I'll ever need. Lemaitre's neatly scribed side notes have me panting in anticipation as my world cracks open wider, allowing me a peek at what lies beyond. He talks of spells, imbuing energies into stones to create charms against heat and cold, breathing underwater, and some sort of travel ability.

Hours pass but seem like minutes as I'm engrossed by the words. His name is French, but the book is so ancient it's unlikely he's alive. Still, maybe I could find a living relative.

Someone clears their throat. "Viola."

A tremble of warmth runs through me at the deep, smoky voice. I'm uncertain how long Boudicca has been standing there, watching me pore over this text, but her amused expression says it's been a while. Of course, she looks immaculately put together in a fitted deep-blue suit that makes her eyes positively glow.

In dismay, I glance at my pile of clothes on the floor. I'm far from indecent, still wearing two layers, but the partlet covering my chest and shoulders has long gone askew, and the lace top of my bodice shows.

"Boudicca." I straighten the partlet and button the high collar. Her eyes drop to my oval pendant, and I quickly tuck it behind the lace before trying to make myself presentable. "I'm sorry. No one ever comes to this room. I... can I help you with something?"

"It must be a good story." She leans forward to pluck one of my ivory hair combs from the floor and hand it to me.

I flush. Goodness, I must look like a swamp goblin. I've

never really cared about my appearance when I'm deep in the stacks, but suddenly, in front of her, I do.

"It is." The squeak I emit is barely recognizable as words.

She smiles even wider. White, straight teeth gleam against her skin. "Monsieur Xander is done with these books and has another list to check out. I was hoping perhaps you could help."

"Already? Were the books not what he needed?" Those books were thick. There's no way he read through them all in one evening.

"Monsieur Xander prefers *they*, not *he*." Boudicca rolls her powerful shoulders with a fluidity that would make anyone swoon.

I puzzle over that statement like it's a complicated treatise to dissect. Our language is so gendered, even down to small items. I've never considered separating it out into neutrality.

"I haven't heard anyone ask to be addressed like that before."

"*They* is a combination of the masculine and feminine pronouns. My employer just prefers to be thought of as *themself* rather than a man or a woman. As for your question, I didn't ask them if the books were useful or what they needed. I was only happy for the excuse to see you again. What are you so caught up in reading that your clothing escaped?"

A laugh erupts from me at Boudicca's teasing tone. "It's so stuffy in here today that I couldn't tolerate all the layers. Sit." I pat the plush chair beside me. "I found some amazing information. Well, first, you said you enjoy fairy tales."

"Yes...?" Boudicca raises a questioning eyebrow.

"Do you believe our world holds real magic?"

Boudicca sits, a pensive look furrowing her high forehead. "I believe there are many undiscovered things in this world. It's such a large place that no one person could ever know everything."

I study her serious expression before my gaze drifts to the long, curly waves of her unbound hair. My fingers ache to touch it. Will it be soft? Springy? What inappropriate thoughts.

I flex my fingers against the page of my book. "Agreed. Well, this author writes about spelling gemstones and mounting them in jewelry. I'm only five chapters in, but the process is riveting."

"Really?" Her brows quirk. "How do you know it's not the wild imaginings of some crazed person? Who wrote it?"

"Lemaitre."

Boudicca gapes in surprise before she swiftly covers it. "Well... he would know."

"Do you know the author?" I lean in, peering intently at her shining blue-gray eyes. The way the light catches them, they appear striped, just like my pendant.

"He's a close friend of my employer."

He's alive, then. Excitement bubbles in me. I bend so far forward I'm nearly spilling into Boudicca's lap.

"I'd love to meet him. What do you do for Xander? Perhaps you can arrange an introduction. Does Lemaitre live here in the city? The book is old. Is he an ancient man?" My fingers curl into the dark velvet of her sleeve.

"Whoa, slow down," Boudicca says, lacing her fingers through mine with a patiently fond look.

What little breath is left in my lungs rushes out as her thumb strokes my palm. Is this magnificent woman flirting with *me?* "Sorry, I get a little excited over books."

"I'll see if he would be agreeable to a meeting. Durant Lemaitre is a very private man."

Her touch sears through me. Featherlight, I trail my fingers down her forearm and watch her expression smolder with desire. She *is* interested in me. Leaning even closer, I slide the book from my lap and curl myself boldly into hers. The move is ridiculously forward, but it's been months since I've had a lover, and this woman would be the perfect escape—even for only a handful of moments. Boudicca's gaze drops, lingering on my cleavage then my lips.

"You are stunning. How lucky am I to have you wander into my life?" I breathe out, close enough now to see my exhalation stir her luxurious curls. I want to know her taste, her feel.

Boudicca's fingers slide along my cheek, her touch enticing, then curl into my hair. Her eyes meet mine, her breath on my lips hot as we draw together. Trembling with anticipation, I rest my hand on her shoulder, feeling the flex of her muscles dance under my palm. My lashes flutter to my cheeks. I want her to kiss me so much the desire burns along my skin. Today is definitely improving.

With a bang, the door opens, and startled, I turn in place. Boudicca's hand clenches my hip, holding me firmly in her lap. Elias strides in. His eyes roam from our linked hands to me snuggled in Boudicca's lap before glancing at the pile of clothing on the floor by my chair.

Shadows of anger sweep over his typically neutral expression, and his fists tighten. "Am I interrupting?"

No one ever uses this room. How is it everyone is finding me here today? I jerk back with a speed that nearly topples us in the chair. "N-No. It's nothing. We were just discussing a fascinating book. Elias, this is my friend Boudicca."

"Friend?" Elias raises a dark eyebrow then looks pointedly at the book on the floor. "I'd heard the rumors that you preferred ladies. I'm certain once you're married, and properly bedded, your tastes will change from these childish crushes."

How dare he. I flush so hard my ears sting as I move back to my chair and gather the heavy layers of brocaded silks onto my lap. "This area is private. Only staff is allowed back here. You need to leave."

"Oh, and is this *lady* part of the staff?" Elias sneers. I don't like the judgmental way he rakes his eyes over Boudicca's body.

Brushing off her crisply tailored pants, Boudicca bristles and stands. "Viola was warm in all those layers. Nothing inappropriate was happening, I assure you, monsieur."

"That's good. I wouldn't want there to be gossip about my fiancée and some lady dressed like a dandy." Elias holds out his hand. "Viola, I'm here to collect you for dinner. I didn't like the idea of you walking across the city unaccompanied."

"I do it all the time," I protest.

His fiancée? My parents haven't announced it yet, and I certainly haven't agreed to anything. It can't possibly be close to dinnertime, but a glance at the nearby wall clock shows the afternoon has flown by.

"Not anymore. The carriage is out front." Elias glowers at Boudicca as if he's ready to strip the flesh from her bones.

Not wanting to cause a fight, I glare at Elias. "Well, then, if you'll both give me a moment of privacy to put myself to rights, I'll be out when I'm done." I gesture toward the door, and Elias begrudgingly steps through it.

Boudicca stands then glances over one shoulder. "I'm sorry if I caused you any problems."

I take a breath, forcing calm through my trembling limbs. "You didn't. I enjoyed meeting you again."

"Chantal said you're arranging a fundraiser ball for the library. Perhaps I could help."

An excuse to see this gorgeous woman again? Yes, please. "I'd love that."

She hums. A secretive little smile curls her lip before she turns and exits the room.

11

BOUDICCA

A buzz of pleasure fills me as I move through the doorway into the hall leading to the main library. Glancing down at the faded red ribbon on my wrist, I smile before tucking it under my cuff. Viola has found a window into my world. It's such a small thing—a beginning. That book reveals just enough that it may open her eyes to more, but it'll also put her in danger. I swear I'll protect my tale spinner with every breath.

The stranger pulls the door closed with an ominous click of the brass latch. This must be the duke's son, the man who wants to steal Viola away. I don't like that he's already attempted to claim her as his fiancée. Roughly, Elias shoves me against a nearby wall and pins me there. Growling, I glance down the darkened hall. There's no one here to see us. I grasp my ring, ready to yank it off and toss this belligerent ass from the library.

Then I inhale, trying to remain calm. There's no way I'm revealing to Viola I'm not human. There has to be another way to handle this. I was always better at fighting than diplomacy.

Grumbling, I look him over. Elias is nearly as tall as I am and powerful enough to threaten this human form. Rust-colored tendrils of blood magic wisp off the man as his dead eyes blaze to life. He appears human, but magic clings to him. He must be a mage like Xander.

"Don't think for one moment I can't smell the stench of earth magic on you, gargoyle. Why are you anywhere near a human?" Elias hisses through clenched teeth.

Startled, I press back against the wall. How can he see through the ring's magic? And what part of the magic world does he belong to that he knows of such things?

"She's mine to protect. Viola claimed me as hers over a decade ago," I snarl.

This puny human body doesn't have the strength my true form does. If I were stone, I'd tower over him and easily toss him down the hall. Elias wouldn't dare try to manhandle me. I fist my hands and shove him away.

He bites off a laugh. "That foolish girl has no idea what you are, does she? You're just a poor beast created for a singular purpose. Did you think she was your friend?"

I flinch at the truth in his words. "She *is* my friend."

"You aren't even real, just a soulless magical construct. Stay away from her," Elias hisses. "Viola no longer needs a stone guardian. I'll take good care of her as my wife." As the door opens, he turns, holding his hand out to Viola.

She's fully dressed again and has pushed her hair up into its decorative combs and braids. There's a parcel tucked under her arm. I'm certain it's the book. Those blue-violet eyes flick between the mage and me.

"Boudicca, I enjoyed seeing you. I need to attend a family dinner with Elias, but I'd like to meet again to discuss..." She swallows, her gaze moving to the mage then back again. "The next few chapters of that book—and the ball of course."

I bow, trying not to glare at the man beside her. "I would like that very much."

"Oh, the books your employer desired—if you go to the front desk, Chantal should be on duty to help you." She lays her gloved hand on Elias's arm. "Good day, Boudicca."

Something inside me cracks as she walks away, and pain floods my chest. I've felt nothing like it before. Elias's implications pollute my thoughts. *Creature. Thing. Construct. Guardian. Beast.* The cruel cadence beats against my skull.

Elias is right. I'm nothing more than a magical stone creation given purpose. What made me think I had any right to try to kiss her? If Viola knew I wasn't human, would she look at me the same way? With a curse, I hike the satchel higher on my shoulder and stride toward the front desk.

XANDER THUMBS through the new books as I stand before them. My wings creak and stretch as I wait. The human form was constraining, and this time, it was a relief to shuck it.

"Are you absolutely certain it was Durant Lemaitre's book? Viola being able to retrieve the books I requested shows she can enter the dimensional space where the magical books are held, but I didn't think Durant had anything there. He's so particular about parting with his knowledge." Xander paces, their long skirt swishing against the polished tile floor. They pull a quill from behind their ear and gnaw on the end pensively before sitting. "Although Viola could always see my tower. That's a curious mystery in itself."

"Yes. I saw the book. She has a room she favors within the magical section of Mazarine. Is it possible Viola is magical? Her stories, the slippers, the way the shades could see her—she must have something in her soul." I strain to keep my voice neutral, but the desire to draw her into my world is so strong I clench my fists until my claws dig into my palms.

"Do you see magic on her?" Xander asks.

All gargoyles can see magic threading through the air. It shines like ribbons of color drifting from everything that carries it. Viola has never radiated magic. The fact that I saw the rust of blood magic on that man deeply concerns me.

I shake my head sadly. If she were of the magical society, I wouldn't have to hold the secret of my true existence from her. "No. Beyond her slippers and gloves, I've never seen magic on her. What about that duke's son, Elias?"

I rumble, hating the way the name feels in my throat and on my tongue. He said he would take good care of her as his wife. The words are like sand, rubbing raw wounds against my stone flesh. It burns.

Xander's quill scritch-scratches across the parchment for moments that last longer than my patience. Thumping my tail, I fidget. My clawed feet scrape the stone floor as my toes curl anxiously.

Finally, Xander looks up with a terse jerk that sends their long earrings swinging. "I'm checking into him. It's possible his magic is learned, not inborn."

It's not enough. "Do you see magic on her?"

Xander observed her that day, with their pale farseeing eye. With that eye, they see magic, like I do, but they also see the future or the past. That's why Xander keeps it covered under a gemmed velvet patch—they say it's too distracting to constantly view things that both have happened and might happen. The mage has explained that the future often changes, and sometimes, it's better not to know.

But my heart thrums with the desire to know Viola's fate. I'm content to have her come to me, telling me stories, until she's old and gray. I don't expect anything beyond that. One day, her body will return to the earth, and I'll still be guarding this tower. I already know my fate as a creature—my purpose. Is it so terrible that I crave the softness of humanity she offers?

I hug my wings around me. No soul resides in my body. I'll never be her equal. Viola calls me friend, and that's all I can aspire to. It was foolish of me to dream anything more could ever be possible.

Xander's hand on my shoulder drags me from my thoughts. "Go to the roof and rest. I'll handle this for you. I'll have more information by the time you wake tonight."

I'm in my stone form, on my usual perch, before I realize they never answered my question.

12

VIOLA

A rainbow shines on the trembling surface of a bubble as it floats with the late-day light through the bathchamber window. This morning was the weekly story time with the younger children. As I read them fairy tales out of an illustrated book, I wondered who would do this if the library closed. Those kids are at the age where they still have wild imaginations and believe in magic. It crushes my heart to think that bit of wonder will be lost to most of them as they become adults. If I can inspire a handful of children to coax something beautiful from this mundane world, it might make it a better place.

Cooling water swirls about my body, but I'm loath to leave the bathtub. Stepping out of it means the start of a dance I don't want to participate in. Dinner last night was awkward enough. Tonight, it's with my entire family. I've always been the odd one among them.

Ignoring yet another light knock on the door, I close my eyes and sink lower into the tub. My chin touches the water, then my lower lip follows. Taking a breath, I submerge completely. Liquid fills my ears with hollow silence. The soft creak of the copper tub is an odd comfort. As the moments tick by, I consider that it may be preferable to inhale a few mouthfuls of water rather than join the dinner party downstairs. Morbid thoughts.

"Viola, if I don't have you dressed and downstairs within the hour, I'll be sacked. Have some pity, and open this door."

Maria's whisper echoes off the brass walls of the tub as I resurface.

Another bubble floats past, echoing the curving pattern of some rainbow-hued dust motes. The locked door jiggles again followed by exasperated sighs.

"I'm coming. I was in the bath."

Water streams down my body as I rise to grab a towel. Feet tap impatiently at my door, their shadows creating a flicker of light along the tiled floor. I cross the room and push the latch open before she can knock again.

Maria eyes my damp hair with exasperation before brushing past me into the chamber. "How do you expect me to get your hair dry before dinner?"

Waving my hands, I gesture her in and relatch the door. "Does it matter?"

"Braids it is. Which dress are you wearing?"

"The red." It's the most comfortable one I own, with soft sleeves and a light skirt.

She opens the double doors to my dressing room. "Too informal. I'll prepare the indigo gown."

There's no point in fighting this. She only asked out of courtesy. It's not like I actually get a choice. I pull a clean chemise from my dresser and draw it over my head, letting the damp towel fall to the carpet. Before too long, I'm being stuffed into heavy velvet I'm likely to drown in. Maybe that's my out—suffocated by fabric and never able to attend this travesty of a meal.

Maria stuffs my arm into a tight sleeve before sorting the lace out above the bodice neckline. Like a doll, I stand there and allow it. A floor below, the clink of kitchen noises echo up through the metal service pipes. I'm briefly tempted by the thought of feigning an illness, maybe cholera as Chantal suggested, and using the calling pipe to ask that my meal be brought to my room. I caress the cool brass wistfully before Maria's stern voice dashes my hopes.

"Don't even dream of pretending to be sick. I'm expected to bring you, fully gussied up, to the dining room, and that's precisely what I'll be doing. Now, take a seat so I can braid your hair."

I close my eyes against the rest of her preparations. The hair, the makeup, the new dress, all for some man I didn't know before yesterday. It makes me want to run along the rooftops of Paris until my thighs ache and my throat is hoarse from screaming. Facing those shadowy ghosts again would be preferable to what is about to happen.

The library has been my shield against having to endure this part of my world. Its loss would be devastating. Mirabelle and Chantal don't have the funds to help, but I bet they have personal connections and wouldn't mind lending a hand.

After Maria finishes tugging my hair into a coronet of braids, I slide my glasses on then pull them off to examine the nose prints left by my gorgeous new acquaintance's almost kiss. The feel of Boudicca's warm touch still lingers on my skin as I clean the lens off. She's definitely a welcome new addition to my life in a sea of unwelcome ones.

I grab a nearby sheaf of paper and a quill to draft an invitation to Mirabelle and Chantal to meet tomorrow at the corner café. After a moment of thought, I pen one to Boudicca and address it to Xander Albright. After all, she did offer her help, and this is the only way I know to reach her.

If I can get the library financed, maybe I can maneuver myself into a more valuable position and be able to refuse this arranged marriage. I can't afford to be cut off financially from my family without some sort of income. The library is my singular hope.

A SMALL TERRIER yaps as the child next to it rubs its white coat with sticky hands. Helena, Charles's young wife, looks on in horror before lifting the dog back onto her lap. Young boys race around the table, so identical I'm honestly not certain which of my siblings they belong to. The children have the standard Archambeau dirty-blond hair and blue eyes. We all look the same. The once-spacious dining room closes in, crowded with almost thirty adults, a dozen children, a squalling infant, and two terrified dogs. All my immediate family is present in this hellscape.

"So, Elias, my son tells me you're a military man." Grandpapa pats his rounded belly as he sits back in his chair. "I was a general back in the day."

Beside me, Elias wipes his mouth then sets the linen napkin between us. "I started at sixteen. My military career has been my entire focus."

I close my eyes. Here we go—an evening packed with talk of battles in countries obscure enough that Grandpapa's truth cannot be questioned. My eldest sister, Angelique, huffs as she fixes the starched lace around her daughter's throat. Her children are the only ones not running about. Glumly, they sit at the table like tiny bereaved adults more suited to attending a funeral than a family meal.

Beside her, Flora slurps through her soup, the only thing she's been able to stomach this pregnancy. Her stomach is so round it appears the babe will join us for dinner. She gives me a sympathetic smile then glances at Elias as he continues reciting his litany of martial pursuits to Grandpapa. I study my other brothers and sisters seated neatly at the table with their spouses. Even they are arranged not only by alternating gender but by age as well. The eldest siblings sit closest to my father at the head of the table, while I, as the youngest, sit at the foot of the table near my mother.

The boys race past the back of my chair, jostling it, and my mother clears her throat. "We've brought you all together this evening to introduce you to Lord Leopold. Your father and I have accepted his suit for Viola's hand in marriage."

My throat tightens. I knew this was coming, but I can't help feeling despair at the whole damn situation. I grit my teeth through the murmur of congratulations until finally I can't remain silent anymore. "I didn't agree to this arrangement yet. What I did agree to was that Elias and I would get to know each other. To my knowledge, that's where we are currently at."

The usual displeased look darkens my mother's face.

Angelique rolls her eyes. "Face it, Viola—it's a done deal. A woman can't survive without family."

One of the boys running around the table trips and starts to wail. The dogs yap in panic at the ruckus, clawing their way up their mistress's bodice. The awkward silence beyond that smothers the room. None of my siblings have ever stood up to my parents. They meekly accepted their fate. It's likely they're wondering who I am to raise such a fuss.

Elias's cool hand slides over mine. "I told Viola we should take time to get to know each other, and if the match isn't suitable, then there's no need to go forward with a wedding."

Mother glares at him. If looks could kill, Elias would be a pile of ash on his chair. He seems unconcerned, though. I'm certain that in his mind, no woman could resist him.

"That hardly seems fair, seeing as I was saddled with this ice queen," Charles grumps as one of the lap dogs snarls at him. Helena snuggles the creature to her bosom with a sob.

"Charles, have some decency," Pauline says over the head of her sleeping infant. She's only five years older than me and just had her third child.

It's like all Archambeau women are created be mothers. My sisters seem happy with their role in life... but I don't think

I would be. Dread settles heavily into my chest. There has to be a way to escape the same fate.

"That seems like a fair arrangement to me," Father says. "With as many battles as you've strategized, you can certainly win over my daughter."

"Win me over? I wasn't aware I was a prize—"

"You're not." A muffled laugh ripples out from the head of the table.

I scan the table for my eldest brother, Claude, and shoot him a glare. "To be won."

Elias winks at me. "I'm up for the challenge."

Realizing his hand still covers mine, I yank mine away. A low, chattering hum rolls around the room, accompanied by the light clink of silverware. Perhaps a change in topic?

"The Bibliothèque Mazarine will be hosting a masked ball on the summer solstice. Fundraising tickets will be available soon."

Angelique's laugh is cruel as usual. Our spread of years has never made it easy for us to see eye to eye. "Are you still working a plebian job in that dreadful place? Honestly, baby sister, this union should be freedom for you. You'll have an entire household to run in a palatial estate."

I frown. "I enjoy books."

Angelique waves her hand as if bored. "I'm certain Lord Leopold can purchase as many as you like. Perhaps a whole room full of the moldy things."

"Now, Angel, sweetheart, don't be so negative about your sister's little hobby." Father smiles, and I stiffen so as not to visibly cringe. "Tell us about the event, dear."

"Well, the library and its community programs need funding to remain open. I'm arranging a ball for solstice eve. If you buy in as a sponsor now, I could have your business listed on the programs. It would be good advertisement."

"That sounds very smart. I'll buy tickets for the entire family. We can settle out the money tomorrow."

Surprise at the offer sings through me, but then, Father has always doted on me as his youngest. Before I can respond, desserts arrive on a large tray, and excited shrieking follows. My nieces and nephews scramble for their seats at the table, far more thrilled about the prospect of cake than about anything served for dinner. It was so easy being a child. Years scrolled by with my freedom unchecked. Perhaps that makes my new reality all the worse.

"Yes, of course," I mutter and stab the slice of cake placed before me. Beside me, Elias continues to regale my family with his extensive travels and military triumphs. Maybe he'll be gone all the time, leaving me to tend to my own needs. That wouldn't be so bad, would it? I'd lose access to the Mazarine, though, and continuing my research would be a challenge.

I need time alone to sort all these thoughts out. As soon as I can escape this house, I'm going to see Iggy, and I'm sleeping on the rooftop tonight. Sorrow grips me at the thought that my freedom to run through the night could also soon be at an end.

13

BOUDICCA

*A*nother person brushes past me as I hurry down the street toward the café, a crumpled invitation in my hand. The magical citrine ring on my index finger gleams in the late-morning sun. Dammit, I'm late. With a nervous yank, I tug the cuff of my sleeve to cover Viola's ribbon on my wrist. Xander keeps the oddest hours, and they didn't read the letter until the time I was supposed to be at the café. I didn't know Viola had invited me until Xander woke me from my daylight slumber and slipped the ring onto my finger.

The facade of human skin chafes against my being, confining to the point of a phantom itch. I tug the collar of my suit, loosening the neckline as I turn onto the street matching the address in the invitation.

My breath catches. Viola sits at a small black iron table with two other women. The light caresses her hair until it shines gold. Rose petals from a trellis arch above them rain around her face in a slow dance. She's the most beautiful person I've ever seen. Leaning toward a curvy brunette I don't recognize, she laughs, and the sound rings through me like a siren song. Beside her sits Chantal, the curly-haired librarian who's helped me when Viola was unable to.

I inhale. She wants me here, helping her to plan an event important to her. The very thought of being part of a human community fills me with both trepidation and excitement. Will they all accept me? I squint at the unfamiliar woman as I notice a faint shimmer of magic around her corsage.

"Boudicca?"

I jerk backward behind a wall of potted greenery, turning to see who said my name. Amber eyes flicker under a long fringe of honey-blond hair. It's Durant Lemaitre. Panic seizes my chest as he smooths the lapels of his immaculate tan suit. I bow low, holding the obsequious pose even as he tuts.

His soft, cultured voice floats around me. "There's no need for that. The council now works for our people, not ruling with an unnecessarily heavy hand as it did in the past. What is a gargoyle doing here in the daylight? Xander doesn't typically let you stray far from their tower."

His knowing gaze follows mine as my eyes slide from the Immortal's ethereally beautiful face to Viola. "Xander has asked that I protect her. The shades have shown an interest."

"Interest in a human?" Durant goes preternaturally still as he studies Viola. "She shows no signs of possessing magic. You know you can never tell her of our world."

I gnaw my lip. As head of the council, can he prevent me from ever seeing Viola again? Frantically, I think of things that could hint at her being part of our world. "She has slippers that allow her to scale buildings, and she tells stories that make pictures in my mind."

I look down at the Immortal, noticing how very human he looks, but I'm certain if I cross him, his eyes will glow red with bloodlust and long sharp fangs will emerge. Vampires, the humans call them. They are the dominant species that rules Paris.

Durant tilts his head upward, moving closer to me. His lips curve into a smile that never graces his eyes. "That's not enough. She's a tender young thing that will get eaten alive by our world if it notices her."

"She's a librarian at the Mazarine. Viola found your book."

One crisp golden eyebrow rises in a perfect arc. "She can enter the bōc-hord?"

I mouth the unfamiliar word letting my lips purse and roll over the letters. It's not French, but the term feels old. "The area with the grimoires? Yes. She found your treatise."

He makes a noise somewhere between a grunt and hum then looks to Viola again with an appraising murmur. Golden magic shimmers around him in a silent wispy dance. "She has no protections. The creatures of our world would slaughter her within a fortnight."

"I'm all the protection Viola ever needs," I growl as my shoulders bunch and flex in this tight skin. Leader or not, he can go straight to hell with that talk.

"You can't even leave the confines of Paris. And how will you protect her in the daylight with that soft human covering you wear? You'll tear like paper. Be reasonable. If Xander set you to protect her, as your kind are created for, then follow their order. But if you breathe a single word to her of the magical world before she finds a way to defend herself, I fear you'll fail in the task set for you."

"Are you threatening her?" Hot rage pours through me, but I know better than to pick a fight with an Immortal this ancient.

"No. It's simply a warning." Durant dips his chin. "Good day, Boudicca."

He turns and ambles off, coattails flapping gently in the light breeze. I take a calming breath as I turn toward Viola again. He's right. I'm just a creature created with a singular purpose—to guard what I'm commanded to protect. In this case, it's her, and I will not fail my duty.

I stride toward the empty chair at Viola's table, and as she notices me, her face blossoms into an expression of pure joy. Warmth pools in my chest. *My tale spinner, I'll guard you until I am dust.*

"Boudicca, you made it! I wasn't sure if Xander would

pass the message along in time." Viola stands, raising her hands to take mine.

As soon as we touch, every tense muscle in my body relaxes. Shoulders unknot, and teeth that ground against each other go slack. I didn't realize I held myself like this until I didn't. Viola guides me to the chair beside her then taps a messy pile of papers before us. I take a moment to read the concise, flowing script. It's orders for flowers and food, proposed floor plans for the ball, and information on the solstice from different cultures. Of course, she deep-dived this. I wouldn't expect anything less.

"You've met Chantal from the Mazarine? This is Mirabelle. She owns an apothecary across from Parc Montsouris. Ladies, this is Boudicca, she works for Monsieur Albright and is a patron of the library. I invited her to help organize the event."

"It's a pleasure to meet you." Warmth bubbles through me at their acceptance. This easy comradery makes me feel so much more human and less like the created thing I am.

Mirabelle beams brightly while Chantal pours me a garnet-colored wine. The café is quiet at this time of day—it's far too early for the chattering lunch crowd. Tables set with cloth-wrapped utensils and overturned clean glasses wait for occupants.

"We have enough money from my family, Elias, and Kensington to at least order the decor and food. I'd like to stick with the theme of summer solstice." Viola shuffles through the papers, dropping some into my lap. Her sun-warmed hand brushes against me, and it takes all my self-control not to fold mine around it and stare into her forget-me-not-colored eyes.

"Who did the art?" I hold up a page with sketches of constellations.

"Oh, me." Chantal looks away shyly. "I thought it might

be fun to incorporate zodiac symbols. You know, do a sun on one side of the room and have it radiate into stars."

"Solstice is the best time to use positive energy to fuel new beginnings." Mirabelle leans her chin into her palm as she takes a sip of wine. "What new beginnings would you like to see in your life, Boudicca?"

I can't help but look at Viola. Her hair escapes its chignon to fall in soft waves around her pointed face. Light shines off the rims of her glasses as her eyes catch mine. She doesn't look away when she flushes as pink as the rose petals around us. I smile, and her mouth curves until tiny dimples form on her cheeks. The insane urge to kiss those dipped spots races over me—not that I've ever kissed anyone before.

Instead, I lean imperceivably closer and inhale the soothing fragrance of her skin. "I think friendship is the best beginning and ending I can ever hope for."

"Oh, I don't know," Viola says with a wink. "Friendship can be the start of an incredible journey. Why limit your life? Write your own brave tale."

Surely, she isn't flirting with me. I continue to watch her as the world falls away. Viola makes me feel real—a person, not a construct. A being with a soul. Maybe with her I can be that, if only for a little while. Viola's hand slides into my lap and wraps around mine with a reassuring squeeze. Her thumb caresses the large citrine ring. How would she feel about me if she knew my true nature as the gargoyle she's adored from a young age? Could Viola love my true form? She hates pretenders and liars. Would she forgive me for fooling her with this human guise?

Chantal clears her throat. "We should probably continue planning."

Viola's blushes red as a sunset as she nods and tears her gaze from mine. Her hand drifts back into her lap. "Yes, of course. You said you know of a printer that can create the tickets. Making them pretty enough to be a collector's item is a stroke of genius."

"I know a few artists on my street that may be happy for the work of designing and creating the lighting. I can help you canvas for participants, as well, and post signs," Mirabelle says, her eyes lighting with glee.

"We still need to figure out the layout in the library and where to move all those tables. I work until close tomorrow. Can you all come by to help plan that?" Viola asks.

Chantal shakes her head as she rises to leave. "I've got family visiting."

"Sorry, I can't either. There's a special midnight market on my street, and all the shops are open, including mine." Mirabelle sighs. "I need to head out to open my shop. Are you busy tomorrow, Boudicca?"

"I can come move tables." Another private meeting with Viola as a human—I'd do anything for that.

"I bet you'd be great at that." Viola eyes my shoulders appreciatively.

Face heating, I run a hand over the back of my neck. That was definitely flirting. Or maybe it was just a compliment. Having a friendship with Viola is more difficult than I envisioned. I thought she'd tell me stories, and I would ask questions and tell her how wonderful the tales are. This is something enchantingly different.

"The library closes at eight. Maybe a half hour to plan? I'd be grateful if you could walk me home afterward." She flags down the waiter before counting some coins out of her purse.

"That sounds perfect." I hope Xander doesn't have any pressing business for me that evening. The thought of spending hours chatting with Viola sends an electric thrill through my body. Every moment in her company is a feeling I want to embrace for eternity.

14

VIOLA

"Mademoiselle, my papa says the library is closing. Is that true?" Emily asks as she looks up from her composition book with mournful, rounded eyes.

I brush back her chestnut hair. She's come so far in the last two years from an illiterate ten-year-old to writing her own stories in the worn book I gave her. I hold back a sniffle.

"I'm trying very hard to make sure that doesn't happen. You keep writing your tales, and we'll discuss them next week. Your brother is here to walk you home. Let's not keep him waiting." I stand and usher her to the door, trying to keep a brave face glued on tight, but it unravels as soon as I'm alone. Needing support, I lean against the wall, bowing my head.

My father took Elias on a tour of his shipping empire today, so at least I didn't have the burden of entertaining him again. I should be getting to know the lord, but every opportunity I can take to avoid him is a welcome one. My moments of freedom are ticking away, and I want to savor each one. Breathing out, I compose myself. *One day at a time. I can do this.*

Heavy footsteps on the parquet floor sound from the foyer. Boudicca cuts such a dashing, dark figure against all the burnished golden wood that my breath hitches. It's been so long since a woman made me feel this flustered—maybe since I was a teen with my first crush. Anne certainly never did. Oh, we had a fun tumble, but I always felt like there was an expiration date on our affections. It would be nice to feel the warmth of a body pressed against mine again. I've been lonely.

"Hello," she says, walking toward me with sure, even steps.

The confident way her broad shoulders sway with the swing of her arms has me staring. What would it be like to be caught up in such muscled arms and pressed against the softness of her breasts? Could she lift me? I nearly swoon at the thought. Boudicca is certainly tall enough to do that. With a dry throat, I croak out a greeting that sounds more like a kitten squeak than a hello.

Boudicca cants her head, swishing her gorgeous coiled locks over the fine fabric of her suit coat. "What were your thoughts on arranging the tables?" She removes her jacket slowly then slides a finger between her cravat and throat, loosening it.

I lick my lips as she moves closer, tilting my head back to keep her stunning features in focus. This is insane. Is Boudicca ensnared by the same level of attraction I'm experiencing? She splays one hand on the polished desk beside me and leans in, the heat of her body licking over mine. Those sky-streaked eyes gaze down at me with a longing that echoes in my soul.

Scratch that. Boudicca is definitely into me. I imagine what it would be like to have her weight above me, our bodies entwined. I cough down a pant of lust and try to push aside thoughts of how and where I'd like to seduce her. Of course, the answer is right here and immediately.

"I thought we could use some of the tables for refreshments and move the rest to one of the side rooms and close that off. Not tonight, of course. Tonight is for planning. To transform the library, special permission will be needed to close it a day or two before the event."

Boudicca rolls her crisp white sleeves up over her forearms, and I come a little undone at the flex of tendons beneath her dark skin. How can she possibly be this gorgeous?

I'm still staring when she clears her throat and smiles down at me. "What would you like to do tonight, then?"

"Research," I squeak.

"Research on...?" Her sensual, inquisitive voice wraps around my thoughts, smothering anything logical.

On how soft your lips are. "Oh, the library is the very best place to research. Maybe solstice customs. I'd love to do a magical woodsy-twilight feel in here to go with Chantal's celestial drawings."

"A forest of books?" she asks, gazing at the second-floor shelves.

"Exactly. We could have attractions to raise money, like a kissing booth." I grin.

Boudicca's brow wrinkles. "A kissing booth? How does that work? Who does the kissing?"

"Like at a fair. People pay a few coins to kiss a pretty girl."

"I've never kissed anyone," she admits.

My entire world grinds to a halt. Boudicca appears to be about the same age as me, certainly no older than her midtwenties. Maybe her family is strict or religious. I'd kissed half a dozen girls by the time I was eighteen—but then, I was an unsupervised youth.

"Never?" I ask.

"I guess the opportunity never came up. How many people have you kissed?"

I flush. "That doesn't matter. You know, the library is an excellent place for research if you wanted to, you know, learn how to kiss."

She laces her fingers through mine. "Is that something that needs to be taught? I always thought the ability would be innate."

I curl my body closer to her chest. Her huge breasts press into my shoulder as they rise and fall. I'd love to bury my face in them, like they're the world's best pillow.

"Research makes everything better. I *am* a librarian. Perhaps if you tell me what you're looking for, I can help you find what you need." Ooo, that was such a cheesy line. I totally deserve it if she laughs it off and backs down.

"Well, if I'm going to participate in a kissing booth, I need a woman with eyes like forget-me-nots to press her lips against mine and show me what it feels like to really be kissed."

Flowers? She thinks my dull-blue Archambeau eyes are that poetic? I gulp down a breath at Boudicca's ardent gaze. Her fingers graze the pulse of my wrist. She's serious. My eyes drop to the curve of her full lips then close as I lean into her, and our mouths brush against each other. She's warm and soft in all the best ways. Her arm circles around my waist, lifting me against her as a quiet moan escapes between us. I'm uncertain if it's hers or mine.

I cup her jaw as the kiss deepens. The line of it feels so damned familiar, like I've held her a hundred times before. Boudicca sits on a table, sweeping me into her lap in one smooth movement that doesn't break the kiss. Her teeth graze my lip before she sucks tenderly at my flesh. This can't possibly be her first kiss. First times are awkward and fumbling.

I pull back, and the wonder in her eyes stops that thought dead. Her arm stays snug around my waist. I let out a wistful sigh, not wanting the kiss to end.

She smiles. "Was that adequate enough?"

"You're a natural."

Releasing my waist, she lets her arm rest on one thick thigh. "Perhaps you're that good a teacher."

Sliding off her lap, I try to refocus on the actual task of setting up a fundraiser for the establishment I love instead of attempting to seduce an attractive woman. If I don't succeed at funding the library, I could lose everything.

I twist my hair into a bun and tug a clasp from my sleeve

to pin it into place. "Ahem. Back to the business at hand. We can add the booth to Mirabelle's list of art items to be created. Come look at the side room to see if you think you can move the tables to here. They're really heavy."

Boudicca follows me through a nearby arch to a mostly empty alcove. The space is smaller than I first envisioned, and I frown. We might be able to stack the tables in here.

A hand slides into mine. "The space is tight, but if I stack the tables three high, they should all fit."

"Will you be able to lift them that high? They're solid oak."

In response, her large hands cup my waist, and she hoists me into the air as if I'm a feather. Air rushes past as we spin, and a laugh of pure joy springs from me.

"It shouldn't be an issue." Boudicca holds me high, her head tilted back so she can see my expression.

I fight to control the flush that seems to be rising from my very toes. "I wouldn't want you to get hurt."

Carefully, she lowers me against her body, still holding my feet from the ground, until our heated breaths intermingle. "You won't hurt me."

I can't resist kissing her again. Her surprised squeal is a delight as her fingers press into my ribs. I wrap my arms around her shoulders, and my smaller body fits against hers like a dream. She holds me tighter, sliding me down her athletic form until my toes touch the hardwood floor. Boudicca pulls back, but I drag her mouth down to mine again, plunging my tongue against hers. A feral groan rips through her, and her fingers dig with rapturous pleasure into my back.

I want to lay her out on one of these tables and show her a completely different kind of kiss. Cupping one gloriously plush breast in my hand, I thumb her nipple through the softness of her linen shirt. Boudicca pulls away again with a frustrated grunt.

"Is everything okay?" I ask. Gone is the velvety look of desire. In its place is swollen black pupils and a stony-faced glare.

She twitches. "I'm sorry. I need to go."

"Right now?" Did I overstep? Dammit—she said she hadn't been kissed before, and here I am ravishing her. I must have misjudged. "Look, I'm sorry if I moved too fast."

She takes a step back and then another. "I'll reach out to you later, but I need to go." With a jerky spin, Boudicca flees the room.

Beyond the arched foyer, a door slams. In disbelief, I fall into a nearby chair. I've never been rejected that fast before. Hell, I'd never been rejected at all before Anne chose a man over me. I must be cursed. Across the room, a faint breeze stirs the papers with my designs on them. I guess I'll get to this alone.

15

BOUDICCA

A hard tug on my chest sends me running down an alley back toward the Tower of Wind. Xander's summon screams through my body. Damn them—this had better be important. I yank the ring from my finger, shredding yet another suit of clothes as my true form tears forth. The lightweight chiton that was tucked under the human clothing billows around me, easily adjusting to my actual size.

Aching wings open, hoisting me into the night sky with a speed a falcon would envy. Fangs erupt painfully from my gums, and my head throbs with the spread of my double horns. The human guise is worth every moment I can spend with Viola, but I'll never get used to this agonizing transition.

Another sharp pull practically drags me home like an errant child. Usually, Xander's summons feels like a light tap on the shoulder. Tonight, it feels like my bones will rip through my skin. I can't begin to imagine what's so urgent that it couldn't wait.

As the usually dark parkway comes into view, a lump clogs my throat. Bright flickers of magic and the glittery explosion of spells light up the night sky around the tower. On the ground, massive, lumbering shades approach—the same type that attacked Viola's home. I bank to the right as a shining arrow pierces one through the head, and it explodes into dust. My sister gargoyle, Cassiopeia, wings through the air with bow in hand, sending more deadly magical arrows toward the attackers. Her pale-feathered wings glow in the moonlight, and her delicate branched antlers gleam silver.

"It's about time you got here," she barks. Streaks of gray ash cover her normally alabaster form. "The twins have taken serious damage from these monstrosities, and my ranged attacks can only do so much. Get in there and smash these things before they get through Xander's shield."

All my fury at the harsh summons melts away at hearing the desperation in my older sister's commands. I inhale then dive over the edge of the tower, charging up the one magical defense I have. I'm going to have to fly close to use it. Choosing the largest of the shambling shadows, I dart forward, avoiding the swing of its clawed hand. A little careful angling gets three of the creatures in a row.

The air splits as I roar, letting loose a sonic boom that knocks the first creature back and vaporizes the other two. It'll have to do. I won't be able to use that breath weapon again for at least an hour. Claws out, I ram into the remaining shade and rip through its neck before its long arms can bash me like one of them did in my last encounter. It seems at close range they have little defense. I ride the thing to the ground, shredding it on the way down.

A radiant arrow zings by my ear, taking out another creature. The silvery shield around the Tower of Wind hums and sparks as a fleet of smaller shades slams into it, only to evaporate. This is the biggest attack we've ever seen. While shades have antagonized Xander for years, they've never shown up as an organized force before.

I fly back up to Cass. "Is Xander safe?"

She nods. "The twins are with our maker in the tower. Xander released the menagerie earlier to chew through the insignificant shades on the ground."

I grimace. Most of the menagerie is made up of smaller gargoyles that are more animalistic. Xander must have felt we'd be overwhelmed if they set the menagerie free from the labyrinth in the depths of the tower. A bright flash has Cass and me soaring toward the south side of the tower, where Xander's balcony overlooks the parkway.

A geyser of shades pours from a rent in the sky to pound against the magical barrier surrounding our home. I'm uncertain how long Xander can hold them off. The mage stands on the balcony, flanked by the lionlike twins, Ariella and Baraq. Clutching her side, Ariella leans against her darker twin. Large chunks of stone are missing from her mica-flecked golden flank, but her expression is still vicious. Baraq lashes his tail and roars at the shades in fury.

"What should we do?" I shout to Cassiopeia.

"You're the muscle. Go handle the shades. I'll make sure no other biggies have shown up."

"How? They're falling out of the sky." I gesture a spiked hand toward the spot just above the balcony.

"Shove something into the hole," Cass calls over her shoulder.

"Like what?"

But she's gone. The shield below me flashes again as the creatures that tumble onto it poof into mist. Xander's face is set in grim, determined lines as their power drains.

I look back up at the midair dimensional rip. What could possibly fill that hole? It's huge. An idea forms, and I dive through the sky toward Viola's home. I know exactly what needs to jam that portal closed.

As I circle closer to the manor house, the dome-shaped orange-and-green carriage lies horseless by the side of the long drive. I dive, claws outspread to spear the roof. Viola hates this thing anyway and has said multiple times it should burn. I'll be doing her a favor.

My claws sink through the soft cloth-and-wood ceiling, anchoring it. With one mighty pump of my wings, I lift the carriage off the ground, dragging it skyward. Below, someone gasps. I glance down only to see Viola, a satchel of books clutched in her hands, watching the "onion of doom" rise into the air in great jerky thrusts. There's no way she can see me against the dark night sky. At least I don't think she can. There's nothing to be done about it now. I tuck the ghastly thing to my chest and soar off.

It's fortunate most folks—even the magically gifted—can't see the tower, because the action around it looks like a damn fireworks display. As I wing closer, great cracks in the magical shell around my home shiver into existence. This doesn't look good.

Shifting my grip, I hoist the onion-dome carriage a little higher. I'm not sure stuffing this thing into an extraplanar hole will work, but it's worth a try. My shoulders strain as I build up enough speed to jam it in there.

Barreling through the sky, I twist at the last moment to shove the carriage into the hole overflowing with shades. It bounces off one side, jarred out of my grasp, and begins a comet-like descent toward the earth. Ugh. There has to be a better way. The sleek leonine shape of Baraq glides toward me, snatching the carriage out of midair. Huge chunks are missing from his back and sides. Crystalline formations cover more than half his body, and his flight is clumsy and slow compared to his usual deadly grace.

"Get back on the balcony. I can handle this!" I shout over the wind roaring in my ears as I hook my claws into the other side.

"It needs to be level," he rumbles. "Go high."

Beating our wings hard, we climb high above the rip in the sky. The carriage is definitely larger than the hole. Baraq nods, and we dive, night air rushing past my skin. Using my tail like a rudder, I maneuver us to be in line with the rift.

"If this pops through the rift, don't follow it!" I shout.

He looks at me as if I'm witless and rolls his eyes. I'm not the one flying around half-stone. Faster, the wind rushes past us. If we miss again at this speed, we'll end up plowing into the earth, possibly smashing the carriage. Not ideal.

I unhook my claws from the stiff fabric and heave the vehicle upward. The carriage lodges into the sky hole with a thump like a cork hammered into a bottle. Baraq peels off to the side, gliding toward the balcony, as he lazily swipes at the remaining small shades. I hover, running a thumb between the carriage and the portal. Half the carriage is suspended in the starry night sky like a moldy moon. It'll definitely give the magic community something to gossip about. Viola saw the carriage fly off. I'm certain I'll hear about that later, either as a statue or a human. Maybe this will be the final catalyst that opens her eyes to the magical world.

***

XANDER RUNS a hand through their wild auburn hair. Soot streaks their pale skin, creating milky rivulets where perspiration washed away the dust of exploded shades. They collapse into the winged-back chair with a sigh that's half relief and half exasperation.

"Where were you tonight? You're the strongest of all my creations and should've been guarding the roof. Ariella took serious damage from those large shades. She likely won't wake for days while she heals."

I turn to face them, flicking one ear in annoyance. "You told me to watch over Viola."

"I meant when she was in possible peril! Not every moment of every day. You know you're needed here." Xander throws their hands up in frustration.

In the corner, Baraq whines softly at the outburst and slinks upstairs to take his stone form in the rooftop sunlight.

Normally, feeling Xander's emotions ripple over me would have sent me packing too. Not this time.

"You never said that. How was I to know?" I shout.

Xander pauses, their face frozen in a sort of blank surprise I'm uncertain how to interpret. I huff and start pacing again, the heavy rasping drag of my tail soothing against the floor. Guilt overwhelms my thoughts. I should have been here, doing my duty—what I was made for. Instead, I was off smooching a woman.

Viola kissed me. *Viola kissed me.*

She likes me as more than a friend. Is that possible? Is that how I like her? My eyes close as I savor the memory of her body sliding against mine. How soft and warm she is. I think of the graze of her teeth on my lower lip. Her hair felt like silken threads pooled in my palm, sliding between my fingers. And her scent...

I inhale as if I could smell her again, that sweet spice of arousal. A faint tug from Xander's pendant brings me out of my sensual musings.

"Boudicca! Are you listening to me?"

"What? Yes, of course."

They growl, fingers fidgeting with the labradorite pendant. "I need you here tonight. Whatever plans you had need to be put on hold. You'll stay until the twins are healed."

"But I promised Viola—"

"You will stay here."

The compulsion washes over me. It's been decades since Xander ordered any of us by using the magic of the pendant, and it chafes.

"Fine." I turn my back on the mage and stomp up the stairs. I have to follow their commands, but I don't have to like it.

16

VIOLA

I poke listlessly at the sweet berry concoction in front of me as twilight paints the sky with violet and dusky rose. Elias is talking to my brothers, Charles and Claude, about some boring military something while I sit at the end of an oval café table with Helena and Davida, their respective spouses. It's like I've already been relegated to attending to the duties of marriage. Helena's terriers yap at a pigeon that alights nearby, and she shushes them with a nibble of piecrust. Will that be me—pretending two small animals are my children until I'm pregnant with my first? Helena doesn't seem happy with her life, and I hate that for her.

I've had a week to mull over my accidental aggressive actions with Boudicca. Two letters to Xander were met with stony silence. I can't believe I overstepped the boundaries of our friendship. Getting tickets sold for the masked solstice ball has filled most of my time and given me an excuse to avoid Elias—well, at least until today. Mother finally cornered all of us with this arranged outing.

I take a sip of my iced lavender lemonade, wishing for all the world there was a drop of spirits in it to make this gathering more bearable. Elias catches my eye over the floral arrangement at the table's center and winks. Gross. I manage a smile before immediately looking away. This will be my future if I don't manage to manifest something better.

I scan the parkway beyond the café. In the distance, the gargoyle tower sits against the lush greenery. I should have asked Boudicca where she lives. My only contact for her is Xander, and all their mail goes to a curiosity shoppe near Les Halles. Maybe I'll catch sight of Boudicca around the city. I could "accidentally" run into her and offer an apology. I'm absolutely mortified I acted the way I did with her.

"Viola, is that all right with you?" Elias eyes me expectantly, like I've been hanging on to his every word with bated breath.

"I'm sorry—I got distracted by the lovely sunset," I simper. I've watched my sisters enough that I've perfected the disgusting affectation.

"Your brothers and I are going to take the carriage for the evening to the local gentleman's club. I'll hail a ride to take you and the wives home."

The wives. Does he even know their names?

"Since my carriage was stolen," Charles says, wailing pitifully for his sweet onion of doom.

I roll my eyes as my thoughts snare on the night I saw the thing jerk its way awkwardly into the sky like a gassy pumpkin. Good riddance to bad rubbish and all. I'm certain I saw dark outspread wings behind it—maybe one of those shade creatures. If so, they must not be completely malevolent.

"Yes, of course." I wave carelessly as I stand. Fortunately, I tucked my climbing slippers into my reticule earlier in the hope of an escape. I'm not spending the night at home with any of these drips. "I can take care of hailing a carriage. Why don't you go off and have fun?"

I don't wait for Elias's response. After gathering the other women, I walk us all around the corner, out of his sight. In minutes, "the wives" are on their way back to the house, and I'm pulling my slippers out to go for a rooftop run. With my parents watching me so closely, it's been days since I've been able to slip away to see my gargoyle, and I'm not going to let this chance pass me by.

THE LIBRARIAN'S GARGOYLE

The fabric of my dress rustles crisply as I pull it between my legs and tuck it into my belt. It's not the best solution, but it will do. Smooth, cool stone chills my heated palms. With a thought, I enable the magical garments and ascend.

Sweat trickles between my shoulder blades as I climb the alley wall toward the clear night sky. Moonlight skims the light-colored rooftops, showing no sign of the shadowy beings that attacked me previously. I've dug through the archive at the Mazarine but haven't found any information on a ghost of that type, not a human one, anyway. I slide down the rooftop close to the tower, preparing to spring into the wind.

What if those things weren't human ghosts at all? I may need to dig into demonic literature. I leap, but the wind doesn't rise to meet me as it has every time before. Panic seizes my chest as I plummet. My hands scramble inches from the stone tower but not close enough to touch it. My dress untucks, billowing around me as I hurtle toward the earth. This is it. I squeeze my eyes shut, still frantically reaching for the stone wall.

A hand closes around mine. The glove immediately attaches, sticking like glue and jarring my shoulder as my body jerks to a halt. Wheezing, I look up.

Carved of creamy-white stone, an upturned hand sits under my palm. It's a gargoyle bending out from one of the many arches, her hands raised as if in supplication. Unlike the others, outstretched feathered wings and branched antlers sprout from her brow. Her doe-like legs end in tiny silver hooves.

Breath rushes out of me, and I swing to catch my one hand on the tower and climb. Thank goodness this statue was so far from the main wall. That fall would have killed me.

I get a foot on the wall and take a moment to tuck in my skirt. Cheating death once a day seems like a good maximum. Within minutes, I'm up over the turret on the roof and in the shade cast by Iggy's gigantic wings. The cool stone of her arm soothes me as I collapse into her embrace.

Is it my imagination, or does her expression look angrier than usual? My gargoyle's deep-set eyes are squinted and slanted in the pale moonlight. Her brow appears furrowed.

"What's wrong, Iggy? I'm sorry I couldn't come for our nightly stories. My parents have watched my every move for weeks, and the library fundraiser has taken up all my spare time."

I stroke her jaw, affectionately running my fingertips over the thick spikes. As silly as it is, touching the statue always soothes me. With one foot on her bent thigh, I haul myself up into her arms. The faded red ribbon I tied around her wrist ages ago flutters in the evening breeze.

"I kissed a friend, and I thought she liked it." I drag a hand through my hair, pulling out the chignon and flinging pins in all directions until it spills in an untidy heap over the gargoyle's brawny biceps. "But she ran."

Unbidden, tears well in my eyes and spill down my cheeks. It's rare for me to find someone I have a true connection with. I hate that I possibly ruined my friendship with Boudicca in a moment of desire.

"I should've kept my hands to myself." I lean into Iggy, pressing my tear-stained cheek against her unmoving chest. "And now I haven't heard from her in a week. I only know how to reach her through her employer, Xander Albright, and I don't even know where he lives. The whole situation is so frustrating."

I sigh as I recline and close my eyes. At least the tickets for the ball are selling well. The novelty of using a library as a ballroom has been the buzz of Paris. Mirabelle has a whole swarm of artists working on the decor, and Chantal knew more people than I ever could have guessed. I assumed she was working at the library for the income, but it appears there are other reasons. Her circle of acquaintances speaks of wealth or, at the very least, high birth in her family.

I turn onto my stomach, letting my body sink into Iggy's stone arms. On the other side of the flat roof is a column with a red door. It's always been locked before, but tonight, it sits ajar. Curiosity gets the best of me, and I slide from Iggy's stone embrace to step lightly across the cobblestone roof.

Who lives here? Maybe they could tell me more about the gargoyles surrounding the tower. As I reach the door and press it inward, a scrambling sounds from the far side. Behind the door? I push it open farther. It's not breaking and entering if the door is open.

"No." The hissed word comes from behind the cylindrical turret.

"Is someone there?" I step around the curved structure, readying myself to leap over the wall and scale down the building if attacked.

A sleek sphynx-like gargoyle crouches on this side as if ready to pounce. I've never seen this one before, but when I've visited Iggy, I've never wandered to the far side of the roof. I run a hand over the gargoyle's powerful flank and curving tufted tail. She's carved of golden stone flecked with mica. A spiral of darker stone marks her left forearm up to her gracefully curved shoulder. Her face is more human than lion, with a close-cropped, spiky haircut and large eyes. She's fierceness incarnate but definitely carved by the same hand as Iggy was.

"Get back." The same hissing voice comes from nearby, along with a rustle over the side of the wall. I peer between the thick crenulations, but there's nothing but some twisting ivy.

Maybe it's the wind. I peer harder into the darkness. "Is someone there?"

A breeze whips behind me, and I turn on my heel. Footsteps skitter on the far side of the tower. The dark spread of fear enters my heart. What if it's those shadow creatures again?

I should go. It's already dark. This is so unfair. The night has been my friend all my life, and now I fear it. Swallowing hard, I rush toward Iggy. My hand slides against hers.

"Sorry, I'm not staying tonight. I'll try to visit again tomorrow."

17

BOUDICCA

"Dammit. What were you two thinking? You scared the life out of her." I growl in frustration.

Baraq rolls his eyes while Ariella files her already sharp nails. "Our job," they state in unison. "She was going to enter the tower."

I frown. Viola shouldn't have been able to see the door. Only those attuned to the tower can detect it. Why it was even open is beyond me. The night of the attack, Xander's magic was so dangerously low that they are still recovering. They've been in their chamber all week, and for the first time in my life, the winds around the tower have been nearly nonexistent. The tower's magical defenses must be lowered as well.

"Watch the roof," I say as I head toward the stairs to the workshop.

"Xander commanded us to guard the tower until they emerged." Ariella lashes her tail.

"Viola thinks I was offended by her touch, but the problem was Xander's irresistible summons. I can't tell her that, so I'm going to reassure her that I still want her."

Baraq raises one tufted eyebrow. "Want her?"

Ariella makes kissing noises and starts doing some ridiculous singsong. These two will be the death of my patience.

"Want her as a friend." I shove the door and turn my back on the snickering twins. Honestly, their immaturity is intolerable sometimes. I'm the youngest. I should be up to that type of antic, not them.

The citrine ring gleams on the cluttered worktable along with yet another suit. I grab both then turn to face a wall of books. Viola is a librarian obsessed with knowledge. What makes a better apology than a book? Scanning the built-in shelves, I find one that specifically includes information on the shades.

There. I can tell Xander I gave it to Viola to better protect her. Surely, they'll understand.

Book in hand, I grab a satchel, shove everything into it, and stride toward the balcony. It's only after I leap from it that I realize Xander's direct command should have magically prevented me from leaving the tower.

"I'M SORRY. Who are you again?" A snooty man in a pressed black suit glares at me. He's a solid head shorter, but somehow, he manages to stare haughtily down his hooked nose.

I inhale deeply. "Boudicca. Here to see Mademoiselle Viola Archambeau on behalf of Monsieur Albright."

Deep hooded eyes study me with curious apprehension. "It's late."

"It's not."

The man straightens his shoulders with a huff. "You may wait in the study."

I bend, giving the man the slightest of bows. I'd rather she come to the door so I can whisk her off on an adventure, but this is better than nothing. "Thank you."

As he leads me through the foyer to the high-arched hall, I'm taken aback by the display of extreme wealth. From perfectly appointed decorations to vases of fresh flowers, everything screams affluence. Viola's family could have taken care of the library's financial woes if they cared about her passions at all. The thought weighs me down as I follow the rude butler. My feet sink into a deep-blue carpet with what must be their family crest woven into it.

He slides a door open. "You may wait here."

A study full of padded leather chairs and card tables sits before a large hearth. Floor-to-ceiling windows stand open to the evening air, but no breeze comes in to help with the stuffiness. I sit on the long couch, absently bending forward to adjust for wings that aren't currently present. Time ticks by, counted off by the tight itch along my skin.

This human form is too small—like cramming twenty pounds of flour into a five-pound sack. I long to lash my tail in agitation and stretch my wings, but both are bound by the ring's magic. Instead, I fidget with the book I selected for Viola, titled *Guardians and Demons: A Guide to Otherworldly Creatures*.

Among its many entries, this book describes shades... and gargoyles. It may be smudging the line, but I want so badly for Viola to know. Giving her a magical book is toeing the boundaries of what's allowed by the council, but she has access to the bōc-hord. In time, she would have discovered this information herself.

"Boudicca?" Viola appears from a side room to the left. A lavender floral dressing gown that highlights her pretty eyes wraps her petite frame.

I let out a sigh, hoping my longing isn't so apparent. "Hello. I'm so sorry I had to leave so abruptly the last time we were together. Does a book make a good apology?"

Viola's lips purse, but a smile wins. "There's no apology needed. However, a new book is always welcome." She steps closer, her brow furrowing. "I was worried I was too forward."

"I enjoyed our kiss." *Gah*. Could I have found a less awkward way to say that? I stand to meet her while my hands still nervously fidget with the book.

Her whole face lights up, and a devilish grin dances over her lips. "Did you?"

I thrust the book at her, hoping to thwart her from making any other embarrassing statements. Viola takes it and turns it over in her hands as she steps even closer. Damp tendrils of hair curl around her face as if she just washed. She can't possibly have been home long.

"Would you like to take a stroll along the river?" I want to put my hand on her waist, to draw her closer. Viola's lemon verbena scent fills my senses until I'm nearly mad with it. Our time together was never like this in all her visits to the tower. I was always stone, aware but unable to smell or breathe. All I want to do now is hold her close and bury my nose in her unbound burnished-gold hair.

A flash of fear crosses her face. "I was getting ready for bed."

I can't help sliding my hand along her cheek. "You've always loved the night."

Her eyes narrow. "I don't recall telling you that. Besides, the riverwalk isn't safe. I got attacked along there recently."

The damned shades. Viola didn't spend the night at the tower, because she's scared now. She's too strong a spirit to go through life like that.

"No harm will ever come to you while I'm by your side."

She bites her lower lip then nods. That wild sparkle in her eyes sends me soaring. "Give me a moment to change clothes?"

"Of course."

What if I came clean tonight—told her I was Iggy, the gargoyle she'd always felt safe with, and I could fly her through the starry sky and show her that every impossible magical thing she'd always dreamed of was real?

Viola leaves with a flutter of her robe and the scuff of house slippers. Impatiently, I pace. If I tell her, the council will come down on my head, and every damn magical creature in the city, from bloodsuckers to brownies, will notice her existence. What would the council do to me? To Xander? What if it affected the very existence of my brothers and sisters? Xander has the largest gargoyle collection in the city—possibly in the world. Would the council feel threatened if they thought Xander didn't have us all under absolute control?

Slumping into a nearby chair, I realize I can't risk that. Worse, Viola might condemn me as a liar for deceiving her into thinking I was human. Would she forsake me?

The lights of Paris twinkle through the large nearby window. This is all too complicated. What I can do is take Viola for a walk by the riverside and show her the night is still safe for her, at least when she's with me.

"I'm ready!" Viola announces with a breathless pant as she races back into the room. She wears the simple gray skirt usually reserved for her librarian work, with a snug vest over it. "I thought maybe we could walk by that little café near the Seine that does boozy desserts, pick up two to go, then head to the library to finish the planning."

"Perfect." I hold my hand out to her. It looks strange and small. The skin is soft over tendon and muscle, and no sharp spikes grace the back.

My mind flicks back to Durant asking how I'll protect her as a human, and my confidence wavers. Viola's hand slides against mine, the heat of her palm glides against my skin, and I relish the lightness of her touch, the tender way her thumb strokes my wrist. Her eyes light with a warmth I want to drown in, and I know I'll do anything to be by her side as long as she lives.

18

BOUDICCA

The door creaks, and light spills from the street lamps into the silent library. The scent of old paper and vanilla fills me as the grandfather clock in the reading area chimes. Wisps of sparkling magic fill the area, some of it earthy and green, the ghosts of long-dead trees.

"Let's head to the antiquities room. The lights won't be visible from the street," Viola says in a hushed tone. She ducks into a side room and returns with a lantern that casts a puddle of golden light on the parquet floor.

I grunt while balancing a box of sweets and two ceramic cups of dark espresso then pull the door closed behind me. The soft clink of cups is the only noise as we creep back through the stacks to the employee rooms beyond. Once again, the way Viola moves reminds me of a cat, with admirable silent grace.

Past the employee lounge and Viola's favorite side room study is an unremarkable black door leading into the antiquities area. Organized in a way that has Viola's touch all over it, the front room is immaculate. She talked to me about working in this area before, when I was stone. It's accessible to staff and to scholars with a permit, not the general public. Those "scholars" are likely magic users, and I wonder how many of that Mazarine staff are as well.

Once I learned from Xander that this is the bōc-hord, I looked up information on it in their personal library. Dangerous for an ungifted human to wander into, the dimensional space is a rabbit warren of small rooms and confusing hallways. The bōc-hord is accessible not only from this library but also from book collections around this world and others. The chance Viola could pass through a door and end up in another world is very real, and she doesn't even know it. Surely, that alone is a reason to tell her about the magical world. How could she not be a part of it if she is able to freely wander in and out?

"Boudicca, did you hear me? There's a table right here we can sit at." Viola flicks on some lights that appear to be electric.

In here? Would someone have brought modern science into a magical world? I squint, shifting my vision, only to realize the lights are magic globes like Xander uses in their study. Maybe Viola sees them as electric.

"Are you all right?" She takes the cups from me and sets them on the nearby table.

I nod. This is it—proof she's magic. Viola has to be to turn on the lights, doesn't she? "I'm fine. Do you come into this area of the library a lot?"

"No, not really. I just finished organizing the front room last month. I took a brief walk through it, but to be honest, I couldn't comprehend the lack of organization, and some of the titles are in unrecognizable languages—and I'm pretty good with languages." Her forehead wrinkles. "Anyway, it was all a bit overwhelming. The front room took me almost two years to organize and catalogue. Just as I started this room, my family dropped the engagement bomb on me."

"Engagement bomb?"

Viola looks horrified. "I'm *not* engaged, no matter what the Paris rumor mill says. It's still in negotiations."

I study her, saying nothing. It seems incredibly unfair that someone else decides her life for her—although my entire existence has been like that, and it didn't bother me until recently.

She's human with a soul. Why should she be compelled to follow the demands of another? What hold could they possibly have over her?

I push the cup of espresso toward her. She takes a sip then opens the box containing some small bites of chocolate and a creamy tiered slice of rum cake. As a gargoyle, I never needed to eat. In this human guise, I'm finding I enjoy all the foods I once only read about in Xander's library. I sip the still-warm beverage, and the smooth, slightly bitter chocolatey flavor coats my tongue.

Viola pushes the cake around with a wooden fork. "The only way I can see out of it, though, is proving my value to this library so I can keep my position and then maybe finding a flat to rent. I don't know. It all seems so impossible when the default in society is to marry a man and have children. How did you find employment with Xander?"

I choke on my drink. I can't tell her the mage carved me from stone and breathed life into me with magic. But I don't want to lie and layer more deceit between us.

I fidget, once again missing the comfort of a good tail lash against the floor. "I guess you can say I was born into it."

"Oh, your family is in servitude? I'm sorry. I didn't realize. Is the debt close to being paid off?" She nibbles at the edge of the square of dark chocolate.

"Goodness no, nothing like that. Xander is an excellent employer who's always trying to expand my world and mind. I've known them since I was young—that was all I meant to say." I stumble over the phrasing. "Anyway, what say does your family have over who you spend your life with? You seem like a free spirit." *Free soul. You have a soul. How could you possibly be controlled?*

"Money. I swear, the whole world comes down to currency—those who have it and those who don't. My family is wealthy. While I obey them, so am I. I'm sure you know how difficult it is for a woman to find reputable work."

I don't, but I nod.

"Well, I thought the library work would be enough to support me, that I could save up until I could live on my own and not have to worry about the confines of what society expects, but it seems that won't be possible. My job here is over at the end of the month, with only the slimmest chance I'll be retained if I pull off this event." She pops the chocolate into her mouth then eyes the other half of the cake before pushing it toward me.

I pick up the fork that touched her lips then scoop a piece of the cake up to savor the buttery sweetness of the frosting. "And if you do make enough at this event?"

She shrugs. "Elias said if we're incompatible he'll release me from the agreement my father made with him. I'm going to have to figure out how to make it on my own. My savings will last about a year if I live frugally. I wish I had some saleable vocation."

"You do. Knowledge." How could she possibly not think she has skills?

"As a woman, it's nearly impossible to entice a scholar to hire me as a research assistant, and unless I use a male pseudonym, any titled scholar will consider research I publish invalid. It's a ridiculously frustrating situation."

I puzzle over the gender inequality that she describes. It doesn't exist in the magical world. This is another reason I need to prove Viola is steeped in magic: so she can exist within my world and be taken seriously. She's brilliant and deserves nothing less.

"We'll just have to ensure the event is a success." I smile and sip my espresso.

"Chantal dropped off the art yesterday." Viola gestures to

a pile of golden wooden cutouts leaning against the wall. "She even made a kissing booth. Will you take a turn in it?"

I laugh. "No."

She smirks. "Not even for charity?"

"There's only one person I ever want to kiss." I stare meaningfully at Viola, attempting to make my intent absolutely clear.

She brushes invisible crumbs from her lips, looking away. A flush creeps up her neck to pinken her ears. "Would you like to see some of the other rooms back here? They aren't open to the general public."

"Sure." Rising, I hold my hand out to her.

For a beat too long, she stares at my palm, and I think I've gone too far. My fingers flex, willing her to place her hand in mine—to give me the chance, if only for this moment, to feel the softness of her palm against me without my stone skin interfering. I look down at my alien hand covered in lined human skin, dark brown instead of the deep obsidian I'm accustomed to. It's mine but not. This isn't me, and the lie burns my tongue. Does she sense it?

Finally, Viola slides her hand into mine, and my breath is released in a relieved whoosh.

She tugs me toward her, her thumb stroking my knuckles. "You have nice hands. Almost too perfect, like an artist carved you from marble. No scars or lines, each nail even and perfectly trimmed. Mine are always such a mess. You'll have to tell me your secret."

I lean in close, breathing in her sweet scent like a balm to my senses. "Maybe someday I will."

She gives me a curious little smile then bumps her shoulder against my arm. "Over here is a hall attached to small rooms."

She leads me out of the entry room, and magic shivers over my skin. The air glows with it—tiny sparkling motes of every type of elemental magic drift around us like a living rainbow. The floor here is beige tile flecked with gold. Books pile in corners and lean against cases like lost orphans clambering for a true space in this world.

I peer into the first doorless arch to see a room crammed floor to ceiling with scroll bins. The waxed emblem of Alexandria marks many of the papers on the nearest rack. Has Viola noticed the rarity of these documents? The next room we pass has globes strung from the ceiling that could be celestial representations. Maps spill over the table, their curled corners weighted by decorative leather bags of sand.

As we move down the hall, each room appears to have some theme. The hall twists, mazelike, and I try to recall which way we went so that we don't get lost. Although being lost with Viola in a magical world would be the perfect excuse to tell her...

Viola stumbles to a halt. "Oh, I haven't seen this before."

A pile of rough stone covers one wall, with a waterfall that streams musically into a clear tile pool. Petite lily pads with delicate pink blooms float on the water's surface. As we move closer, orange flashes of koi sparkle in the depths of the pool.

"A fountain in a library?"

"It's absurd." Viola wrinkles her nose. "The humidity will turn these books into a mold buffet."

I pull a book from a nearby shelf and flip through its crisp illustrated pages. "The books seem to be unaffected." The glimmer of protective magic dusts my fingers. I wait for her logical mind to process the clues—to rectify the illogical with the conclusion of heavy magic use. But instead, Viola sighs.

"The damn French rulers of old were so impractical. I bet library fountains were all the rage at some point. I suppose I should be happy I haven't found any forgotten caged animals withered away to bone dust."

I smother a groan then swallow hard. *C'mon, Viola. Put it*

together. Could a dangerous creature from another dimension wander in here? Probably not. This place should be linked to various libraries, and who keeps a live animal in a library?

Images of Xander's menagerie flash through my thoughts. Tiny obsidian dogs and thorny toads. Salamanders with six legs and snakes thicker than my thigh. They carved so many animals, and all of them have wandered the tower library at one point or another. There's nothing to say someone else's pet couldn't end up here.

A curved stone bench with fluffy pink cushions sits along the fountain's edge. I tug her toward it and sit down. To my surprise, Viola curls herself into my lap. I almost purr at how sensuously intimate our bodies feel together. Before, I was unyielding, unfeeling stone. I never knew we would fit together like this. Her body eases into mine like I'm the safest of harbors. Viola's hips settle deliciously against the tops of my thighs.

My hand naturally moves to cup her side and strokes the ripple of her ribs. Viola's hand caresses my jaw as it has a million times before, but now, I feel it. I feel everything, and a soaring sensation tightens my throat.

Before I can voice anything, her lips hesitate against mine, fluttering like the lightest of feathers. I pull her to me, deepening the kiss. Viola's shoulders relax, and the comforting weight of her body nestles into the curve of my arm. Accepted. I want her to know I want this. I desire her more than anything in my centuries of existence.

I slide my fingers through her long, silken hair, luxuriating in the texture. I never imagined I'd be so blessed as to touch Viola like this and that she'd allow it—that she'd want me this way. She moans a little and twists on my lap, squirming closer.

Pressing her body to mine, she nips along my ear, sending delightful shivers of pleasure through me. I never knew it could be like this, never dared to dream. I pull back to look into eyes like drowning pools of indigo. Viola smiles up at me then toys with the coils of dark hair that spill over my shoulders.

"Too fast?" she asks in a husky whisper.

I tremble. "No. You're perfect."

Our lips meet again, heated and hungry. Her tongue laps along my skin, and all reasonable thought scatters from my mind. My hand skims her thigh, feeling her muscles flex beneath the thin fabric. I need something: this. Overwhelming urges pound through me, muddying all coherent thought with the driving need to consume her, and my lack of experience cripples my desire.

I press my forehead to hers. "I don't know how to do this."

The whispered words hang in the air between us for an eternity of seconds. Her murmured response nearly sends me to my knees.

"Would you like me to show you?"

19

Viola

As the words leave my lips, I want to haul them back. *Slow down, dammit. You already rushed her once.* My parents are forcing me into an engagement. It's utterly unfair of me to seduce a woman and leave her—like Anne did to me. My heart hammers, and the press of Boudicca's body feels so good against mine that I'm swept away. She kisses me again, and I let myself drown in the heat and the slow slide of her skin against mine.

Boudicca removes my spectacles with a tenderness that swells my heart. Her other hand slides along the edge of my skirt, lifting it to graze my thigh with her fingers. I tremble against the touch, wanting more but still afraid to ask that of her. Would she be furious with me later and ghost me? Boudicca squeezes my thigh in her strong hands, and I can't help but moan against her lips. Everything about her is familiar and compelling. I've never fallen so hard for a woman this inexplicably fast. It's just so easy with her.

"Show me," she whispers.

Boudicca's voice is so quiet and hesitant I'm uncertain if it's a question or a request. That thought shakes me out of my lustful state. The whole moment seems surreal. Behind us, water burbles down the rock wall to splash gently into the pool. Where is the water even coming from? How are fish surviving here, and why hasn't the humidity destroyed these books?

Focus. I'm in a gorgeous woman's arms, and the desire is so thick I can't breathe.

A frog croaks out its amphibian love song, snapping me out of my confused haze. This has to be a dream. It has the same uncanny feeling as when I look for my grandmother's study only to end up facing a blank wall. A frog in a library? This can't be real.

"Viola? I need to tell you something." Boudicca gently grasps my chin, turning my face to hers. The low light gleams from electric orbs around the room to caress her sharp cheekbones and high forehead.

Something about the lights seems off, but I can't quite place it. The color maybe? The lights in this part of the library are always a soft violet as opposed to the yellow glow in the main room. Boudicca squeezes my thigh again, dragging my attention back to her. Dust motes float through the air, turning to sparkling rainbows in the dim lights. The feel of this room is familiar but not. My head spins, and lights flash along the edges of my vision. Something isn't right, but my mind grows hazy every time I focus on the details that bother me.

"I'm sorry." A nervous laugh squeezes out as I slide from her lap to sit beside her. Unable to look her in the eye, I fidget with my emerald ring. "I got caught up in the moment, and now I feel a little strange. We should go back. It's late."

Disappointment flares across Boudicca's face, but she covers it with a quick smile as she stands and offers her hand. "Of course. I'll escort you home."

I STARE at the blank wall in my home, the one I always come back to when I think I've found my grandmother's study. That feel in the library was the same—ethereal, not quite of this world. It had an otherness about it that I need to get to the bottom of.

Placing one hand on the wall, I close my eyes. Maybe I've been going about this all wrong, trying to start from the beginning of where my grandmother led me. What if I start from the end? I focus, remembering the white room with the cloth-draped furniture and the way the raised decorations on the wall felt under my hand. I slide my hand along the wall, and the coils almost seem to grow under my touch.

Excited, I press on. This has to be correct. I'm certain my grandmother not only was aware of the existence of magic but was an active practitioner. The molding with the latch to the door was the tail of a winged creature. If I find that, I find the way down. The curl is under my hand. I open my eyes.

To face a blank wall.

A shriek of frustration echoes down the hall as I crumple to the carpet. I didn't ruin an evening with Boudicca just to fail here. The library had the same feel as my grandmother's study. If I can just hold onto that feeling long enough, I'm certain I can get there.

Pulling myself up from the floor, I glare at the smooth walls then pace. There has to be some part missing in this. The study has to be magic, just like that waterfall pool in the library was obviously magic. My feet still on the plush hallway runner.

The room in the antiquities area is magic. How did I not realize that immediately? There's no way a room like that could exist without careful tending, and none of the staff have ever complained about cleaning the pool or feeding the fish.

Unravel this from the end. I rarely see anyone in that area of the library. Not even Master Frederick passes beyond the main room. Maybe it's like my grandmother's study, and he's unable to enter the room in the antiquities area. If the magic works the same, what's keeping me from finding the study in this house if I can pass through the room at the library? What vital information am I missing?

I run my hand along the wall again. Then I close my eyes and feel the texture change. It's an illusion. It has to be.

"Viola? Well, this is a pleasant surprise to see you up so late. Did you miss me?"

Startled, I turn. Elias stands in the doorway, his collar undone around his throat and a cravat hanging limply against his suit coat. His eyes are unfocused and sleepy looking as if he's drunk. Why on earth would I miss him?

I fold my arms. "No. I couldn't sleep. Sometimes I walk the halls."

"Looks more like you're staring at the wall." He strides forward, listing slightly to the left. His fingers drag over the wall, but they trace the air in places, like he, too, can feel the curls of molding. Does he sense the magic cloaking this place?

I touch the wall again, but it's flat. "Does this wall seem at all odd to you?"

A creepy smile slides over his face, like he knows something I don't. "Odd? What do you think is odd about it?"

"Say nothing," a voice hisses into my ear, startling me.

"Is something wrong?" Elias leans closer, and the whiskey on his breath washes over me.

"Nothing. I should get to bed. Goodnight, Elias." Not waiting for a response, I flee down the hall toward my room.

That voice. I heard it before as a child. I'm certain it was my grandmother's, but that can't be possible, can it? I twist the emerald band around my finger, wishing she could be here to advise me—or that any reasonable, mature adult could offer a modicum of help.

Reaching my room, I spy the book Boudicca offered me, tossed carelessly onto the bed. The gold-foil typography on the cover gleams in the room's low light. *Guardians and Demons:*

A Guide To Otherworldly Creatures. Where would she have found this?

I open the book and puzzle over the odd script on the bookplate within, which should have an owner's name or a library stamp of some sort. Instead, there are three wavy lines and some writing that might be old Greek. I flip open the book to a random page.

On it is a cartoonish black dragon-like creature with a small body and large head that seems to be mostly made of teeth—an impossible number of teeth. I scan the facing page.

The Sera is a singular being considered a demonic symbiotic parasite that can reside in multiple hosts simultaneously. However, it protects its host with unmatched ferocity and is considered a blessing by certain hereditary lines.

A shiver runs down my spine. How could possession be considered a blessing? I flip through several more pages describing creatures of folklore in such a way that they seem real, until a dark, scratchy illustration falls under my hand. Shadows with claws and teeth. I run a finger along the drawing, remembering the attack along the Seine and the way the creature grabbed at my neck and tore open my blouse. Terror wells up in my throat at the clarity of the memory, and I choke it down as I read the passage.

A shade is a summoned creature from the nether realm that remains completely under the control of the summoner for the duration of the spell. They need shadows to survive and are frequently used in nighttime warfare.

Magic is real, and it's far more dangerous than I ever imagined. This book seems to be an alphabetical catalogue. I rifle through the pages toward the beginning, admiring the illustrations, until a heading catches my attention.

Gargoyles. The illustration is of Le Stryge, a famous gargoyle perched on the Notre-Dame Cathedral. Maybe this book is a collection of folklore. Heart in my throat, I read the passage.

Gargoyles—elemental stone guardians. These beings are created by skilled mages and brought to life for the purpose of guarding either a place or a person. They are nearly indestructible and can survive long past their original creator's lifespan, often permanently returning to a statue-like form if they lack a purpose. Gargoyles are only active at night, preferring their stone form during the day.

Is Iggy alive or one of the gargoyles who reverted to stone? What about the others on that tower? There are so many.

It's possible that the mage who created them lives there. *A mage.* My heart races. I have to know. I glance at the wall clock. It's well after two in the morning, but I can't sleep without knowing if this is real.

In minutes, I'm changed and have my climbing shoes on. I'll start at the bottom of the tower this time in case the wind is strange again. A thrill zings through my soul. This could be the window into the magic world I've been seeking all my life.

20

BOUDICCA

*I*t's close to three bells when the familiar grunt and patter of Viola scaling the walls echoes nearby. My ear flicks against my mane as I pull myself from slumber. Baraq stretches his lionlike body at my feet. His twin sister, Ariella, curls next to him, her golden stone gleaming against his darkness. In an instant, they wake and launch into the sky so Viola won't see them.

"Iggy, I need to know something," she whispers as she hauls herself up into my arms.

I'm surprised to see her this late at night after our trip to the Mazarine. A soft breeze blows past my cheek as she makes herself comfortable. Her bottom presses against the curve of my wrist, and her legs drape over my forearm.

The wind teases her long loose hair. It tickles under my chin then caresses my stone breasts. If only we could be skin to skin. I'd sigh if I could, but I remain still, made of the obsidian of which Xander first carved me. Quiet settles between us like a weary beast too tired to prowl. Her cheek rests against my shoulder, and every warm breath whispers over my mane.

"Are you real?" She grips the short, thick spikes on my jaw and stares into my eyes with an earnest, longing expression.

I ache. I can't move—can't tell her. It was risky enough giving her Xander's book. Unblinking, I stare as her frown of impatience grows.

"I've told you every story I've ever heard, all the secrets of my life. You know what I seek. If you're alive, speak to me now." Her demanding tone echoes over the cobblestones.

I pray Xander will hear her and come up to see what this ruckus is. They were up and out of their chambers for the first time since the attack. Xander still looked terrible, but at least they were able to make some tea.

"I know!" Viola leaps from me and runs across the cobblestones toward the door.

Sheer panic hits me at the thought that she'll enter the tower, then I recall that Cass locked the door earlier. Viola doesn't bother with the door, though. She runs around the squat tower to the far side. I resist twisting in place to watch her.

"Ha!" she cries from out of view and then comes charging back toward me, springing through the air at the last moment and leaping into my arms. She grasps the thick curl of my lower horns and presses her forehead to mine. "You can't keep this from me! The sphynx statue isn't there. She's too huge to move, so you all must be real. Tell me! Say something! Say anything!" She pounds one fist against my stone chest then whimpers. "Please."

I want to. I want to hold her in my arms and tell her I'm alive. Would she be amazed? Terrified? I'm not sure. People often ask for what they think they want only to refuse it later. And if the council hears that I gave a book of magic to an ungifted human... that will get sticky. I need proof she's of my world, and I have none.

Defeated, Viola slumps into my arms, staring up into the starry sky. "I guess I'll do what I've always done to make myself feel better and less alone. I'll tell you a story."

After minutes—or hours or maybe days—Viola's chest rises, and the magic of her tale begins its soulful dance through my mind.

"Once upon a time, there was a little girl who lived in a

beautiful palace. She had everything a little girl could want except companionship. You see, her mother and father were very important people, always busy, busy, busy, and she was their seventh child..."

Gleaming white walls arched high above the little blonde girl. Material things were insignificant when there was no one to share them with. But one day, when she was wandering through a closed wing of the palace, her grandmother arrived to visit.

The woman looked just like her portrait in the great hall. Her snowy hair was braided simply in a thick tail, and her silvery gown with long, flowing sleeves rippled in some unfelt breeze. "I have a gift for you. Come see."

Viola thought her grandmother looked like a radiant fairy queen. She'd never met her before but had no reason not to follow her as the woman gestured temptingly, leading her through a series of bright-white rooms. Billowing sheer cloth was draped over all the furniture. Lumpy shapes covered the floor, and shining dust motes danced in the air. Even the scent was different from everywhere else in the manor, the whisper of dreams mingling with the heady fragrance of spring hyacinths. Never mind that snow had graced the gardens for months.

Down a long, unfamiliar hall, they walked until her grandmother paused. "Touch the wall right here, where this golden gargoyle spits flame."

Viola looked up at her grandmother, who was ever so much taller than she was and, in her squeaky little girl voice, said, "I'm too small and can't reach it."

Her grandmother smiled and pointed to a chair-shaped sheet. With great effort, Viola swept the sheet to the side then dragged the heavy chair to the wall, leaving scuffs in the polished wood floor. Carefully, she grasped the arms of the chair, hauling herself up into it before leaning against the back to touch the carved relief on the wall.

"That's it. Now twist," the old woman said, and a panel of the wall slid open. Not much, just a crack, a sliver of shadow against all the white.

"It's so dark," the little girl whispered as she climbed off the chair to peer through the secret door.

Her grandmother chuckled quietly. "I'll be your light, sweet girl."

With diligent caution, Viola followed her silvery grandmother down a steep, spiraling passage. The elderly woman shone in the dark like she was lit from within. Soon, they came to a small room laden with books and tables and scrolls. All sorts of cabinets with tiny drawers lined the walls, and herbs hung from the low ceiling. It smelled of dust and a sweet, peppery spice. Viola sneezed violently.

Her grandmother sighed. "I'm sorry it's been so long. I had to wait until you were old enough. Open this cabinet right here."

Standing on her very tippy toes, Viola tugged the door open. She fell backward as it swung toward her. The wood was heavy and dark, but inside the cabinet, many colorful boxes sat on shelves.

"Take this box here." A wizened finger pointed to a pale wooden box carved with spiraling winged creatures.

Viola reached up again, not quite so high this time, and pulled the box toward her. The box was neither big nor small, and when she opened it, Viola saw, nestled in velvet, a pair of gossamer gloves with crimson ribbons tucked into a transparent pair of slippers that shimmered like threads of spider silk. A large gray pendant on a fine golden chain sat between the shoes.

"They're so beautiful. Are these for me?" Viola blinked up at her.

Her grandmother's eyes were the exact same shade of blue-violet as her own, but smile lines creased them, granting her the wise look of the aged. "They are indeed. They belonged to me when I was a girl, and now I want you to have them."

"Thank you," Viola squeaked, clutching the box to her narrow chest.

"There's one more thing." Her grandmother glided forward so gracefully it seemed her feet didn't touch the floor.

The light followed her, casting long shadows in the room. Viola's eyes skated over the shelved books, but it was difficult to read fat books with lots of tiny words, and she doubted these were the type with interesting pictures.

"Pull open this drawer, and take the green ring," her grandmother said, tapping her fingernail soundlessly on a desk covered in parchment and scrolls.

Viola strained to tug the drawer open. It took a few tries as the desk was stiff with age. Inside was an assortment of quills and nibs. Vials of different-colored inks and little boxes lined one side. A ribbon-tied notebook was to the left, and on top of it sat a thin gold band with a small emerald.

"We're special, you and I. Both of us are the seventh child. Until you're older, I want you to wear that ring." Her grandmother hovered closer, and the ring sparkled gloriously in her silvery light.

"Why?" Viola picked the ring up. It was adult sized and much too large for her tiny hand. She slid it onto her finger anyway, and to her delight, it shrank until it was a perfect fit.

Her grandmother chuckled. "You'll know when it's time to remove it."

Viola twists in my lap to look up at me, her lovely eyes magnified by her lenses. She traces my forehead and brow, then light fingers skate down my cheek. "I told my older brother that story once. Not what I found, of course, but that I spoke to our grandmother." Viola's face screws up as she rubs the emerald ring on her finger. "He said it was impossible and that it must have been a dream because she died the year I was born. He also said there were no rooms like that in our home. I never found that room again."

She spins the ring thoughtfully. "I've tried to find that room so many times over the years. Earlier this week, I was reading this book all about imbuing things with magic. I came upon one entry detailing how to make a ring that blocks magic from being detected by creatures made of magic. And I wondered if my grandmother's ghost was somehow trying to protect me. But those shadow things attacked me, so it seems magic found me anyway."

Viola sits a little taller so that we're face-to-face. "I can find my way to my grandmother's world if I try a little harder."

Blue-violet eyes sparkle in the starlight, and my heart lurches. I want to hug her—to go soft so she can feel my warmth and how important she is to me. Her knuckles brush the sharp edge of my cheek before trailing along the thick coils of my mane.

"Everything is moving so fast. The ball is in just a few days, and I've barely slept—I'm so busy organizing it. My parents plan to throw a party next week announcing my engagement to Elias." She blows out a breathy sigh. "He didn't even court me—not that I've ever been attracted to men. I've never even kissed one. I'm going to have to conform just like Anne did."

Viola stares out over the light-lined streets of Paris with a wistful sigh. "There's this woman. I just met her, but she feels like home. I wish I could kiss her right now, just like this."

Oh-so tenderly, Viola touches her lips to mine. Her kiss is

full of passionate fire. I want to roar forward and embrace her —kiss her with all the ardor I feel for my tale spinner and tell her I'll always protect her.

She withdraws and slides from my arms. "I'll likely never get the chance to explore what I feel for her, though. It's too late for me."

Everything in me aches to move, to breathe, to show her I'm alive—not stone.

"Grandmother said I'd know when it was time to take the ring off. I'm ready now." Viola slides her ring off and places it on the tip of my index finger then turns and walks away.

Viola glows silvery like the moon, like the brightest star. I can see it now—the magic in her runs deep and wild. The ring must have muffled it, but now it sings to me, roaring like a symphony in my ears. Threads of magic spin around her, blindingly bright. As I break away from my resting form, she leaps from the roof.

21

VIOLA

Tears blind me as I race from building to building in the cool night air. Sparkling mist drifts through the city, making the illusion of bright lines stream from the lamps below. The taste of stone still lingers on my lips. How ridiculous am I? Did I expect her to somehow come to life with a kiss, like in one of my tales? Even if magic is real, there's no reason to think a statue would be. That book is likely just folklore.

There was no change when I removed the ring. Nothing about me feels or looks any different from how it did moments before. I hit the side of a building and scamper upward two stories before leaping toward the next one. I'll go back tomorrow and get my ring off Iggy's finger. It's not like she'll be going anywhere.

I drop to my rump, slide off a steep roof, and am preparing to land on the next building when a shimmer of purple nearby catches my attention. It surrounds part of a nearby parkway, looking for all the world like a portal. I leap toward it, intending to take a closer look, but a shadow hits me as I zing through the air, knocking me sideways. I spin in place, gripping a nearby flagpole with one hand, then plant a foot on a wall. *What on earth?*

Another shadow is on me, teeth and claws and fangs and darkness. Dammit, shades. How could I be so distracted as to forget these creatures still stalk the night? I've traveled the rooftops of this city in safety for years, and it's made me careless. The creature's strange chittering is like nails on a chalkboard. Twisting away from it, I drop, allowing myself to fall a story before enabling the slippers and gloves to adhere to the wall. I don't know how to fight these things, and I sure don't want to hang around. My slippers stick and release as I bound from one building to the next, losing height with each leap.

A glance over my shoulder shows the shadows gathering. Inky and dark, they leach out of the surrounding buildings. Terror swells in my chest. Without help, I'll never outrun them. I sprint up the side of a building, trying to lose them, then twist and leap again. Claws pluck at my clothing, and teeth snap near my cheek. I'm not going to have to worry about marrying some stranger, because my body will be found shredded in the alley. I charge up another wall and jump then climb higher, trying to get back to the rooftops.

The harsh chattering gets louder. Claws swipe my arm, tearing my sleeve. Screaming, I tumble. Wind rushes past me, and I stretch out my limbs, desperately trying to grip something, anything. I'm going to be a smear on the cobblestones. Involuntarily, my eyes squeeze shut as my painful end comes closer.

Then I'm weightlessly moving upward faster than any breeze has ever buoyed me. Something hot holds me close, and I open one eye. Black, shining obsidian rests against my cheek, and wild waves of coiled, silky hair whip against my face. No, not hair—a mane. The beating of wings fills the night as we shoot at an impossible speed toward the stars.

"Hold on tight—I've got you," a husky contralto voice says.

It's... it's Iggy. My gargoyle.

My head goes light, and all the air rushes from my lungs. We're flying. *She's real*.

Shoving her mane to the side, I look over her shoulder at

the pinprick lights of Paris. I can't see if those shades are following us. I can't see much at all at the speed we're traveling. The wind burns my eyes.

I place my lips next to her pointed ear. Iggy trembles. "Can they follow us this high?"

"Not likely. But I'm going to take you a little higher just to make sure," she rumbles.

Mist clings to us as she wings through the clouds and then levels out, soaring over the city. Her powerful arms wrap around me, cradling me in her strength, and I take that moment to stroke her shoulder with my fingers. It doesn't feel like skin—it's too smooth—but she's warmer and softer than I expected.

I look up into bright-blue eyes streaked with gray. "You're alive."

Iggy chuckles. "I am."

I quickly shake off the dizzy feeling threatening to overwhelm me. "Why do those things keep attacking me? What do they want?"

"Shades," she growls. "I'm uncertain why they focused on you."

The deep bass of her words reverberates against me, sending a crazy thrill through my body. I gulp down some air, still reeling at the idea that Iggy is a living, breathing being. Some super-inappropriate thoughts are happening as I feel her breasts—which are no longer stone—pushing against my shoulder. Covertly, I glance at her cleavage and hear her low chuckle. Ugh, I'm such a creep.

To cover my embarrassment, I blurt, "You saved me."

"Most likely."

"Are you a gargoyle?"

At that, she side-eyes me and shifts her grip so we can see each other better. "Did you hit your head?"

"No." I peer at her.

Sensual lips curl in a smile over sharp white fangs—she's teasing me. A giggle wells up as I slide my arms up around her thick neck, burying them in her curly mane. Iggy's hair is so much softer than I ever thought it would be. A contented purr moves through her chest as she beats her wings then glides. Moonlight gleams off her barely covered torso, highlighting every ripple of muscle along with the firm curve of her large breasts. In the wind, the silky fabric of her dress snaps tight over her nipples. Faintness steals over me.

"Where would you like me to take you, Viola?" Her broad nostrils flare as she inhales on the next wingbeat.

My mind swims. "Your home... the tower."

She touches the lightest of kisses to my forehead. Iggy's lips are warm, almost hot, and there is the slightest hard press of her fang before the air whips against my skin again. Oh, heavens above... I kissed her. On. The. Mouth. Because I thought she was stone, or maybe I didn't. Was I pretending she was Boudicca? That's even more embarrassing. My skin flames as I bury my face in her shoulder.

"It'll be all right. I'll always protect you." Iggy's arms tighten around me.

She's taking my mortification as fear of being attacked. Relief sweeps through me.

Iggy shifts me into a bridal carry as she lands on the familiar rooftop. A shorter gargoyle with a feline face and sharply barbed wings perches near where Iggy usually sits. With a gasp, I recognize her as the sphynx statue. She hisses at us before disappearing around a turret.

My eyes widen. I was right! There's more than one. Is every gargoyle on this tower alive? What about in the city? The red door creaks when Iggy swings it open to carry me down a flight of stairs into the tower.

Realizing I'm holding my breath, I let it out in a rush of air as we enter what looks like a workshop or study. Tiny violet flames illuminate globes around the room. The oddest-dressed person I've ever seen stands from behind a desk covered in baubles and parts. Multicolored jewelry gleams in the dim light, illuminating the turquoise ribbons and beads in the person's beard. *This could be a mage.* Mismatched and strange, this potential magic user's clothing is a riot of color that burns afterimages into my vision.

"Is she hurt? Was it the shades again?" the person asks, striding across the room as long purple jacket tails whip in an unfelt breeze.

"I didn't have time to check if the shades hurt her." Iggy sets me on my feet.

I wobble, and Iggy steadies me with an arm gently around my waist. For all the gargoyle's size, her touch is exceedingly light. "I'm Viola."

"You may call me Xander. Welcome to the *inside* of the Tower of Wind." They give me a wry grin.

That heat returns to my cheeks and my mind spins with the implications. "You're Boudicca's boss!"

Xander nods as they gather gauze and several bottles of liquids.

Questions burn on my tongue, spilling out before I can stop them. "Did you create the gargoyles? Are you a mage?" They obviously know I've been using the rooftop for years.

"I did, and I am." Xander tuts as they take in my ripped blouse and filthy pants. Their fingers lightly move the fabric aside, their eyes lingering on my pendant before sweeping over my stinging claw wounds.

"Does Boudicca live here? Is she here now?" I could really

use a hug from her. This whole anxiety-fraught night has my palms sweaty and my heart pounding.

"Move her to the couch, please," Xander says. "Cassiopeia may have some clothing that will fit. Could you please check with her? I believe she's on the east balcony." Xander turns and starts rooting through a cabinet full of small drawers, completely ignoring my questions.

"I won't leave Viola." Iggy settles me gently on the couch. Tenderly, she brushes my windblown hair back from my face. "Are you thirsty?"

I nod, still in shock as she drapes a blanket over my shoulders. Xander sighs as they pick up a cup. "Baraq, could you please see if Cass has a dress we can borrow?"

Claws click down the spiraling stairs from the roof, and an obsidian gargoyle enters the study on four huge paws. His face is far less human-looking than Iggy's, with a broad lionlike muzzle and sharply pointed slitted eyes. Long fangs extend down past his jaw, and his dark horns curl on the sides of his head, much like a ram.

"I'm on it," Baraq says.

I try not to stare. "H-How many are there?"

"A few. Don't worry—no one here will hurt you." Iggy twists in place, takes a cup from Xander, and gives it to me.

Sipping it, I try to adjust to this. "Do you have a real name?"

She hesitates and glances at Xander, but then her lips stretch wide, and those thick, thorny spikes on her jawline flex. "Iggy is fine."

Xander snorts softly. "How cute. Here, take this potion. It will help with the pain but make you sleepy. You're welcome to stay here for the night."

Affronted, I huff before sipping the bluish liquid down. "She looked like she was made from igneous rock."

A low growl emanates from my gargoyle. "Viola was young when she named me, and I find it endearing."

Endearing. Heavens, every time I crawled into her arms—and I told her my stories and my troubles—she was listening.

"You heard everything," I murmur.

Her labradorite-colored eyes flash with concern then a tender warmth. So similar to Boudicca's. "And it meant the world to me."

22

BOUDICCA

*V*iola sleeps with her head propped on my thigh and the blanket drawn up around her curved shoulders. Cassiopeia's dress hangs loosely around her slim form, billowing over her legs in a pool of lavender silk. The medicinal smell of the salve Xander covered her scratches with stings my nose as they lean over us to study the pendant Viola wears.

"She'll be out for a while with the drops I gave her for the pain. The wounds weren't deep enough to need stitches, and the salve should take care of them in a few hours." Xander touches the pendant resting at the base of Viola's throat. "You're right. Her pendant is from the same maker as my own."

"Do you see her magic now? This ring blocked it." I wiggle the emerald ring from my little finger and place it in Xander's calloused palm.

"I do." Flipping down a golden lens from their hinged spectacles and then a blue one, Xander hums. "It appears to have a similar magical signature as the pendants. You said her grandmother gave it to her?"

"That was the odd part." I stroke Viola's golden hair. She's fallen asleep draped over me so many times, but this time is different. I can touch her in my true form without my stone shell between us. "Her brother told her their grandmother died shortly after Viola was born, but somehow, Viola met her. Viola said she's a seventh daughter."

My maker studies the ring carefully. "Her family's name?"

"Archambeau."

"Hmmm. No, that's not one of the magically gifted families." Xander drums restless fingers briefly on their jeweled eye patch before lifting it to gaze at Viola. "Oh my. Her grandmother was a Bichler, a family of makers and creators of wonderful arcane objects. As a seventh child, she would have been quite powerful... as Viola will be when she learns. No wonder those shades could see her. The objects have drawn them even though the ring hid her."

"But who sent the shades?"

Flipping down their patch, Xander lounges in a beat-up armchair. "That is an excellent question. One I'm afraid I have no answer for. She'll be safe enough here for the night." Xander's brow bunches, and they tug at their beard. "Although this situation... it's not ideal. When do you plan to tell her?"

I gnaw my lip. "I didn't. She doesn't need to know. Please don't tell her."

Xander's frown deepens. "It's not like you to be deceitful."

"I know. I really enjoy her company, and if I can pretend to be real just a little longer... what could it hurt? I don't want her to know I'm a creature." *Thing. Construct. Soulless.* I push the harsh litany of words from my mind.

"Daughter, you *are* real. You never needed to pretend that. I'll leave the choice up to you whether to tell her or not, but I urge you to do so now that she's entered our world."

I give Xander an uncomfortable shrug. "Anyway, her family has arranged a marriage to Elias from Austria. The engagement is about to become public. I think he's involved in some bad things."

Xander rakes a hand through their hair. "Such as...?"

"Blood magic. Maybe even the shades. I don't want her to have to marry a man, especially not him."

Xander quirks an eyebrow, their lips lifting. "I'll look into it. But if Viola agrees to the marriage, that's her choice."

Every spike on my body flexes straight. I don't like the idea of Elias being anywhere near her. I growl. "He smelled like blood magic. The threads of it drifted from him in dark waves."

"There're mages who use blood magic to boost spells that are perfectly harmless. I'll leave you to think about why you feel Viola shouldn't know your truth. In the meantime, I'm headed to bed, and you can stay here and watch over her."

The violet lights around the room dim, and some wink out, leaving us in shadow as Xander departs the study. I sigh. Baraq, Ariella, and Cassiopeia will guard the roof tonight, but I should join them. Gently, I lift Viola so I can slide out from under her, but she twists in her sleep.

"No, Iggy. Stay with me. No monsters." She wraps her arms as much around my waist as she can.

I groan quietly and flex my wings behind the couch. My tail is half-asleep, pinned behind the cushion, and my leg is bent at an odd angle. I'm not used to sitting on furniture like this. Grabbing a pillow, I carefully slide it under her, then slip away. I need to think, and it's too hard to do that while she's so close.

Creeping silently, I climb the stairs from Xander's study to the rooftop. Cass and Baraq lounge there, a chessboard set up between them. Ariella balances lightly on the nearby wall, buffing her nails. Cassiopeia looks up first. Lithe and delicate, her feathered wings drape in an artistically fluffy swirl around her. The stone Xander carved her from was different from mine—cream-striped alabaster instead of obsidian.

Cassiopeia smirks, indigo eyes dancing with glee. "Shouldn't you be downstairs, tending to your little tale spinner?" She moves a piece. "Check."

Baraq groans as he slides his king out of the vulnerable position.

Ariella flicks her tail lazily, her toothy mouth stretching into a feline grin as she studies the board. "I don't know why you bother, Baraq. If you want to win something, challenge Cass to a sparring session."

"We have enough problems with those annoying shades. There's no reason to needle each other," I say.

Cass studies the board for the briefest of moments then moves a piece again. It's inevitable that she'll win—she always does. "Viola smells divine. All that shining silvery celestial magic flowing around her like a river. I'm shocked none of us scented her before. Check."

Nodding, Ariella kicks out her back paws as she reclines. Sharp claws drag against the stone, sparking. "I bet she tastes delicious. Do you think she'd mind if I licked her? I could sneak one in while she's asleep."

I shoot Ariella an *absolutely not* look. Clearing my throat, I refocus on a scowling Baraq. "Have you seen any more shades tonight?"

"Just one," Baraq mutters. "It appeared to be a scout, though, and disappeared as quickly as it arrived." He taps a thick claw against the edge of the board then moves his king again. He has already lost—Cass has checkmate in two moves. Baraq always was stronger than he was smart, and chess is a game of strategy.

"Have you told her yet?" Cass slides the piece that will pin the black king in place.

"Told her what?" I feign ignorance, already knowing what she's about to ask.

Ariella shoots me a look, flattening her pointed ears. "That you're the woman she met as Boudicca. The ring's illusion isn't very different from you. Your human face is thinner and less chiseled, and you have hair instead of a mane. The browner tone to your skin and lack of horns, wings, and tail won't throw her off for long. You have the same eyes. She's a scholar, not a fool."

"There hasn't been time. We really just met." I gaze at the expanse of the starry night sky over Paris.

"Baby sister," Cass chides. "What is it?"

I can't look at her. "Xander created us. We don't possess souls like humans do. As creatures made for a singular purpose, we simply exist. Don't you ever wonder if there's more?"

Baraq flicks his tufted tail and snorts. "Look at you, being all philosophical like our maker."

Ariella tackles him. Her fingers dig into his thick, lionlike mane, tugging him around. Baraq tucks his wings around his leonine body, and they go rolling across the rooftop.

Cass nudges my shoulder. "You'll figure it out, Boudicca. We've got the roof for tonight. Go back to the study."

My sister is not the oldest, but Xander gave her a little something more when they made her. I guess the mage did that with all of us, as if they held a specific purpose in their mind as they carved our bodies. Baraq and Ariella are quick, vicious fighters, and Cassiopeia was always the brains. Lysander was the first of us, but he hasn't woken in years. Then there are the menagerie creatures: wyverns, griffins, snakes, and the long-legged dogs and spiraling dragons. They protect this tower as much as we do. Xander says I'm the most sensitive, but I'm not really sure what they mean by that—or what they intended when they made me.

My thick reptilian tail drags along the stairs as I descend to the study. Viola still sleeps on the couch. I stand over her, gazing down at her marred skin. The wounds are barely red lines now against her pale, freckled flesh. I crouch beside her, tucking my wings snug to my back. Her blue-violet eyes flutter open.

"You're real," Viola whispers as she takes my hand. Her thumb rubs against the red ribbon she tied there long ago on the night she claimed me as hers. "You've always been my very best friend."

Friend. My heart squeezes as her eyes drift shut again. The pleasure-pain seeps through me. I'm not real. Just like the little red fox and the wolf in her stories, we're too different. Viola is alive, a human with her whole life ahead of her. She can be anything she wants and go anywhere she desires. I'm a creature bound to this tower with the sole purpose of keeping it safe. As a created thing, I have no purpose beyond that.

Tentatively, I touch my lower lip, remembering the thrilling sensation of her kiss. Shaking my head, I sigh. I can't ask Viola to stay in this tower. It means having to come clean that I'm Boudicca, and she's already said how much she hates liars and pretenders. That creep, Elias, must be steeped in the magical world. What if he means her harm? Durant was right —I can't protect her beyond the boundaries of Paris as I'm tied to this city. Besides, she's attracted to me as a human, and that's it. If I tell her I'm a gargoyle I'll lose everything we've built. She's flesh, and I'm stone—as a gargoyle, I can never be more than her friend.

A thought flits through my mind, and the realization fills me with hope. As a human, perhaps I can continue to be more.

23

VIOLA

"Good morning, my dear," Xander says kindly as they wake me. The fragrance of pastries and the sharp scent of herbal tea come from a tray on a table nearby. Xander appears different, and then I realize their beard is gone. Without it, their face is narrow with a pointed chin and pale, thin lips.

Xander's loose shirt is the exact same shade of green as their uncovered eye. The neckline gapes, and I catch the barest glimpse of a turquoise bandage around their chest. Long, colorful skirts swish over the floor around their bejeweled slippers.

"Were you injured last night? The bandage on your chest..."

They sit near me. My pendant is around Xander's neck, among a jumble of chains and charms. My hand flies to my chest, gripping the cool stone. Not my pendant, then. How do they have one exactly like mine?

"Me? No. Oh, you mean this?" They tap the silky turquoise fabric. "It's just a bit of binding. I prefer to not be perceived for my physical traits but rather for what I provide to this world."

Daylight streams through the windows nearby, but it's difficult to tell what time it is. I shake off the grogginess as I rub my sleep-crusted eyes. "Where's Iggy?"

"Resting."

"Is Boudicca working today?" I sit up.

"We need to talk." Xander drops four lumps of sugar into their teacup before stirring it pensively. "You've attracted quite a bit of trouble to my home, and I suspect your presence is what has drawn the shade attacks here over the last decade."

"Me? Why would they want me?" I lift the steaming cup of tea to my lips and take the tiniest sip, trying not to scald my tongue.

"Because, my dear, you have magic within you. Your emerald ring hid it, but now that they have your scent, the shades won't stop coming as long as you're in Paris." Xander holds out their palm with my ring at its center. Then they flip the golden band pensively over their knuckles. "You have some options—"

"You have the same pendant as me."

"I do. And that is where our talk begins." Xander takes a long gulp of tea. It must be cooler than mine as all I can do is sip. Exhaling, they sink into a nearby armchair. "Many years ago, I created the gargoyles that reside here and used this earth-magic-imbued pendant to give them life."

I gasp. "Like Lemaitre's book. It *is* possible to store magic in gems." This is incredible. If everything I've read about in that book can actually be done, it would improve the world immensely.

Xander nods. "The pendant can also control stone creations, and while I don't use it for that purpose unless under duress, it's possible. You're in possession of a similar pendant, and I'm afraid over time you've bent—Iggy, you called her—to be the companion you needed in your life."

"S-She's my friend." A lump forms in my throat. "I thought she was a statue. I didn't know."

Xander leans forward, patting my hand consolingly. "I know it wasn't intentional. You were a lonely child and unaware of what you did. But over the last decade, she's become far more than the being I created. You shaped that, and she cares deeply for you because you needed a friend. I believe she became that by your will. Created creatures have no souls, Viola. They shouldn't be able to feel to the extent that Iggy does."

I can't breathe. Not only do I have magic, but it affected another without her permission? I squeeze the cold pendant. "Did she even have a choice?"

Xander arches one thick russet eyebrow but doesn't answer.

No... oh no. Somehow, in my childish desperation for attention, I've remolded someone else's will. The room spins, and my chest heaves.

Dizzy, I snatch my hand back as I stumble from the couch. "Where is she? I need to talk to her."

"I can offer you two choices. One, you put this ring back on your finger and give me your pendant for safekeeping. I believe the shades are in pursuit of the pendant, not you, and the ring's magic wasn't quite enough to cloak the pendant. The ring will dampen your personal magic so you'll be undetectable again. However, the ring also cuts you off from the magical world. All the new things you could see will be gone again. I detect a minor mind-altering effect on the item as well. It could make it difficult to believe in magic, let alone see it."

"New things?" I remember the purple sparkling lights from last night.

"The glittery dust you see is magic. Last night, when you were flying above Paris, the bright lines were ley lines, the channels that magic flows through. You saw them, didn't you?"

"Yeah." Stunned, I stare off into middle space. Magic is real. It's all real.

"If you put the ring on, you'll be able to go about your life and not draw attention from Mageía, the magical world. You could marry and live a quiet life, especially if you leave for the countryside. Once there is some distance between you and Iggy, I believe she will return to her natural state as a guardian of the Tower of Wind."

I don't want to lose magic now that I found it. I squint. "Or...?"

"Or you stay here. I could use an apprentice. I'll help you hone your magic skill and protect you from the shades. However, your magic and proximity means Iggy will likely continue to change, and that could possibly hurt her. In my experience, the level of control you've exerted on her will eventually drive her mad."

"What? No!" Tears wet my cheek. "I wouldn't do that to her. There has to be another way. Is she aware this is happening?"

Xander runs a hand through their wild tangle of long hair. "I always had the best of intentions when I created my stone guardians. I started small with the beasts, some fanciful and some mundane. Snakes, then dogs. Later, I carved some intricate wyverns and griffins. Then one day, I carved my first gargoyle, and he was magnificent. I named him Lysander."

"'Was'? What happened to him?" I gnaw my lip.

"I used the pendant to breathe life into him and then to command him—to bend him and shape him into a son for me. It was my early days in this city so far from my home, and I was lonely. That was my error. Instead of giving him a suggestion and the free will to figure things out, I controlled him. Over time, Lysander became unstable." Xander pauses, staring forlornly into their tea. "And that is what I fear you've done to Iggy."

My voice cracks. "What did you do with Lysander?"

Eyes averted, Xander rubs their forehead. "I laid him to rest in a room under the tower. I haven't made that error with the others."

"I haven't commanded Iggy to do anything. I don't even know how to use the pendant," I protest.

"It's all a matter of will. Iggy is obviously overly fond of you. To the point that she forsook guarding this tower—the purpose I created her for—to guard you. I'm afraid even if you got rid of your pendant, it wouldn't be enough. It's possible she'd eventually become an empty shell, only existing to serve you. With you close, she'll continue to bend to your will. If you stay, I'll have to ask you to limit your contact with her to prolong the inevitable."

I inhale, my racing mind tumbling over solutions. "I see. Are you certain? Is there a way around this? It's just—I can't imagine my life without her."

Xander hesitates, their gaze dropping to the floor. "I'll speak to her about it after I know your choice. I'm sorry, Viola. You've been through a lot."

I stand and move through the open arches to a curved balcony. There's an invisible barrier here that allows in light but not the elements. I run my fingertips over it in wonder. My heart pounds as I suffocate in my thoughts. "What about my family?"

"I looked into that this morning. Your mother doesn't have the gift, and neither do any of your siblings. The magic came through your paternal line. You could never tell them. There are strictly enforced rules that keep the magic world separate from the world you grew up in."

"Oh." I stare out into the bright-blue sky and green parkway beyond the tower.

Everything magical I ever dreamed of finding is slipping away like a fading dream. Xander joins me on the balcony. An unfelt breeze teases wisps of their hair and tugs at their colorful skirt. They flip the gold band hypnotically over their knuckles, and it gleams, leaving a faint trail of glittering light in its wake. I could be Xander's apprentice, but that would cost Iggy her life. The price is too dear.

This is so unfair. I just find out she's alive, and I have to let her go. Maybe there's a way around it. I'm the top researcher at the Mazarine, and a whole room of magic books is available for me to study. This is one more reason to fight to keep the library open.

"What if there's a third option?"

Xander leans toward me with an expression of keen interest. "Go on."

"I'm fighting to keep the Mazarine public. I suspect you know about the magical books in the back room."

They nod.

"Give me a few days to research this and think it over. I won't hurt Iggy by staying, but I refuse to believe there isn't a way around this. If magic harms, it should also help. In the meantime, I'll limit my visits to the tower so as not to affect her." Those last words send a knife through my heart. I've talked to Iggy almost every day for over fifteen years, and even though she was inanimate, I loved every moment. The thought of letting go is tearing me apart.

"And if you don't find a solution?" Xander asks.

"Then I'll turn in my pendant, and you won't see me again." I bite my lip as hot tears burn to be shed. "I should go home. My parents will be looking for me."

"Do you want me to walk you home?" Xander asks.

"No. I need some time to myself."

"Viola? Viola, wait up!" Boudicca calls from across the wooded park.

I peer toward her with blurry, tear-streaked eyes. She's all undone, running across the rolling emerald hills of the park.

Her shirt flaps, held over her bouncing tits by one valiantly straining button. Boudicca rumples her suit coat in one hand as if it were an afterthought, and the top button of her pants lies undone against the muscled expanse of her abdomen. As sad as I am, she still takes my breath away. As she jogs closer, I sit on the marble edge of the decorative fountain.

My head hurts from crying, and I can't seem to make my feet move toward home. It all feels too heavy and not right. All my life, I wanted to find more magic in this world, using my slippers as proof that it exists, and now that I finally have my foot in that world, I have to give it all up.

Panting, she gives me a warm smile. Boudicca works for Xander. She must know about Mageía and the gargoyles.

I push my loose hair behind one ear and try to smile. "Hey."

"Hey." Boudicca frowns a little as she studies my face. "I wasn't expecting to see you out here this morning. I was, um... on the way to the tower. Xander usually has some errands for me in the morning."

"Oh, you don't live there? What can you tell me about Xander?" I force an attempt at polite conversation to avoid dragging Boudicca down into my depression. My mind rolls and buzzes. All I want is for my thoughts to go blank as I skim the cool fountain water with my hand.

"Xander has an innate affinity for wind magic. They make things mostly. Mechanical curiosities, carvings, and jewelry. They peddle their wares at a market once a month here in Paris. Sometimes, Xander takes on private commissions." Boudicca cups my chin, lifting my face to hers. "Are you all right? Your eyes look a little red."

The gesture is shockingly intimate, but touch starved, I lean into it. I could use a little comfort right now. "I'm not. But it'll be fine. I ran into a bit of trouble last night, and

Xander sheltered me. I really need to get home before my family realizes I'm gone."

"Wouldn't they have already?" Her brow knots with concern. "It's nearly midmorning."

I shrug. "Unless there is some specific event, I'm typically ignored. The spare heir."

The joke falls flat as Boudicca takes my hand. "I'll walk you home."

I shake my head. "No, I was just steeling myself to go. Elias will probably be waiting, and I don't need any further friction with him."

Boudicca shifts her weight from one foot to the other. Her hand drops. "Do you like him?"

"I don't even know him." I fling my hand up in frustration, splashing the fountain water all over Boudicca. "Oh!"

The water glistens on her face, instantly soaking the front of her white shirt. Heat flushes over my cheeks at the sight of those stunning dark curves. Realizing I'm staring, I blink away, but magnetically, I'm drawn back.

A bemused grin crosses her lips, followed by her hand sliding into mine. "Let's get some breakfast."

I sniffle. "I'm not hungry."

Boudicca takes a deep breath, shoulders flexing, and then lets it out. "What would you like to do?"

Words tumble through my mind, and I bite my lip. I'd like to live in a tower the rest of the world apparently ignores, with an eccentric mage and a gargoyle I adore. One I just found out is alive—even though my very presence could harm her. I'm not sure what to do with my feelings yet.

I tug on my braid then look up into Boudicca's familiar eyes. "Has it ever felt like the entire world is too large and everything is overwhelming? So much has happened to me since yesterday, and I don't know what to do with it all. I mean, if you work for Xander, you must know all about Mageía, right?"

Boudicca takes a seat beside me on the fountain's edge, folding her hands into her lap. "I do."

"It's just, I have a dinner party I don't want to attend. The ball is in four days, and while we've made half the money needed on ticket sales, the auction and kissing booth will have to make up the rest." I inhale a choked, frantic breath. "Shades keep attacking me. I found out there are beings in this world that are every bit as smart as humans—maybe more so. And as elated as I was by that discovery, it all came crashing down, and I'm still not sure what to do with the knowledge."

"I know what you need." Boudicca buttons her damp shirt then slides on her rumpled jacket before offering me her hand.

I look at it doubtfully, struck again by how beautifully flawless her skin is and the way each finger is perfect with nary a scar or callus. "What?"

"Gelato."

24

VIOLA

Boudicca hands me a glass cup full of the sweet, creamy treat as we sit at an outdoor café on a quiet side street. She held my hand the entire way here, and by the time we arrived, my thoughts had finally settled from swirling chaos into something that was at least adjacent to order. Maybe. Sort of.

Pushing up my spectacles, I sneak a sideways look at her as she spoons the pistachio-flavored gelato into her mouth. Why couldn't I have met her a month sooner? It's so easy to be around Boudicca, and I wouldn't mind her pursuing my attention. My family might actually consider my attraction to women less of a phase if I seriously courted someone instead of sneaking around for a casual tumble.

From our handful of conversations, I know that Boudicca is smart, funny, and sweet. If I'd only met her sooner, I'm certain I wouldn't be in the awkward place I am now. I would've picked her and declared myself taken, saving myself from my parents' random choice of *male with pedigree*. It's not like they need more heirs.

At that moment, I spy the deliciously curvy figure of the brunette who held my attentions, if not my heart, less than two months ago. Anne strides closer, her black eyes flicking from me to Boudicca and back again. I used to think her eyes were so pretty, but now they look tired and a little mean.

"Viola, what a surprise to see you out and about. Congratulations on your engagement." She gazes at Boudicca appraisingly before focusing her attention back on me.

"I'm not engaged yet. It's still in negotiations." I try not to stare at her stomach, but Anne stands right in front of me with one hand cupped under her curved belly.

She can't possibly be showing already, can she? It's only been a bit over a month since her wedding, and I was in her bed the week before she told me she was marrying. I clang the spoon against the edge of the cup. Unless she was sleeping with both of us at the same time. How long would it take to show the way she is—three months, maybe four? Was she fucking him the entire year she was with me? I'm going to spew gelato all over the street if I think about that too much.

"You might as well be married already." She rolls her eyes, tipping her wide-brimmed hat against the sun. "It's inevitable. You can play at whatever this is..." Anne gestures to Boudicca. "Like we did. But eventually, we all have to fall in line to birth the next generation for our family name."

Is that why she married so fast—because she was busy "creating the next generation" with that brainless lump of suet while still "playing" with me?

I stuff my fury down. "I thought, with all your lofty talk of owning your own cakeshop and catering to all-female intellectual events, that you were different, but obviously, it was just a bunch of hot air."

Anne huffs. "Well, at least I know my place. You'll never get anywhere with your ink-stained hands and clothes full of book dust." She rakes her eyes over Boudicca's rumpled suit with a disdainful glare. "At least I passed in society. Is this really what you want to be seen with? People will talk."

Oh, she does not *get to speak to Boudicca like that.* "Be civil. Jealousy doesn't suit you." I cover Boudicca's hand with my own. "I always intended to leave my mark on this world with my knowledge, not my offspring. You made your choices."

"Ha, you absolute child. You think women have a choice? We're locked into our stations from birth to death, stealing only brief moments of pleasure for ourselves." She grits her shining white teeth at me.

Exhaustion and sorrow overwhelm me. She never had the courage to break from the mold of society. I'm uncertain if I do either, but I'll still try. I'm not sliding on an engagement band yet. Over the metal rim of my spectacles, Anne seems out of focus and distant. She and I never lived in the same world.

"I don't think we have anything constructive left to say to each other. The life you chose is waiting for you." Dismissing her, I turn to face Boudicca, then dip my spoon back into my half-melted gelato.

Anne stomps off with all the furious vigor with which she arrived. I manage to hold my shoulders still until she's out of sight, but then the tears course down my cheeks. I thought I was all dried up after this morning's crying jag, but apparently, that well is endless.

Frustrated by the outpouring of emotion, I tear off my spectacles to dab at my eyes. "I'm sorry you had to see that. I hate fake people. She wasn't always like that, or maybe she was and just pretended to feel kindness toward me."

Boudicca's arm goes around me. "You have the power to be anyone you dare to be."

I sniffle. "Yeah?"

"Always. Say, the ball is coming up. Do you have an escort?"

She's likely asking if Elias is my date. "No. I'm the one running it, so I haven't even considered a partner for the evening. It would be rude to leave my date alone while I make sure everything goes smoothly."

"May I escort you? I'll be helping run the event anyway."

She traces a slow circle on my shoulder while waiting for an answer.

It's a little unorthodox, with the rumor mill saying I'm already engaged and all. "I wouldn't want to put you in danger if Elias takes offense."

Boudicca strokes my cheek. It's tender in a way I can't help but lean into. "I can take care of myself."

My eyes skate over the broad expanse of Boudicca's shoulders and down the thickness of her biceps. "I'm sure you can physically, but there's plenty that people in power can do to make your life miserable."

"Viola Archambeau..." Boudicca takes a knee before me. She's so tall we still nearly see eye to eye. "Please do me the honor of allowing me to escort you to the Mazarine ball. I hear it's going to be this season's most amazing event."

I smile at her gleaming grin. "Yes, I'd love to go with you. What's the worst anyone could do? They're already trying to force me into marriage."

She shrugs then sits beside me. "It's too bad you can't find another job."

I think about Xander's offer and then the possible damage to Iggy. Can I even stay in this city without harming my dearest friend?

"Do you like it?" I ask, trying to change the subject.

Boudicca twirls her spoon in the air. "Like what?"

"Working for Xander. Are they good to work for?" I swallow another mouthful of the sweet, creamy dessert then suck thoughtfully on my spoon.

All the moments of my life are slipping away too fast. I hope there's time to research how to keep from hurting Iggy. If I can understand the mechanics of exactly how magic works, there may be an alternative to this. It didn't take me long to figure out the slippers. There's got to be a way to stay here.

Boudicca stops playing with her spoon and stares at me intently. Her eyes appear more gray than blue today, like storm clouds rolling over the ocean. She gives me a lopsided grin. "Xander doesn't ask much of me, and all my needs are met."

I scrape my spoon along the side of my cup. "They aren't from here—the accent is a giveaway. They sound a little... Greek maybe?"

"Xander moved to Paris ages ago when they had a vision that they'd meet their soulmate here. But so far, no luck. They can see into the past and people's possible futures with their covered eye."

I mull over that information. That must be how Xander knows I'll hurt Iggy. Is future sight always accurate, though? So many factors could affect events that haven't happened yet. I lean against Boudicca's shoulder as we sit in comfortable silence, finishing our treats. A flock of pigeons lands in the street, cooing and pecking at crumbs between the cobblestones.

"I don't want to leave Paris," I whisper.

"Then don't." Boldly, Boudicca slides both her hands over mine. "I don't want you to leave Paris either. We finally met, and you're too wonderful to give up."

My heart skips, and I can't help but move a little closer. I'm not giving up this feeling. She's so warm and comfortable. It feels like I've known her for years. I don't want to marry Elias and lead a life like that of my sisters or, worse, become like Anne, full of bitterness. I'll dive into researching magic— it's my only ticket out of this situation.

I sigh. Why is life so difficult? "I wish I'd known you sooner."

She lets out a contented little hum as her lips curl into a secretive smile. "What would you do if you knew me sooner?"

"Well, get to know you better, for one. But my family is pushing this engagement with Elias that I don't want. And I just found out I may have unintentionally hurt someone I care for deeply, and if I stay, I may continue to hurt her, and well…" I inhale then let out a breath, trying to hold in the sob. "She means a lot to me. If me leaving Paris means she can't be hurt, then, as a last resort, I may have to do that."

"Oh. I didn't realize you had another suitor." Boudicca frowns a little.

The tears threaten again. "Oh, she's not a suitor exactly. She's a person I love, but my presence is hurting her. Our relationship is… unconventional. My parents would never accept her." I look back out at the cooing birds. It's tempting to spend the entire afternoon sitting beside Boudicca, watching the pigeons, but I can't dodge my family forever.

Boudicca's jaw tightens. "I see."

With a sigh, I stand and brush off the pretty lavender dress that Cassiopeia lent me. "I suppose I'm ready to face my family now. I'll take you up on that offer to walk me home if you're still willing."

Boudicca clasps my hand loosely as we walk back toward my family's manor.

25

VIOLA

I slump against the back wall of the kissing booth, facing away from the long line of patrons waiting their turn with money in hand. This was an excellent fundraising idea if a bit gross, although Mirabelle seems to be having a good time.

"My lips are positively chapped." She giggles as her shift ends and another woman takes her place.

Not surprisingly, Charles offered to help with the booth and is at the far end of the stall with an extensive line of ladies waiting for his smooch. Flipping through the cash drawer, I smile. We've already made enough here to cover the projected costs. I might be able to keep my job after all. I've just begun to research how my pendant works and whether it's really affecting Iggy.

I tug my gold-lace mask a little tighter. It was hard to find something that fit over my glasses, and at the last minute I settled on this. Boudicca was supposed to meet me here, but it's been over an hour, and unless her mask is particularly clever, I haven't seen her yet.

"Here's some balm." I pass a small blue pot to Mirabelle. "Have you seen Boudicca?"

"No, but here comes tall, dark, and creepy. I thought you'd escaped that prearrangement." She takes the pot, unscrews the lid, and dabs a little of the pink-tinged balm on her lips.

I look up. Elias strides toward the booth, pushing past the waiting patrons. His large-nosed black mask looks villainous, and his clothing is barely a step above his usual plain uniform. At least I'm not up in the booth. I only had to do five cheek kisses and was thankful he wasn't one of them.

Brushing off the skirt of my deep-purple gown, I look past the approaching man to the library beyond. The transformation is stunning. Planets and stars hang suspended from the ceiling with tiny lights twinkling between them. Large cut-out trees lie against the bookcases, giving the appearance that a forest grew in the Mazarine overnight.

It didn't of course. Mirabelle, Chantal, Boudicca, and I worked through the day and half the night preparing the room. Totally worth it.

"Viola, would you do me the honor of a dance?" Elias lifts the counter entrance to the booth and holds out his hand.

I give one last look around the room, seeking Boudicca's familiar height, before placing my hand in his. Elias's palm holds the chill of a corpse, and I make a concerted effort not to flinch. "Sure. I wanted to talk to you anyway."

With the library funded, I should be able to get my job back. Or maybe work for Xander if I can prove it's safe for me to be near Boudicca. I don't need to marry. I've proved beyond a doubt that I'm worth more than an alliance. Letting Elias lead me onto the dance floor, I can't help but continue to scan for Boudicca. Where is she?

"I haven't seen you much." He sets his hand on my waist, deftly moving me in line with the other dancers.

"I'm sorry. I've been so busy arranging this fundraiser ball. I really haven't had time for the usual frivolous outings."

"Well, I'm certain you will now that the event is over. Our engagement announcement dinner is in two days." He smiles down at me.

"Elias, that's what I wanted to talk to you about. I really love my work here in the city and wouldn't make an ideal wife, let alone mother, in the countryside. You said before if we found this pairing unsuitable, you'd bow out. I'm asking if you'll keep your word." I hold my breath, hoping the public setting is enough for him to be civil.

"I hardly think we've had enough time together to determine if we are compatible. Perhaps think this over. How will you support yourself without marriage? Your family certainly won't condone your unorthodox lifestyle."

Unorthodox. Well, I suppose that's a polite way of saying sapphist. I let him lead me through a few complicated steps. Infuriatingly, the man still smiles as if this is all under his control and always will be.

"I want out, and I'm demanding, on your honor, that you keep your word and make some excuse up to back off."

Elias glances around. No one is close enough to hear him. "And I'm telling you that time is far past," he hisses. "The upper crust of this city already believe the deal is sealed. I'm certainly not going to back down now, and your father's shipping empire will be greatly advantageous to me in the near future. I'm expected to produce heirs, and you will be the one bearing them. At the very least, our children will be intelligent, if a bit plain. Hopefully, you'll get it right on the first try and give me a son. After that, I could care less who you fuck. It's not like your choice of bed partners will get you pregnant."

I gasp at his bluntness, not able to pull together a coherent response after being blasted by such cruelty. The music winds to a close, and I stumble to a halt, tearing my hand from his.

"How charmingly said." A dashing figure in a coal-black suit appears beside me. Over their face is a curling snarl of a golden dragon. I recognize those lips. Heavens know I've fantasized about them enough over the last few days. "Viola, may I have the next dance?"

"She's with me." Elias blocks Boudicca from taking my hand.

"Actually, I think I could use a drink. There suddenly

seems to be a lot of hot air here." I brush past Elias, taking Boudicca's arm. "You look amazing, I love your mask. Who's the artist?"

Boudicca grins as we quickly stride away from the dancefloor. "Xander made it. Watch." The nostrils emit a tiny puff of smoke in delicate rings.

"Clever." I sink into the comfortable feeling I always have when Boudicca is close and try to forget Elias's possessive words.

I want to enjoy the little freedom I have while I have it. I glance back to see Mirabelle has waylaid Elias with her cheerful chatter. Then I breathe a sigh of relief as she guilts him into a dance.

Boudicca hands me a glass of sparkling lemonade from the buffet table then takes one for herself. "I'm sorry I'm later than you expected. Is everything running well? Can I steal you away to somewhere quieter?"

I glance to where Chantal is directing the booths of games and prizes along one wall. She looks like she has it all handled. Elias watches me from across the room, but I doubt he'd damage his reputation by making a public scene. To most attendees, I'm simply speaking with another woman. People always see what they want to.

On a small platform, the musicians play on. A harpist will step in during their break. It certainly doesn't appear that anyone needs me. I slide my hand into hers, enjoying the smooth warmth of her palm and the way her fingers curl around mine.

"I'd love that." I tip my head, gazing up into Boudicca's beatific expression. No one has ever looked at me the way she does. That touch of awe in her gaze makes it hard to breathe.

"Come on, I found a place I want you to see."

She leads me past the crowds to the silence of the antiquities room. Her shoulders brush the edge of a narrow archway I hadn't noticed before, and beyond it is a metal spiral staircase. I pause to glide my hand along the twist of metal roses twining around the ascending banister.

"I didn't realize there was a second level in here." I follow her upward.

"There isn't. This goes to the roof. I think you'll like the view." Boudicca pushes a hatch open above her head and crawls through the ceiling.

Reaching back, she offers me a hand up. I enable my slippers, which gives me a firmer grip to haul myself up through the hatch. This would be far easier if I weren't in a ball gown. Carefully, I hike up my skirt, gathering it into one hand before I take Boudicca's. She neatly lifts me as if I weigh nothing then sets me down gently beside the metal hatch.

My breath catches. We're at the center of a rooftop garden. Green vines and fragrant flowers twine around domes of latticework. Geometric beds spiral outward in a mazelike pattern. Boudicca leads me to a large lounge complete with fluffy pillows. Four posts around it support a transparent canopy.

"This isn't possible," I whisper as she nestles me among the tasseled pillows. "I've run across this roof before. I would've seen this."

Boudicca reclines next to me, folding her arms above her head to gaze up at the stars. "You asked me once if I believed in magic in this world, and I said yes. I wanted to show you a little bit of magic."

"The antiquities room..."

"Is a portal not everyone can pass through. Only those with magic in their veins."

"So I..." I sit up to hover over Boudicca.

Her hand threads through my hair. "Are so very magical. This is the world you belong in."

Her fingers curl against my scalp, dragging me down into a

welcomingly rough kiss. Warm lips move over mine with a hunger that leaves me breathless. The feel of her breasts against mine draws a sigh from me that she eagerly swallows down. Powerful shoulders flex, sending a tremor of desire through me as her hands skate down my back. I love how hard and soft she is all at once.

"You feel divine," Boudicca murmurs. "I never thought it would feel like this. Our bodies fit together like I was made for you."

I draw back gazing into her darkened eyes. "Can anyone else wander up here from the ball?"

"It's unlikely." She grins. "And I locked the hatch."

A laugh bubbles forth as I sit up, one hand on her chest for balance on this fluffy pile of pillows. "Why, Boudicca, what do you have planned?"

"Me?" She tugs me back toward her. "Well, the cutest librarian I know said that this was the best place for research."

I can't help it. Our lips meet again, bodies melting together as I breathe her in. How does she smell so good? It's nothing identifiable, not a perfume or soap, just purely her. I nuzzle into the side of her neck, relishing the scent.

Finally, I come up for air. "I could help you research."

I slide my fingers down her taut stomach and hook them just above the fastening to her trousers. Boudicca watches me, eyes wide with anticipation. I don't want to push this time. I need her to tell me she wants this.

"Can I touch you?" I brush my hand along her waist, untucking her shirt as I go. My mouth goes dry at the feel of her even through clothing. I want to press my lips to her skin and hear the breathy noises she'll make. "I don't mean to be so forward, but you're gorgeous I can't believe you'd desire me."

"I want you enough that I'm willing to completely disrespect our friendship to have you." Boudicca traces my cheek, meeting my eyes. "You can touch me wherever you like."

26

BOUDICCA

When Viola doesn't immediately unfasten my trousers, I reach one hand down, flicking them open, then undo the top button of my shirt to make it perfectly clear that I want her. Bold. Maybe too bold, but I want no mistakes this time. My hand slides against hers, palm to palm, begging for her touch. I'll treasure any moment she's willing to give me. The slow glide of her tongue against her lower lip sends a thrill tickling over my skin.

"You are the most stunning woman I've ever seen." I breathe out, trying to compose myself enough to not crush her to me and kiss her senseless. I can still feel the heat of her breasts on mine, and the thought of us being skin to skin drives me to distraction.

Viola hums approvingly as she unbuttons my crisp white shirt. Her hands are so soft against my flesh. No one has touched me with such tenderness. She tugs the garment over my shoulders, taking the suit jacket with it. I panic. She's going to see the red ribbon on my wrist and put together who I really am. I can't bear to take it off. But then she abandons my clothing. Relief sweeps through me as I strip one sleeve off, leaving on the other to conceal my secret.

"How are you so unbelievably perfect?" Viola's gaze drops to my nipples, which are tight against the cool air.

I gasp as her mouth finds one dark areola, then the other, licking and teasing with playful sensuality. The wet heat and slow lap of her tongue has my head spinning with the sensation. Stone doesn't feel like this.

Her lips are on mine again, and the whole world slows down to that sweet touch. The lightest flutter of her fingertips skates along my collarbone to graze upward. I tremble under the intensity of her attention.

"I want you," I murmur as her mouth moves to my cheek.

Playful teeth close over my earlobe, and the sharpness sends me reeling. Viola crawls into my lap, straddling my hips. When did she get my trousers off? Heavens above, her thighs are bare against mine. The silken whisper of her gown against my bare abdomen tears a groan from me. The feelings are too much and not enough. I need more.

I sink my fingers into her hips, hauling her against me. Viola's breathy laugh teases my neck, sending a delightful shiver along my skin. Had I known it would be like this, I might have moved years ago to show her I'm real.

But I'm not. I'm a created thing.

That dark thought creeps insidiously into my pleasure, dampening it. She only does this because I appear human. She'd never love a creature. A thing. A construct. I should tell her before this goes too far.

"Viola, you should know..."

"That I'm crazy about you?" Her lips curve in a wicked grin as she grinds herself against my thigh, leaving a smear of arousal there. Viola removes her wire rimmed spectacles then tosses them to the side. Her fingers go to the laces at her neckline to slowly loosen them, and I can't help but stare in anticipation.

"I mean, yes, but I'm..."

"Gorgeous." Her lips cover mine again, and then her bare breasts press to my flesh, nipples on my skin, and I can't think.

Soft, so unbelievably soft. Sweet musk fills my senses, and I inhale her desire deeper, filling my lungs with it. This is more than I dared to imagine. With a teasing grace, her tongue flicks over mine, and my low groan gets swallowed by her eager mouth. Still, I should tell her.

Viola's hand slides between us, cupping me. The heat drives away all thoughts except the feel of her. I drown in the deep violet of her eyes as she pulls away to look up at me. "Can I touch you here?"

Unable to speak, I nod and part my legs wider, leaning back against the cushions to watch her through hooded eyes. The night itself stills, slowing as if the entire existence of the universe holds its breath in the magic of this singular moment. The wind catches her hair, and the long gossamer strands brush teasingly against my chest.

Viola's fingers move, and the thrill zings through me, hot and molten. I'm wet, so surprisingly wet. I've read about this as a curiosity but never thought I'd be participating. As her fingers slide through my folds, my hips rise to meet her stroke, eliciting a groan as my thigh presses into her.

"Yes," Viola whispers.

Her teeth scrape my lower lip as her hands thread through my hair then grip, pulling me into a seamless press against her. The fit is exquisite—the way her lithe form melds so perfectly to my larger frame. Like we were made for each other. I look down at the hunger in her eyes tinged with something familiar. Fondness? Desire?

Her smile sweeps all of my nagging doubts away. Viola wants me in the way lovers do. I brush my knuckles against her cheek, boldly holding her gaze as her fingers curl within me. My hand flexes on her undulating, and her sharp cry echoes over the heady scent of the roses.

She grasps my hair again, riding my thigh harder as her fingers thrust against me, rubbing along my opening in a way that makes my flesh thrum in pleasure. Viola caresses my jaw as she lures me into another kiss, and it reminds me of every time she's traced my spikes as a gargoyle. The sensation is familiar, even loving. She's always held such tenderness for me, and now that I'm flesh, not stone, my veins sing in desire for her.

I flex my thigh under her, cording the muscle. She moans into my shoulder, her hips grinding more urgently against my soaked skin. I can't help but smile. Later, I'll smell of her sweet perfume and relish it. Her palm grinds against my center, and the sharp, sudden pleasure tears a loud cry from me. My panting gasps follow, yet she continues mercilessly.

Everything about her glows. Magic radiates from her skin in low, thrumming pulses. I study every line of her face until explosions of light flash, forcing my lashes to fall to my cheeks, and I spasm and pound in time with my racing heart. This is sorcery—life and death all at the same moment.

Viola seals her mouth over mine, swallowing a cry that belongs to us both. Then her body slows as her forehead presses to my shoulder. Our hair mingles in a fall of light and dark. Instinctively, my arms cradle her limp form, drawing her against my chest as her fingers slide from my body.

She licks them off, her pink tongue darting languidly along long, elegant digits. I tremble. It's so personal, almost too close. A sensuality I never expected.

"You're delicious," Viola murmurs, nuzzling me sleepily. "As I thought you'd be."

I close my eyes. Instinct has me wanting to encase us in my protective wings, but in this soft human disguise, all I can offer my tale spinner are my arms.

27

BOUDICCA

*D*arkness flickers over my half-shaded eyes like sunlight through leaves. Pleasure surrounds me, my body still pulsing with intense feeling. Viola's head rests on my chest. Her hair spills over my torso like a shining river. Each breath draws the silken strands over my flesh in the most exquisite of tortures.

She licks her lips then laughs quietly as she pulls her clothing back around her, straightening with a blush. "Sorry. I guess I fell asleep."

Shadows flash behind her, blotting out the stars for a moment. I shake my head to clear my vision. We're in a pocket dimension. Shades shouldn't be able to enter it without the summoner being present. It must be a trick of the light.

Viola squeezes my hip as she rises, and my attention returns to her. Her eyes are so dark they look twilight purple against the ivory of her skin. Pink lips swollen with lust seek mine. I gasp, tasting myself on her mouth, then close my eyes, sinking into the kiss. Nothing could've prepared me for this feeling. The intensity of us coming together isn't like anything I've ever experienced. Is this what love feels like?

She jerks back from me with a startled cry. My eyes fly open to see her hair stretched above us, caught up in shadowy claws. Dammit, the shades are here. I swipe, but these human hands have no claws and pass right through the apparition. A low ticking growl crawls from my throat. I don't have enough magic in this form to affect them. How am I going to fight something I can't touch?

Viola scrabbles at the shade, her hands passing through the transparent form. She yanks her hair away, leaving pale strands hanging in the air.

"The shades!" she pants as I tuck her under my arm.

I try to shove one back, but again, my hand passes through it. If I pull off the ring now, she'll know I'm not human. I roar in frustration and sweep Viola behind me. Claws rake down my shoulder, leaving bloody furrows. I scan the area, seeking a way out.

"The hatch," I grunt as one pummels me with rocklike fists. "I'll block them. Move toward the hatch."

I wish I had my wings to shield us right now. I try to tug on my shirt, but the fabric rips as another shadow claws me. The damn wounds aren't closing. Blood trickles down my forehead. I don't heal in this form. This lack of magic in a magical skin is more than frustrating. I bunch my shirt then grab my pants from a nearby cushion.

"Boudicca, they're hurting you." Viola turns as drops of my blood splash onto her arm and cheek.

"I'll be fine. Keep moving." I shove her ahead of me.

Wind rushes over my back, and the clawing stops. I risk a glance up to see the shining golden body of Ariella streaking past me, eviscerating the shades.

"Why are you naked?" she hisses through long fangs.

Relief and fear rip through me in equal parts. "Stay hidden!" I hiss back. "She's not wearing the ring. Viola will piece together I'm a gargoyle if she sees me with you."

Ariella rolls her eyes. "Inconvenient."

"Don't let her see you!"

"Let who see what?" Viola yanks on the hatch, and it clangs with protest. "It's locked. Someone must have barred it from below."

I hover over her. "Let me try."

My hand closes over the handle covered in chipped white paint as a swarm of shades dives from the sky. Swallowing hard, I brace myself for the impact even as I tug. The hatch groans and creaks in protest, but it's been locked from the inside.

Viola twists toward me, eyes wide. "I can go down the wall, but you're too heavy for me to carry. And maybe get your pants on?"

She flinches as a feral catlike scream rips through the night. I'd know that call anywhere—it's Baraq. I'm not sure how the twins got here, but I'm certainly happy they're handling the onslaught. If I can just keep Viola safe and out of view, we might get through this without any awkward explanations.

"I'm working on it." An arrow zings past me, spearing an errant shadow to the nearby wall. I tug my suit coat over Viola's head as I push her toward an arch of roses.

"Was that an arrow? Is someone firing at us?" She tries to wrestle her way out of my coat but I hold it firmly over her head as I search the skies for Cassiopeia. That was definitely one of her arrows.

"I'll get us under some cover. You can't go down the wall. We're in a different dimension. I'm not sure where you'll end up."

"A different dimension?" Viola pokes her head above the collar. Her mussed blonde hair stands out in all directions, and her glasses sit askew on her pert nose. "What sort of dimension? Is it an entirely different world or just the size of the roof?"

A shade dives at me. Baraq plucks it neatly from the air then ducks behind a spiraling column. "This is hardly the time to contemplate such things."

She squints at the sky, attempting to wiggle from my hold. "But what if we could use that dimension to our advantage?"

Another arrow soars behind Viola's head to thud solidly into a shade. I glare up at the feathered form of Cass. "Watch it!"

"Nice butt." Cass smirks.

Viola tries to tug the suit out of the way. "Who's there?"

I pull her closer and glare at my sister, who shrugs before hiding behind a flowering tree. "I think we need to focus on staying alive right now and getting back down to the library."

"Is there another way down?"

Is there? Portals can be tricky, but there's typically more than one way out. Tucking her under a bench, I scan the rooftop. There's a skylight on the top of the main staircase. If that's present here...

The arched glass dome sits on the far side of the garden, decorated in a golden-filigree swirl. That's got to be it. Viola pants beside me, staring at the same spot. She bites her lip with fierce determination then nods.

"Excellent—the skylight." Viola pulls the back of her gown through her legs and tucks it up into her sash. "My slippers may not hold both of us, but I can probably slow us down enough to fall to the uppermost landing."

She tears off, dodging around the grasping shades that immediately pursue her. That wasn't the plan I had in mind at all. "Clear the way for her!" I growl to the gargoyles secreted around us.

Ariella glares down from her perch on a high archway then dives behind Viola, where the shades are trailing her, and swipes them out of existence. Viola turns as Ariella tucks and rolls under some greenery.

"Hurry up! Those things could come back soon." Viola runs her fingers along the edge of the glass panels. "One of these has got to be a vent."

The glow of magic pours from Viola's skin. The damn shades are going to throw themselves at her like moths to a flame. I tug my trousers back on then rush forward to protect her.

A loud thunk and crash come from behind us, and I grasp the ring on my finger. I can guard her in my true form. This human guise is nothing but trouble. She may be shocked, but it's better than her being dead.

"There should be a panel that opens—they always make it so seamless." A side swings open on a soundless hinge. "Ah, here we go."

Viola pops through the opening of the domed skylight, her feet sticking to the underside. Her purple gown swishes around her, obscuring the platform below. My fingers slide from the ring's warm band. Not yet. I sit on the stone roof and scoot forward, dangling my legs into the hole. It's not a terrible drop, maybe fifteen feet, but I'm not sure what this body can handle. I glance up, and my blood chills.

Across the terrace, Elias watches us with fury in his golden-brown eyes. How long has he been up here?

"Boudicca, don't be afraid. Just jump." Viola tugs my hand.

The edge of the dimension wavers around the skylight, flickering like cinders in a breeze. This portal should take us back to the world as she knows it. I move forward, my gaze still pinned to the menacing form of Elias. "Go ahead. I'll follow you."

Right after I take care of him.

A snarl curls my lip. There's no way he doesn't have something to do with these shades. No matter what Xander said, anyone tied to blood magic is bad news. As I stand, Ariella's golden body streaks across the roof and tackles Elias into the tall shrubbery.

"We'll get him back to Xander. Take care of your tale spinner," Cassiopeia whispers.

I nod as Viola tugs my hand hard again, and I follow her

through the skylight. When we step over the edge, the world spins in a way it doesn't in the bōc-hord. An unanchored portal. That wasn't the safest of passages.

"I can jump from here. Close the skylight." I glance at our joined hands, and Viola releases me. Below is the marble landing of the third-floor staircase, farther away than I initially thought. It would be nothing to glide that distance, but without wings, the best I can hope for is not to break anything.

"I'll hand you down. It will halve the fall. The slippers should hold." Viola braces herself against the ceiling, upside down, and reaches for me like a trapeze artist. This idea is dubious at best, but I place both hands in hers and let myself down slowly.

We hang in the air a long moment with her straining above me and the floor below waiting to welcome my soon-to-be-broken body. "Are you sure about this?"

"Well, I've never tried it before," Viola admits as her slippers release from the ceiling with a sickening pop.

She flails frantically in the air as I plummet the last ten feet, my arms outstretched to catch her. The floor cracks in protest as my feet strike it, but I remain standing, and Viola falls into my arms. A relieved breath rushes from my chest as I hold her against me. We're all right. No one is broken.

I glance down at the spiderwebbed marble tile. Well, except the floor.

"Whew, good catch. I guess the slippers do have a weight limit. Back to the ball for a dance, then? We should be safe from the shades there." She flashes me a grin as if we hadn't just run from magical monsters and popped through a dimensional hole. But I can feel her heart hammering in her chest and her breath pushing, fast and shallow, from her lungs.

I hold Viola closer, tucking my face into the curve of her

shoulder. "You never have to put on a brave face for me. Why don't we stay here a moment longer?"

28

VIOLA

The clock chimes as we enter the main hall of the Mazarine. It's well past midnight, and only the dregs of participants are left, talking quietly in small groups. The musicians are packing up, and Chantal seems to be directing a cleaning staff I don't recall hiring. I hope we can afford them.

"I guess we were on the roof longer than I thought," I murmur, gazing around the dimly glittering decorations of an event I barely got to enjoy. Ah well. As long as it made the funds needed...

Mirabelle sweeps across the floor toward us in her stylishly outdated gown, full skirts swishing with each stride. "Viola, where have you been hiding? I still need to tally up the proceeds. Can you stop by my shop in the morning, and I'll give you the final documents?"

"How does it look so far?" Apprehension worms through my gut. My future hinges on the library staying public. I can't marry Elias. I need Boudicca in my life.

Mira beams. "Oh, very successful. If you held a ball every year, it would likely continue to support the library, staff, and community programs without an issue."

"A success." I inhale then let it out slowly. It feels like the first free lungful of air I've had in weeks. "Do you need help cleaning up?"

"No, we've got all that handled." Mirabelle glances at

Boudicca with a speculative glint in her eye. "Why don't you head home, and I'll see you both tomorrow?"

Exhaustion seeps into my bones. Boudicca's hand tightens against my waist. "I'll see her home safely. Thank you for closing up here."

"Of course," Mirabelle chirps, far too jovial for the late hour, then turns away.

Stepping outside, I look up, expecting to see a gibbous moon, but instead, there's a strangely colored half orb in the sky that looks suspiciously like...

"Is that my brother's carriage?"

Boudicca tips her head upward with a grin to look at the monstrous cart plugging the sky like the world's ugliest cork. "Huh, seems to be. Well, it's late. Let's get you home."

Shapes flicker across the ceiling of my bedchamber, chasing the hours of the night toward dawn. I should be able to sleep, between lack of rest and the events at the ball, but the whole casual way Boudicca handled the shades and explained dimensions—not to mention my brother's abomination of a carriage hanging in the air—keeps running through my mind. She said she believes in magic, but she seems more steeped in it than she's letting on. She's never actually detailed what she does for Xander beyond "run errands."

My fingers graze the spot where my emerald ring sat for years. The ring hangs on the chain around my neck, with my pendant, until I figure out my best course of action. Poor Iggy. Are her affections genuine, or is what Xander said true? I swallow the bittersweet feeling and turn onto my side, curling into a ball. She'll be alive if I choose to stay in Paris, but for how long? The whole situation is grossly unfair. I haven't found any useful books on the topic yet. Even the book on magic I found says nothing about gargoyles. I'm running out of time. There must be a way to solve this problem.

Images of floor-to-ceiling leatherbound books spring to mind. My grandmother's room has to be somewhere in the bowels of this house. I navigated through dimensions in the Mazarine. How much harder could it possibly be to find my way to my grandmother's study? It must be in some side pocket of space—a place that most people wouldn't or couldn't notice.

My robe is on, and I'm out the door before my thoughts get sidetracked again. I don't bother closing my eyes this time. I know the feel of passing through the dimensional pockets now, that subtle shimmy of space as it glides over my soul. I race down the darkened hallway and nearly trip when the sound of my footsteps changes from scuffs on carpet to clacking on a wooden floor.

My body vibrates with excitement. I'm not wearing the ring. What if that was why I could never find my grandmother's sanctum?

Moonlight fills the room, making the white-sheet-covered furniture look like a herd of forlorn ghosts. On the nearby wall, tiny sculptures of gargoyles spiral among the gilt curls of molding. My grandmother must have known about gargoyles. Are these small ones alive or just decoration? Do they guard the secrets this portal hides?

Stepping closer, my feet brush against long gouges in the wood floor. This is the spot where I dragged the chair as a child. *This is real.*

I rest my hand on the long tail of a beast with twisting horns and push down. A click echoes in the stillness of the room as if the apparitions of this place are all holding their breath, waiting for the next moment of eternity. A portion of the wall glides soundlessly inward, and moonlight shines on the top of a spiral stone staircase.

This is it. I've found my grandmother's study. After all these years of searching, it's real, and I'm here. I race down the stairs but stumble in the dark after only a few steps. Blacker than black—there's no gleaming woman to light my way this time.

I'm not going back to find a light. What if I can't locate the entrance again? With a hand against the rough stone wall, I feel my way down. I'm not sure what I'll do at the bottom of the stairs, but I recall a light down there somewhere.

After a few moments, my eyes adjust, and a dim glow comes from below. It's just enough for me to make out the curve of the wall and edge of each shallow step. A spicy scent tickles my nose, and dust drifts thickly through the air.

The cool light grows brighter as I step off the staircase into a short hall with a stone arch at the end. Anticipation ripples over my skin, and excitement quickens my step. Everything feels and smells exactly as it did all those years ago.

I enter the room. Pale-violet globes dangle in silvery casings against the walls. They stir to life, and dust glitters like mica in the air, swirling around me with each forward step. Not dust. Magic.

As if suspended in time, everything looks exactly the same as the first time I saw the room as a child. A desk littered with scrolls and books faces outward from a tall apothecary cabinet. A green-painted bookcase is along the wall, filled to the brim with tomes my fingers itch to explore. An arm with a small cauldron extends over an unlit fireplace surrounded by comfortable-looking wing-backed chairs. A silvery halo of mist encapsulates the left chair.

Curious, I step toward it. The light shines brighter, coalescing with a shimmering brilliance into the shape of a woman with snowy white hair.

"Grandmother?"

The woman smiles and stands. The chair wavers through

her translucent form as if passing through water, and my eyes burn as her visage shines impossibly bright. "That's right, Viola. It took you a little longer to work it out than I expected."

I squint. "You didn't exactly leave crystal-clear directions. I've been looking for this room for years. Are you a ghost?"

"Something like that," she says, continuing her history of vagueness. "I wish I could've been present for your education, but as I passed from your world earlier than expected, I had to wait until you were old enough to find your own way here."

I swallow hard. She's here now, and I've found my way into the world of magic outside the mundane casing that has mired me all my life. "The ring," I whisper, realizing that the tiny piece of metal had some larger role in this.

"Our world can be extremely predatory to those who can't protect themselves. I gave you the ring to shield your magic so nonhumans wouldn't notice you until you were old enough to handle yourself. Of course, that also interfered with you being able to sense magic."

"I've looked for magic my entire life. Do you know how alone I've been?"

"I'm sorry, my dear. It's so unfortunate everyone alive in our family is ungifted. Everything has a cost, and I felt protecting you with the ring was for the best." She hovers close to me, flickering around the edges like a candle caught in a breeze. "But now we can begin your education—well, to some degree, anyway. You come from a long line of magical artificers called makers. It really is a shame your father lacked our gifts, but such is life. I made the slippers and ring I gave to you in the hope that one day they would lead you back to me."

"And the pendant—the one that controls the gargoyles?" Impatience to know everything at once wells in me. I was in the dark for so long.

Her brow furrows. "The labradorite pendant is not of my

making. I gave it to you to keep it hidden and safe. The ring's magic should have kept it cloaked. What do you mean by controlling gargoyles?"

Expecting her to enlighten me about everything, I gnaw my lip. "Gargoyles are alive."

"Well, some are. It depends on their maker. Do you know a maker?" Grandmother asks.

"Xander Albright. The mage in the tower in the park area."

She brushes the long, full skirt of her antique-styled gown, leaving a trail of glittering dust. "Huh. They're still alive and puttering around that old tower? How curious. Yes, I'm aware the stone guardians of that tower are alive. Xander is an eccentric sort, but I'm willing to bet they'd help out with your tutelage if you asked. At least then you'd have a teacher able to leave this study."

My heart drops. "You can't leave here?"

"Afraid not, dear. Nestled between your world and the afterlife, this is where I anchored myself when I was alive. However, I can direct you to some books here, and you have access to all my supplies. I'll get you able to defend yourself before the creatures in the magic world notice you."

I frown. "They've already noticed me. Am I safe here? Shades have been attacking me. So far, a gargoyle has protected me, but magic creatures noticed me even before I took my ring off."

"Shades?" Grandmother hisses through her teeth. "Those things could kill you. You'll need a magic weapon to harm them."

"Well, I certainly don't have that unless kicking them with a slipper will work." The gravity of everything hits me. Words bubble forth in a tumble. "My parents are marrying me off to some random minor nobleman to pop out heirs, so your teaching time is going to be quite limited." My voice rises a hysterical octave. "I mean, it's possible I'll retain my job and avoid marriage briefly, but it doesn't sound like Elias is willing to let me go. I wish I'd found you sooner. It's a shame I didn't know about a lot of things earlier in life."

Grandmother tries to put her arms around me, but they pass through with a cool tingle. A frenzied laugh crawls out of my throat. There's a ghost in the nonexistent basement of my parents' manor, and the door to the magic world is finally wide open, but the things on the other side are going to kill me.

"What should I do?" I ask.

"I think you need to talk to Maker Xander. They may be able to help, especially by using their gargoyle guardians."

I hold back a groan of frustration. "I did. I mean, I'm still working things out with them. Do you have any books on how the pendant functions?"

Grandmother floats to the bookcase. "This one here should give you a good start. Everything in this room is my gift to you. Use it as you will."

The multicolored spines of the books gleam softly in the low light. I can only hope the answer to my problem is among them.

29

BOUDICCA

"What do you mean you didn't catch Elias? I saw you tackle him." I lash my tail in agitation as I pace the familiar worn stone floors of Xander's study.

Baraq shrugs while Ariella leans against the bookshelf, filing her already sharp nails. Out the window, the first edge of dawn creeps over the horizon, and we're all exhausted and ready for stone sleep. I won't even get that today. I promised Viola I'd meet her at the café near the library to deliver the good news to Master Frederick.

"Xander sent us to keep an eye on you because they foresaw you'd have problems." Ariella flicks me the barest of glances. "We weren't expecting you to be smooching a human up on the roof. *Anyway*, Elias disappeared just like a shade. Poof."

"Where's Cass?" I ask. The last thing I need is Ariella's flippant attitude. I comb my fingers through my already tangled mane, causing the curls to frizz into an unmanageable snarl.

"She's already in stone sleep." Baraq sighs. "Like we should be."

I wave my hand dismissively. "Go, then. I need to speak to Xander."

"They're in the kitchen." Ariella prowls up the stairs to the roof.

Sighing, I walk to the other side of the room then down the spiral staircase. I pass the level mostly taken up by Xander's bedroom and continue downward to where the tower widens into a kitchen and dining area along with a sprawling living area and library. I never questioned before how this level is so much larger than it looks from the outside. It never occurred to me that Xander has dimensional pockets built all over their living quarters until I experienced the Mazarine Library.

A sharp clang from the kitchen, followed by muttering, draws me into the cozy space. It's obvious that Matilda, the brownie who usually sees to the cooking, isn't present. The scent of burned bread wafts on the air along with another swear.

Xander stands at the sink, scraping charred eggs out of a pan. They stop and rest their hand on a forehead beaded with sweat. A half-open rumpled robe hangs from the mage's narrow shoulders. Visible beneath is a short cloth wrap around their chest and billowing turquoise pants.

I clear my throat. "Do you have a moment to talk?"

"I don't suppose you've learned how to cook in your forays into the human world." They dump the pan into the sink, then grab an apple from a bowl on the table and sink their teeth into it with a chomp of frustration.

"No. Look, I think Elias is the one behind the shade attacks. He was on the roof last night at the ball."

Xander makes a muffled grunt then takes another huge bite of apple. They chew it thoughtfully and swallow. "You mean the rooftop garden only accessed from the bōc-hord. The one you took Viola to."

"Well, yes, but we knew he was a magic user of some sort—"

"The rooftop you... *romanced* her on." Xander levels a look at me that I do my best to avoid.

"What she and I did up there is of no concern to you. I believe Elias is behind the shade attacks we've been experiencing for decades. We have to investigate this. Especially before Viola is forced to marry him."

"Do you love her?" Xander takes another bite of the apple.

"I—what? Yes. I mean no. I've known her for years—there's certainly familiar affection there—" I sputter on awkwardly. *Love her?* How can a soulless creature love?

"But last night you made love to her." They glare.

I lash my tail. "I was in human form."

Xander's voice rises to a pitch they've never uttered before. "You are a *gargoyle*."

"And *you*," I snap, "carved us all to be anatomically correct. Why would you do that if you never expected us to have sex?"

Xander's mouth clamps shut. They glare at me before answering. "Because the female form is an artistic delight to gaze upon."

"You've carved males as well. That sounds like a load of—"

"This little experiment has gone on long enough to become tedious. Viola is obviously distracting you from your duties of guarding this tower. You're bound to this city, Boudicca. When she leaves, you won't be able to follow her."

"Leaves?" My wings droop. "Why would she leave?"

"Elias isn't going to settle here in Paris. I'm certain he'll be hauling her back to Austria shortly."

"But the shades..." My voice trails off to a squeak of protest.

"He's not nearly powerful enough to summon so many. That would take a lot of magical skill." Xander sits on a kitchen stool. "Let me worry about Elias. While my farseeing around him is clouded, that's not unusual for reads I get off fellow magic users."

"Viola isn't safe," I growl.

"That isn't your concern. She's a human—you're a

gargoyle. You never should've indulged in what you did last night while wearing your human guise."

Rage pours through me. "Were you spying on me?"

"I am your maker, and you're absolutely forbidden to leave Paris. At the edge of the city, you'll simply become lifeless stone."

My eyes drop to the labradorite pendant around Xander's neck. They've always behaved like a parental figure, to the point of being doting. The very fact they'd lay this on me now, when Viola's life is at risk, makes hot fury run through my veins.

I straighten, pulling my wings tight against my back, and grab the ring from Xander's desk. "I promised Viola I'd accompany her to her meeting at the library this morning. I need to go, or I'll be late."

"She won't need you. Go take your stone sleep on the roof."

"No. I already promised."

"Boudicca!"

Xander's shout falls on deaf ears as I exit the room via a nearby balcony. I leap, allowing myself to fall a short distance before unfurling my wings to catch the updraft. There's just enough twilight left before the sun rises and I become too heavy to fly. Cold, wet rivulets streak my face. Raising a hand to my cheek, I realize they're tears. I've never cried before—I didn't even know I could.

I hover in the air, staring at my damp fingertips. This sensation feels both wrong and wonderful all at the same time. The first ray of dawn skims the city, and I dip as my weight increases. I need to land and change back to my human form. Viola needs me, and I'll always be there for her.

30

VIOLA

My bright-periwinkle skirt flares as I skip down the street on the way to the Mazarine, with the paperwork from Mirabelle clutched under one arm. Twirling playfully, I spin the skirt higher. *We did it.* The ball raised enough funds to keep the library open for at least a couple years. In the meantime, with the books in my grandmother's study, I'm sure I can find a way to stay here and not hurt Iggy.

Take that, you crusty old men. Knowledge is for everyone.

I turn down the street and see Boudicca's tall, broad form sprawled in a metal chair outside the café. Last night comes back to me in a rush of heated pleasure. The touches, the whispered moans that left her lips—being with her was so exquisite it scarcely felt real.

"Boudicca! We did it!" I race breathlessly toward her. "I just got the final tally sheets from Mirabelle. She's headed to the bank now."

She stands and holds her hand out to me, and I put mine in hers, reveling in the smooth comfort of her palm. I tip my chin, but my smile falters when I see her red-rimmed eyes. Boudicca looks away, her long curly hair falling forward to hide the strong planes of her face.

"That's wonderful. So you'll stay in Paris now and work in the library?" She squeezes my hand and leads us down the street.

"Maybe. I'm not sure yet. I'm still trying to work that out."

My heart swells as we enter the square before the library. I've proven I'm useful. Hell, I'm essential. I've taken a bad situation and not only turned it around but also took the initiative to spearhead this endeavor—something none of the scholars who use this facility even bothered to try. Not all of them are wealthy. They would've lost access to all this knowledge unless they had some connection to Kensington.

Lifting the hem of my skirt, I jog up the steps while Boudicca takes them by twos. The library is closed to the public today to allow time to clean up. Mirabelle hired a crew for that, and they should be nearly done.

I pause in the vestibule, allowing my eyes to adjust to the light. Low voices murmur over the tables lining the long room. The cleaning crew has already stripped anything remotely decorative from the building, making it look as if the event never happened. Half a dozen elderly scholars sit at the table at the far end of the room, arguing among themselves. I slide my hand from Boudicca's and approach.

Standing before them, bent shouldered and defeated, is the head librarian, Master Frederick. He's not wearing his usual black robes today but is in a threadbare sweater and patched trousers. I've never seen him out of uniform, and the sight sends a cold lump straight to the pit of my gut. Something's wrong. It doesn't make any sense. Why would there already be a council called to decide on the fate of the library before I even had a chance to present the proceeds.

As I stride forward, the unwelcome form of Lord Kensington comes into view. He leans against a wood column, a knowing smirk on his face as he watches me. Like he's already won. Not today. The funds are in the bank, and the proof is on these papers. These books are safe from him and his hoarding.

"Master Frederick, I have wonderful news. With the fundraising accomplished from last night's ball, there is more than enough money to run a fully staffed Mazarine for two years. Now, I know it's not enough to keep the doors open indefinitely, but I have some ideas to discuss with you that could make that a possibility." I stand before the master librarian with my back to Kensington. His smug glare continues to burn my skin.

"Ah, Viola." Master Frederick gives me a weak smile. "You've worked so hard for this establishment, and I want you to know how grateful we are for your efforts."

A rumbling starts up from the men at the table, and shouts of "Waste of time!" and "Just marry her off!" hit my ears with unexpected force. Frustration overwhelms me. I'm literally handing them the ability to keep this place public.

"What our former master librarian is saying is it has come to light that there are back taxes owed by the library because of the new laws that came into effect this month, and the money you raised won't even begin to cover that."

Lord Kensington's words ring in my head as I attempt to make sense of them. No. That isn't fair—we worked so hard. Boudicca rests her hand on my shoulder, but I shake it off.

"How much more do we need? I can raise it."

I hand the documentation to Master Frederick, who peers through his thick lenses to peruse it. "I'm sorry, dear. It would take twenty times this to break even. At this point, Lord Kensington has graciously offered to pay off our debts and allow scholars to apply for membership to the Mazarine."

Desperately, I try to save some of my life's work. "What about the philanthropy programs the library offers to the community?" Despair clogs my throat. I'll lose access to the magical parts of the Mazarine. There's no way His Lordship will ever allow me membership.

"The schools of Paris are good enough for the street rats you teach. There was never any need to subject these books to their grubby little hands." Kensington's patronizing tone grates on my last nerve.

"He means to turn the Mazarine into a social club for the male privileged," I spit, attempting to appeal to the scholars present, who will never be able to claim membership. "Kensington will sell off the collection piecemeal, leaving only the most mundane of texts for the ultrawealthy to peruse. Enjoy your conformity, and death to critical thinking."

"Now, Viola, that seems rather harsh." Kensington smiles, but it doesn't reach his eyes. "Perhaps this is your chance to see a different part of the world. I've heard the mountains of Austria are breathtaking."

The nerve. I grab Boudicca's hand and storm out of the building. She stumbles behind me as I stop midstep on the stairs. Rain pours down beyond the overhang of the roof, obscuring the city beyond. "Xander can help."

"What?" Boudicca peers down at me, a quizzical expression on her face that would be adorable if I weren't so pissed off.

"Xander is a mage that creates gargoyles. Surely, they have social ties and deep pockets. They're your employer—you can ask them to help."

Thunder cracks across the sky, and the wind kicks up, tossing Boudicca's mussed curls. "Viola, I can't. It wouldn't be appropriate."

"Appropriate? Is it appropriate that I'm about to get shipped off to Austria with some military buffoon after we—" I bite my tongue, trying to control my temper. "Please, at least try."

Boudicca chews her lower lip, sucking the flesh between her teeth, before looking out into the deluge. "I can't."

"As a wealthy recluse, Xander has to be able to do something. Their name is practically legendary in the upper-crust circles. Surely, you could convince them—"

"We had an argument this morning." She scuffs her boot tip against the damp cobblestones. "I can't ask for that."

"I know Xander is a mage and a powerful one. There has to be some way they can help."

Boudicca throws her hands up, her voice deepening to a growl. "What part of *no* is hard for you to understand?"

I reel back. It would have hurt less if she'd slapped me. It doesn't matter anymore. My job is gone. I'm about to be married off, and there isn't a damn thing I can do about it. I'm on my own, just like I always was.

"No, sure, I get it. I need to get going." I step away then turn and head out into the downpour.

Boudicca grabs my arm. "Viola, wait, you don't understand."

I shake off her hand and stride down the street. Unfortunately, I understand being on my own all too well.

31

BOUDICCA

Rain pours down from the gray sky, filling my boots with a sea almost as deep as my sorrow. Viola disappears down the street, leaving me reeling with loss. After weeks of dishonesty, I can't tell Viola that I don't just work for Xander but I was created by them—or that I'm not even human. As a soulless creature, how dare I even dream to partner with her? With the argument I had with Xander this morning, I could never ask for their help. Xander's asking me for one thing, Viola for another, and it's tearing me apart. What about what I want? How could Xander possibly expect me to just be a tower guardian again after I've experienced love?

Love. There's no other word for the tenderness I feel for Viola. I'm in love with her.

I strip off my human clothes in the middle of the street then stuff them in a satchel and tug down my chiton. Removing the ring, I burst into the air without caring whether anyone sees me. Lightning darts across the sky, and thunder echoes the mighty clap of my wings that sends me soaring higher. I love Viola, which means I can't possibly be soulless. Not anymore.

I shoot up above the storm clouds, winging my way through rays of sunlight. I don't feel the usual stiffness the light brings. There's one way to prove all of this. I'll fly over the boundary of Paris. If I crash like lifeless stone, then Xander was right, and it's all over anyway. If I survive, then I'll come clean to Viola about my true nature and hope she returns my feelings. My heart sings at the thought of being with her for the rest of our days. I'll offer to fly her anywhere in the world she wants. She'll never have to marry a man she hates.

I wing east, clutching my fists so tight my claws dig into my palms. Dark clouds blanket Paris, forcing me to dip beneath them to see what part of the city I'm flying over. Remains of the old wall that used to surround the city mingle with newer buildings. This could be the height of foolishness, but in my heart—my heart that loves—I'm certain I will survive.

Rain soaks my skin, plastering my chiton to it. My mane whips around my shoulders in sodden tendrils as I fly closer to where the city stops and the countryside starts. Low clouds roll in, obscuring the buildings and forcing me to glide even lower. What controls when or if I turn to stone? Is it the old boundaries or the new ones, where the city outgrew its walls?

I press on, sensing rather than seeing the edge of Paris. The growing push of wind against my wings strains my already abused body. Pumping hard, I bank in the clouds to avoid a tall building. Saint Mandé and the castle directly south of it pass under my belly. It's outside the city borders. Maybe it's a suburb of Paris. My muscles tense in anticipation. Where's the line? Will I even feel it?

As I skim lower, I can almost touch verdant treetops when my wings stiffen. But it's daylight—this doesn't mean a stone fate. Rolling storm clouds prevent the sun's rays from touching my body, yet my weight increases, dragging me lower.

It's unfair. I was so certain the new, soft emotions I felt for Viola were proof I was something more than a created being. I glide lower to the earth and land in a field of forget-me-nots that remind me of the vivid blue of Viola's eyes. A skin of stone creeps up my arms as I breathe in the wet, earthy smell around me.

I hope Viola has a good life free from the confines of the society she rebelled against. She's so strong. She never needed me to forge her path forward, but it was my honor to be included on her journey. My wings grow too heavy to lift, falling to the earth to pin me in place. As my vision dims, I play out a future in my mind's eye: Viola surrounded by children in the library as she reads fairy tales to them. Maybe sometime, she'll tell the story of a gargoyle friend she named Iggy.

Stone creeps up my neck, and I bow my head. This life was good. I tried my best. Closing my eyes, I remember the warmth and comfort of Viola's body against mine—the tenderness that she showed me and how much I loved her for it. I hold my arms out before me as I've always done to cradle her. Stone stiffens my limbs until my breathing slows and my heart gives one last thump.

32

Viola

As I scale the tower seeking Iggy's comfort, tears sting my eyes. Today didn't go the way I thought it would at all. It started out so perfect, and I actually thought things were finally working out in my favor. And then that whole thing with Boudicca. Ugh, it's fine. I'll just ask Xander myself. The worst they can say is no.

Scraping my hands on the abrasive stone, I haul myself up over the tower's crenulations. I just need to talk to someone who will understand, and my body screams to be in the comfort of my gargoyle's arms.

I stare across the rain-slick rooftop at the blank space where Iggy usually stands. Numbness coats my mind. She's always been right here. Perched nearby is Baraq, wings extended to the stormy sky.

Grasping his wild stone mane, I bring my face to his. "Where's Iggy?"

He doesn't flinch. Baraq's eyes have the thousand-mile stare all stone statues have. I shove his shoulder. "I know you're alive, dammit. Tell me where my gargoyle is."

Nothing. Not even a ripple over his granite hide.

I race across the stone tiles and yank open the red wooden door to the study below. "Xander!" I choke out, racing down the stairs at breakneck speed.

The mage sits behind their large, cluttered worktable. Their hand pauses in midair, with a metal device pinched between two fingers. Xander's beard is inexplicably back—

wild, braided with ribbons, and tossed casually over one shoulder like a shawl. They blink several times through colored lenses that magnify their green eye to a gargantuan size before flipping the gadget back over their head.

"Viola, to what do I owe the pleasure of your—"

"Where's Iggy? She's not on the roof," I pant.

Xander takes a moment to remove the magnifying headset and pick up their glasses. "I don't know, my dear. We had an argument this morning, and she took off. She's been disobedient more and more lately, to the point where I fear she may no longer be viable as a guardian."

"No longer?" I clutch the pendant at my throat. "But I've stayed away. Where is she?"

"It doesn't seem to be enough. Iggy is making her own decisions now. She's no longer under my magic." Xander stands and crosses the study toward me. "I wish I could help you, but I can't even feel where she is anymore."

I sigh. "The fundraiser ball I threw for the library failed. Lord Kensington said there were some back taxes the Mazarine owed that were far more than the proceeds."

"Kensington? The English lord?" Xander arches one auburn eyebrow. "What does he have to do with all of this?"

"He's buying the library and making it private. I think he just wants to get his hands on the rare books. It doesn't matter. I failed. I failed in everything." I tug my pendant from my neck and slide the emerald ring off the chain. "Here, take the pendant so I can't harm Iggy anymore. At least that's the one thing I can fix."

Xander holds out their hand, and I pool the pendant and chain into it. I try to hold back my tears as I close their fingers around it. This was inevitable. I reached too far.

"I need to go," I mutter. Clutching the ring, I head back up the stairs.

THE LIBRARIAN'S GARGOYLE

THE DOOR to my bedchamber bangs open as Mother storms in. I stayed out all day and most of the night, running from rooftop to rooftop, until I finally settled into my own bed well after dawn. My eyes burn, and my head throbs, but I'm all cried out. All that is left to this husk of my soul is my resolve.

Blearily, I blink at Mother. "Can this wait?"

"Viola, where have you been? In your absence, your father and brothers took Elias out into the countryside to entertain him with a hunt. How am I supposed to explain to your future husband that you were out all night like some"—she takes a dramatic breath—"like some trollop?"

I roll my eyes. What exactly does she think I do at the library—flirt with the decrepit old scholars? I try not to giggle as my mother continues her hysterical tirade.

"I'm sorry, Mother. I got caught up in the library and lost track of time. I fell asleep on the chair there, and with no windows in the room, I didn't realize how late it was. I assure you—

it was nothing scandalous. Just a bunch of old, dusty books."

It's a lie, but I don't care. I roll out of the bed, still wearing my clothes from the night before. I already regret how Boudicca and I parted. Sure, I was angry about the situation with Kensington, but I shouldn't have taken it out on her or pressured her into something she was uncomfortable with. Boudicca usually sets my anxious heart at ease. I stare at my reflection in the vanity to avoid my mother's glare. The truth is, Boudicca makes me feel more at peace than I ever felt at home.

Mother huffs. "You are absolutely forbidden to leave this house without notifying either me or your father. We have guests coming over tonight for dinner to celebrate your engagement. Maria will be in shortly to help you get dressed."

I swallow down my rage. I've been escaping this house for most of my life, and she never even noticed before now. "I forgot that's tonight. I didn't agree to this arrangement. Can we move it? I'm not hungry."

"Most of us actually eat an evening meal every night. You'll need a plumper figure if you ever expect to be a mother." She waves her hand dismissively. "The men should return by sunset."

"What if I don't want to marry Elias?" I blurt. "What if there's someone else that's caught my eye?"

"Is there?" Her thin eyebrow arches so high it will permanently attach to her hairline.

My neck heats. The burn rapidly travels to the tips of my ears. "Maybe, yes. I mean, I just met her."

"Her? I don't have time for this foolishness. You may have had your whimsical phase of playing with women, but it's time to put that all behind you. Your future is raising heirs for your father's trading empire. Make yourself presentable, and I expect you to spend the evening getting better acquainted with the duke's son—your future husband." She slams the door hard enough that the sound reverberates with her final word.

Great. I pick up my brush and drag it through the length of my hair. Why did I even mention that? I might as well have announced I'm in love with a gargoyle.

The brush stills in my hair. It's true, though. Discovering that Iggy was not only alive but had been there for me for my whole life warmed my entire being. Just hearing Xander saying I created that feeling within Iggy, out of loneliness, crushed me. Is it even possible for a created being to feel love? I wonder where my gargoyle is now. Will Xander put her down like he did Lysander? A shiver spikes down my back.

And what about Boudicca? I toss my brush onto the vanity and stand. This is ridiculous. I've gone my entire life without having more than a casual dalliance with anyone, and now that I'm *betrothed*—I try not to gag at the thought—I'm falling for Boudicca *and* a stone woman, neither of whom are the person I'm engaged to. This is insane. I should've stuck to books.

A hesitant knock comes from the door as it opens a sliver. Maria pokes her head into the room cautiously, a deep-blue gown draped over one arm. "May I come in? I'm here to help you prepare for tonight."

I answer her with a wave of my hand, not able to articulate anything beyond a garbled bleat. My eyes dart to the stack of books on the table nearby—my grandmother's is on top. Maybe there's something in there I can use. It couldn't hurt. My situation couldn't possibly get any worse.

Maria holds up a corset a handsbreadth wide.

I snort. "Is my mother insane? That doesn't look like it will fit a small dog, let alone my torso." How is it that I'm supposed to be both sturdy enough to bear children and tiny enough to fit into a toothpick-sized dress? I hate society's ideas of what's acceptable.

"It's a Paquin gown, mademoiselle. She's the premier designer in Paris right now. Your mother insisted on something to show off your womanly assets tonight."

"Of which I have none," I grumble as I reluctantly hold my arms up for Maria to attend to me. It's not her fault, and there's no point in making her job any more difficult.

"That's why there is strategic padding." She shows me the interior of the garment.

Thick pads line the bust and hip, built into the garment itself and supported by the ruffled underpinnings. Well, at least it will be impossible to get out of if Elias gets any premarital notions of the frisky variety.

"Fine." I let my mind go blank as Maria tugs and lifts various parts of my body into the confinements of fashion. It's as fake as the relationship my family is forcing me to endure.

While Maria fusses with lacings and fluffs parts I don't have, my lips twist. It surprises me that Xander didn't know exactly how the pendant effects gargoyles. Or is the use of magic nebulous and not that scientific? I'm running out of time, and *this* needs more research. I don't want to go to this ridiculous dinner. I need to be plundering my grandmother's study for knowledge.

"Have a seat, and I'll do your hair and makeup." Maria presses a hand firmly on my bare shoulder. Turning, I catch my hourglass-shaped reflection in the mirror.

Heavens, but Madam Paquin could design a dress. The brilliant-blue hue somehow makes my eyes look dark violet. My waist is positively nonexistent, and my small breasts are pushed nearly out of the corset with all the padding under them. I look like a piece of art, not a person. I can't decide if I love the unique artistry of the gown and the skill it took to create it or hate how artificial it is.

Frowning, I poke at my outrageously padded hips before taking a seat. The pillows on my bed have less cushioning. God forbid anyone should touch me and mistake me for furniture.

"It's lovely, isn't it?" Maria combs my hair and then starts the intricate twists and braids.

"I'm certain my parents will be delighted." I'm more like a thing than a person. An item to be traded for value, with less will and autonomy than a beautifully carved gargoyle.

33

VIOLA

"You look positively stunning." Elias bows before me.

Taking my hand, he brushes a light kiss over my knuckles. His gaze moves over my bare shoulders to my upper chest, where a choker of sapphires lies against my skin. A slight frown ripples over his face, but it smooths quickly. Perhaps I imagined it.

Our ballroom is positively packed with people, and the hum of conversation is enough to make me want to run back to the quiet sanctuary of my chamber. I had no idea my mother invited so many guests. She said there'd be a dozen—this is more than twice that. My eyes widen as a woman sits by a harp near the entrance to the dining room and begins to play. My parents are flaunting their wealth more than usual. Staff in their best livery serve trays of bite-sized food and glasses of champagne. The press of the gathering is too much.

"Can we talk?" I whisper to Elias as the high knell sounds for dinner.

"Perhaps after the meal." His hand drifts to the small of my back. I step forward, trying to avoid his invasive touch as Elias maneuvers me toward the dining room.

Mother and Father beam at us, and looking around, I realize what this is. These are all their business partners—the people they negotiate with. They're introducing Elias to their elite circle as a reciprocal trade contact, most likely.

My stomach knots. I glance around the room in search of

a friend—someone, anyone—but I'm alone in this crowd. A thing. A bargaining chip. Another daughter to use for prestige and power.

My dress is too tight. The ruffles swish, making far too much noise, and the fabric irritates my skin, rubbing against my shoulders until I'm ready to scream. Can people tell I'm padded out like a chaise longue? Too much of my chest is showing, and I want to hide. I'd give my left hand to be in breeches and a loose shirt. Well, not the entire hand—that could make climbing difficult. Maybe just a pinky.

"Viola, breathe," Elias murmurs. "You'll be fine."

This. Is. Not. *Fine.*

Pulling out a chair, Elias gestures for me to sit before taking his seat beside me. The conversation turns into a dull, unintelligible roar. I clasp my hands in my lap, knuckles turning white as my grip tightens. It's too loud. The music of the harp sounds discordant with the chatter of the gathered crowd.

"Viola, breathe, or you'll pass out," Elias hisses, staring at me in what could be concern.

A plate with a swirl of crimson and some fancy frill-cut artistic something appears before me. I'm not sure if it's a vegetable or meat, but it has a weird herbal smell that has my nose twitching. My lungs refuse to fill. I can't make sense of the dish as it floats upward toward me.

Elias's hands curl around my shoulders, pulling me back against the chair. "Good heavens, woman, you nearly put your face in the appetizer. What's wrong?"

I pull in a jerky breath and look around the table. No one else noticed. "I'm dizzy."

"Scoot forward," Elias mutters. "Cripes, they have you trussed up and padded like a Christmas goose. Come, we'll find a private room and get that loosened up."

Well, *that's* flattering. "I won't be seen going somewhere with you privately. I'm fine."

"No woman in the history of forever has ever meant she's fine when she says that word."

Elias angrily plucks my stays while moving his body to block the view of his endeavors.

They weren't actually that tight to begin with, but it's easier to let him believe my clothing is the issue. With agility I find questionable, he has the laces loosened all the way up the back of my bodice in seconds. I'm not sure if I should be shocked or impressed as he somehow unties the bow of my corset through a gap in the bodice lacings, allowing it to slip a fraction wider.

"Done this a few times before, have you?" I lift my glass and take some healthy swallows of wine.

"I wouldn't make much of a lover if I didn't know my way around ladies' garments," he purrs into my ear before settling back and lifting his fork from the table.

My brain grinds to a full halt, certain I didn't hear those words in that order, but I did. Fire lights in me, burning off the panic from earlier. "A bit experienced, are you?"

Elias's hazel eyes slide to mine over his glass of wine. He takes a sip and sets it down before leaning close enough to block our conversation from onlookers. "You'll thank me on our wedding night."

"Creep." I narrow my eyes. "What happened to giving me a choice in this engagement?"

"That ended the moment I saw the company you kept." His low growl prickles my skin. "You're one of the rare artificers of the Bichler family. I thought you were completely unaware of that world and I'd be introducing you to it, but quite obviously, that was an incorrect assumption on my part. Now, smile, my Christmas goose. They're about to toast our engagement."

I gape as his heavy hand presses to my back and his fingers curl around my hip, lifting me to rise. *The nerve.*

Elias raises his glass. "The honor is mine to have a wife this lovely returning with me to my homeland."

It takes every ounce of politeness in me not to stomp on the arch of his foot. "I will never marry you," I hiss through my teeth. Cheers of applause and clinking glasses sound around us.

"Challenge accepted. I do relish a good fight." Elias dips his head, pressing his lips to my cheek. His mustache prickles my skin, and I endure it, disgust rippling over me to settle low in my gut.

"We are so pleased to have made such a wonderful match for our youngest daughter." Father raises his glass.

This is a done deal, the only choice I have left. I've lost the Mazarine and alienated Boudicca with our argument, and Iggy is gone—possibly insane, if Xander is to be believed. For a moment, I contemplate putting on the emerald ring and forgetting the magic world ever existed.

Elias squeezes my hip, and I can't jerk away. It would mortify my parents and embarrass them in front of their guests. It's enough to jar me out of my funk. I don't know where my life is going, but this isn't it. There's no way I'm giving Elias the satisfaction of seeing me as the blushing maiden. I take a page from Mother's book, faking a swoon back into my chair then slumping dramatically to the floor. Elias of the bazillion names wants to play a game? None of this will be easy for him. I'll play to win.

34

Boudicca

A sliver of light beats back the absolute velvety dark of my consciousness. I'm weary, and it's so easy to stay in the comfort of this eternal sleep. The coolness of stone soothes my aching heart. Stone doesn't feel. Stone doesn't hurt. Stone doesn't love.

But I do. I love my life and adore my family. If Viola loves me the way I do her, she'll forgive my evasiveness with my identity. The worst she can do is reject me. To do that, I need to be alive, to breathe, to be my own being. I stretch. First, it's only a finger that moves. Obsidian crumbles from my skin in a hail of tiny pebbles.

I open my eyes.

The world is bathed in silvery moonlight that kisses each blue-violet flower in the field in an ethereal glow. Magic swirls around me—the cool greens of earth, the silver of the heavens, the warm salmon color of life. I'm alive. With effort, I inhale, and the stone shell cracks further. It's never been this difficult to shift from my stone sleep. The stone drops away in huge chunks like the shell of an egg.

Flexing my thighs and lashing my tail out of its prison, I pull my legs free of the surrounding stone. Quickly it crumbles, and the eddies of magic twirling around me devour it. Experimentally, I fully extend my wings. They ache from immobility as dust sprinkles fall off them, but they don't appear to be damaged.

Flowers ripple below me as I take off into the night sky.

Moments later the old, crumbling wall of the city comes into view. The twins anxiously pace the boundary, stopping only when I alight on the stone nearby.

"Huh. Looks like I lost that bet. You're not dead." Ariella prowls closer then sniffs at me. Her wide nose wrinkles. "You smell weird."

I rest a hand on her strong shoulder. "Thanks. I was worried about you too."

Nearby, Baraq stretches his long catlike body then lifts his nose to the air. "We came looking for you as soon as the sun set. Xander's drunk, thinking you ended up like Lysander—crazy and dangerous. But you smell..." He sniffs the air again. "Not like stone. You smell like magic and something sweet... maple? Are you insane?"

"No. I'm not insane. We should let Xander know I'm all right."

And then I need to find Viola. I hate that we parted like we did. As soon as the twins are ready, we take flight together.

Something in the air tonight feels wrong, like the tension on the surface of a soap bubble before it pops. Lights over Paris sparkle against the velvet-dark sky. It's deceptively peaceful, and I scan the horizon for the trouble reverberating in my bones. I fly through the windless night toward the tower we've always considered home. Xander never used to drink to the point of being drunk, and that they've done so worries me. I land on the familiar empty rooftop, noting that the red-painted door to Xander's workshop is ajar.

Wind whips around us as Baraq and Ariella wing close then land with outstretched talons beside me. After shaking out his feathered mane, Baraq carefully folds his scaled wings to his back as he prowls forward on four feet. Ariella, the more human sculpted of the twins, leans back against the stone torrent, examining her long fingernails.

Baraq's slitted blue eyes narrow. "You feel it too?"

I nod. "Any shades?"

He shakes his head as Cassiopeia's hooves ring quietly with each step behind us. She rests a marbled cream-colored hand against my shoulder. "Xander wants to speak to you."

I turn and stoop to press my forehead to hers, careful of her branched horns. She tiptoes on her cloven feet to give me a gentle hug. Cass has always been a sister-mother to us, and right now, with this unease in my heart, I need her comfort.

"Watch the roof for me," I say, releasing her.

The only entrance to the tower is the roof. There is no door at the ground level. Well, that's not true. There's a door that leads to a menagerie of obsidian beasts in a labyrinth of stone. The few intrusions foolish outsiders have made through there haven't ended well for them.

The spiraling limestone steps down to Xander's study take longer than usual to traverse, and it's dim when I get there. I touch two of the violet globes near the stairwell door, brightening them, before moving forward. Papers tumble across the floor and spin around the room in an endless dance. The mage's control of the wind must have slipped to allow it inside the tower.

Xander has moved their favorite battered old chair out onto the balcony behind the desk. A bottle sits beside it with another on its side, already emptied. This doesn't look good.

I step forward until the stars shine over the nearby trees. Then I crouch beside the chair. "You wanted to speak to me?"

Their chin tilts toward the sky, and their eye patch dangles down around their beardless neck to tangle with the multitude of pendants and medallions. The glass clinks against their rings as Xander lifts it to their lips. Even from here, the potent smell of the spirits stings my nose.

Their voice quavers. "When the night's clear like this, I can almost see her. My wind dancer. Three hundred forty-two years I've been in this city, waiting for her." Xander takes another long, slow sip. "She's here somewhere. I feel it in my bones."

"You're drunk, Xander. Let me help you to your bed." I move to lift them into my arms.

Xander stops me with a look. Their mismatched eyes gleam feverishly in the moonlight. "You're alive." They give me a wan smile. "I'm sorry I tested you so hard, Boudicca, but I had to know if you could disobey me and think for yourself. I made a mistake interpreting what I saw the day Viola was curled in your arms on the roof. I saw devastation, change. I thought it meant she controlled you through the pendant. But you love her, don't you, my daughter? You have genuine feelings for the girl. I don't know how she did it. Viola doesn't possess the blood of a deity needed to create life."

I frown as the wind mage studies my face. "Viola has never controlled me. We feel the touch of the pendant that made us, Xander. It's not a subtle thing."

"I've made a mistake. Forgive me—it's already done." Tears stream down Xander's cheeks. "I didn't realize Kensington was involved. At this point, I don't think I can stop Elias from leaving with Viola."

"What?" My voice rises. "Where is she?"

Xander shakes their head. "I thought you'd been controlled by her use of the pendant—molded to be a friend the way I tried to mold Lysander—but that's not what happened, is it?" They take another long swig, draining the cup. "It was her stories that brought you to hold the life you have now, the soul within you. Because unlike the others here, Boudicca, somehow, you have a soul."

The pain not only of losing Viola to this forced marriage but of her leaving because of hurting someone she cares about tears through me. Of course I have a soul. How could I feel such love and such pain without one? My hands fist, spikes bristling.

"What did you say to her?" I whisper because there's a strange tugging in my chest, an ache. The night swells darker, and the thin press of magic shimmers against my skin.

"I told her if she stayed, she'd hurt you. That you only cared for her because she willed it into being. That you'd become an empty shell only existing to serve her. Or you'd go insane, like Lysander."

Oh no... She's leaving because I'm the one she's afraid to hurt. She called this friend a person, but she meant me. I tip my head back to the stars. My breath seizes in my lungs. I can't lose her to Elias.

"It's never been like that. What have you done? I'm more real around her than I've ever felt. Every moment Viola is near me, my heart sings. I don't want a life without her." My wings flex as I stand.

"I'm sorry. I'm not infallible, and in this, I was so wrong. I'm done underestimating you. Perhaps it's not too late. You should find her." Xander covers their face with a hand then slides the eye patch back up over their pale-blue eye.

I enter the study and grab the satchel of clothes off the couch. Viola said she had a dinner party in her home that she didn't want to attend. That must be tonight. Two steps out the balcony arch, my wings scoop the wind as I leap into the air, pushing high and fast toward the northern side of the city. I have no idea what I'll say to her or how I'll say it. Hopefully, I can get close enough to ask her to talk—to explain that Iggy and Boudicca are one person.

Person. I'm a person.

My wings snap again, beating once then twice until I catch another current and soar high above the city. Mind racing, I bank around the brighter lights of the Louvre and beeline toward the Archambeau manor. The immense house is festively lit, and through the large glass windows, people in fine clothes mingle, drinking from fluted glasses.

I'll never fit in with that gathering. The clothing I have isn't formal enough. I land behind a clump of young trees and study the front of the house. Balconies dot the second and third stories, but I'm not sure which room is hers. Is it creepy to find her room and wait until the party ends? Possibly. Probably.

I groan and jam the citrine ring onto my finger, losing a third of my size as my wings and horns are absorbed uncomfortably into my skin. The pants go on first and then the shirt. In my rush, I misbutton it with shaking fingers. Cursing, I take the whole thing apart and start over. The red ribbon slips out from behind the loose cuff and I stuff it back under again. I need to tell Viola what I am and that I love her. I don't know what happens after that, but she has to know this is all of my own free will.

I stride to the side of the house where I saw Viola enter the first night I followed her home. Luckily, the door is open, and within minutes, I'm hurrying down the long corridor. Laughter comes from my left, and farther down the hall, the unmistakable kitchen sounds of dishes clanking and a cook shouting orders shatter the silence. Her room should be upstairs.

I duck around the corner and find a narrow staircase. After pausing briefly to listen, I rush up the stairs. Frustrated, I run a hand over my jaw as I gaze down the hall. There are so many doors. Which room is hers? Turning the other way, I cry out with relief.

Tendrils of faint magic wisp around a door toward the end of the hall. That has to be her room. I tap on the door then enter. One inhalation in the dark room tells me everything I need to know. Viola's familiar lemon verbena scent permeates it. A silvery echo of magic threads from an open closet, and a sliver of moonlight shines through the glass balcony doors to detail a spacious room with a large bed situated across from a fireplace. Voices come from the hall, and quickly, I cross the room and step outside to the balcony.

The door opens. I duck behind a stone arch as a man enters, carrying Viola slumped against his chest. A maid scurries behind him.

"Set her on the bed, if you please, and I'll take care of the rest. It must've been all the excitement." The woman turns back the thick blankets.

Not wanting to be discovered, I move deeper into the shadows when I recognize the man. It's Elias. He holds Viola gently against his chest. Crimson tendrils of magic drift from him. I don't like him touching her. Is she hurt? Elias lays her down, and Viola moans softly.

"I'll stay here with her." Elias pours a cup of water from a pitcher and brings it to the bed.

"And have a man in her room? That would be highly inappropriate." The woman glares at him, drawing herself up to appear about as threatening as a stuffed teddy bear. "I'm more than capable of taking care of her. You can rejoin the dinner below."

Elias sits on the bed, and I nearly spring from my hiding place to knock him from it. "She's my betrothed, and I should be here to care for her." He tips the cup to her lips, and Viola sputters.

"Oh, my head hurts," Viola moans. "It's very kind of you to want to stay, but please rejoin the party. Everything is too bright. Dim the lamp as you leave. I'll be better in the morning."

Elias's eyes narrow, but Viola gives him a pained, pleading look. He rises from her bed then lowers the lights and leaves with the other woman in tow. Viola waits a mere moment before leaping from the bed, tugging the pins from her hair, and vigorously attempting to wrestle her way out of the dress.

The door opens again, and the woman stands there with

one hand on her hip. "I hope you know what you're doing," she chides before helping Viola shimmy off the gown.

I turn away, giving her privacy, until the low click of the door tells me Viola is alone. The gentle glow of a lamp flickers, casting shadows on the balcony. When I turn to look back into the room, Viola frantically flips through a book as she paces. I flush as the lamplight briefly outlines her body through her thin chemise. A shadow of her high, pointed breasts and the subtle curve of her hip leave me heated. Viola crawls into her bed, dragging two more books with her. Inhaling to steady my nerves, I tap on the glass.

Her head jerks up, lips pulled tight into a frown as she bounces back out of her bed. She grabs a long floral dressing robe and wraps it around her body before opening the doors. Viola peers into the dark, not seeing me.

She bites her lip. "Iggy, is that you? Where have you been? I've been so worried, but I stayed away because Xander said I was hurting you."

My heart twists, and I step forward. "I'm sorry for the impropriety, but I needed to see you."

She grips the neck of her robe tight as her lips part. Her long hair tumbles around her shoulders, and my hand flexes at my side. I want nothing more than to run my hands through it again and feel the warmth of her kiss, skin on skin. I take a hesitant step forward, trying to arrange my thoughts into something that sounds more romantic than creepy, but my limited experience isn't helping.

"Boudicca? What are you doing on my balcony?"

35

VIOLA

For a moment, striated blue eyes peer out of the darkness, and I think it's Iggy on my balcony. Boudicca's and Iggy's eyes are so similar. I noticed that before, but never remembered to ask about it. My heart slams into my throat, but as the figure steps from the shadows, she's too short to be my gargoyle.

I inhale in surprise, clutching my robe. "Boudicca? What are you doing on my balcony?"

She must've come through the house. It's a long way down from here, and there isn't a way to climb up. Well, unless she has magical slippers.

"I need to talk to you. Viola, please don't marry Elias and move away. I couldn't bear it." As she reaches for me, a shadow detaches itself from the wall, knocking her hand to the side.

I fall back onto my bottom and scramble toward the door as another shadow strikes her chest, drawing a thin line of blood. "Boudicca, no! Get inside!"

Boudicca growls fiercely, swiping at the shadows as more swarm her. No, not shadows—shades. I need something magical to fight these. I run inside and grab my slippers then charge back outside, brandishing one shoe fiercely. They aren't attacking me this time, though—only her. Twisting around her head in a flurry of claws and teeth, the damned things have her blinded. I swing at some in the air nearby, but the soft slipper doesn't seem to do much damage. In desperation, I huck my shoe at one but it bounces off and tumbles under the bed.

I frantically grab Boudicca by the wrist and drag her into my room—not that it helps. Now I have monsters in my bedchamber. Lemaitre's book has to be magical, and it has more heft than a slipper. Grimacing, I pick up the thick tome and smack it across the one chewing on Boudicca's shoulder. The beastie flies across the room to land in the fireplace with a satisfying thump and squeal.

Right. The book seems solid enough to club these things into submission. Clenching my jaw, I take aim at the next one, and swing with all my might. The shade shrieks as it bounces off the ceiling.

Boudicca flings her hands into the air and dodges. Wide-eyed, she looks at me. "Are you hurt?"

I shake my head then slam my book into another of the creatures, sending it soaring through the open balcony door. My chamber door opens, and huffing, I spin in place.

"A headache, hmmm? Or a secret rendezvous with your lover." Elias steps into the room, closing the door behind him. The same shades cling to his shoulders like obscene black crows. Their claws click against the leather straps on his suit coat. "It's no matter, Viola, dear. While seducing you to use your magic would have been useful, the most important thing I need from you is the Alluvium pendant. Hand it over."

Boudicca steps in front of me, her eyes darting wildly from the shades to the man before us. "You. Have you sent the shades all these years?"

"I thought Xander held the last known pendant made by the earth mage Mizah. However, my research showed the Bichler family also had a pendant that could make and control stone creatures. Commanding shades to attack a human with magic potential was much easier than trying to break through Xander's defenses. Imagine using an army made of stone to fight wars instead of sacrificing human lives."

I try to swallow, but my mouth has gone dry. Elias is a mage? Boudicca presses me back as she steps away. "We're living creatures too. You have no right to sacrifice us for your wars."

We? I glance down at Boudicca's wrist. A faded crimson ribbon peeks out of her jacket cuff. My ribbon. The one I tied to my gargoyle. A squeal of realization squeaks out of me as all the pieces come together.

"You're created, a thing, a beast made only to do the bidding of your maker." Elias's amused gaze flicks to me. "Does Viola even know what you are? Have you told her?"

Boudicca's spines stiffen as she pushes me back another step.

"She's not a thing." I step forward, past Boudicca. "Gargoyles are every bit as alive as you or me and have more virtue than you could ever dream of. I don't have the pendant. I gave it to Xander. This engagement is over, Elias. Get out of my room."

There's a ripping noise from behind me, and heat flares along my back as two webbed obsidian wings curve high above me. Iggy—no, Boudicca—protectively curls an arm around my waist, pulling my back to her chest. I clench the thick book to me, waiting for the shades to attack again.

Elias snarls. "That thing only lives for the will of its creator. It's not real, you foolish girl."

"You're wrong. She's as real and true as they come, and I'll spend my life loving her. Get out unless you want to cause a scene. I'm certain there are some sort of enforced rules against using magic in public, though... aren't there?" I clasp Boudicca's wrist above the crimson ribbon, trying not to shake.

I'm totally bluffing. I have no idea how this all works or who the magicians' governing body is, but given the firm separation between the magic world and the ungifted one, logic dictates there *must* be something that keeps the chaos in line. Besides, if I'm going to bluff, the best time to do it is with a massive guardian at my back.

The shades twirl around Elias's shoulders as his expression locks into one of pure rage. "Don't think I'm not bold enough to take you down right here, girl. One untrained mage isn't a match for me."

Silently, Boudicca moves me behind her. As she straightens, the spines on her hands and shoulder flick upward into daggerlike points. She tenses her toes, leaving six deep gouges in the hardwood floor.

Oh, Mother is not going to like that.

Boudicca's wings flare out, blocking Elias's view of me. "You'll have to go through me first."

The rumbling challenge sends a tingle of pure pleasure through me. I duck, peeking around Boudicca's waist. Elias seems undecided, eyeing my gargoyle as if he's uncertain of the outcome of an altercation. More shadows gather, and then a knock comes at the door.

"Viola, sweetheart, Maria said you had a headache." Mother pauses then knocks again. "I have some of my powders for you. It would be nice if you would return to the dinner, dear. I'll get your maid to dress you, and then you can come join us."

The shades instantly dissipate. Elias smirks and holds out his hand. "Yes, my betrothed. We should return to our celebration dinner."

I purse my lips. "No, I don't think I will. I won't be part of this farce any longer." That only leaves one choice. I tug on Boudicca, careful to avoid her spikes. "Let's go back to the tower."

Boudicca turns and scoops me into her arms. In two long strides, she leaps from the balcony and soars into the night. I hope Elias has a blast explaining to my mother why he's in my bedchamber, gouging up the floor.

Tingling warmth like a hundred butterflies fills my chest. Being in Boudicca's arms while flying through the moonlit sky is the most soothing experience I've ever had in my life. I always wondered why her gargoyle arms were bent as if to cradle something. I'm certain now it was me that was missing. This is where I belong. Now that I know Boudicca and Iggy are one and the same, my confused attraction to both of them makes sense.

I'm the most efficient researcher at the Mazarine. We'll figure out a way for her and me to be together without fear of changing her. There has to be a way—I love her too much to lose her. Clutching Lemaitre's book to my chest, I wish I'd grabbed my slippers and gloves. I sigh. Eventually, I'll have to explain myself to my parents.

"Don't be sad," Boudicca murmurs. Her lips brush my forehead with a tenderness that both ties me up in knots and makes me feel like I'm finally home. "We'll get this all sorted together."

She doesn't take me to the tower, though. We land on the rooftop of an ancient cathedral. As Boudicca releases me, I give her a questioning look.

An awkward cough follows a sheepish smile that's nothing short of adorable. "I wanted to talk to you alone first, before I took you home. Sometimes, my siblings can be intrusive."

We take a moment to look each other over. She doesn't appear injured. I reach out, touching her shoulder where I saw those shades claw her earlier, but the skin is firm and warm.

"They hurt you." I look from the smooth skin to her gray-blue eyes.

"I'm fine. The shift healed it. Are you all right?"

I nod. "You've been Boudicca this whole time. I'm embarrassed I didn't see it sooner. Your eyes, your smile—it's all the same."

She curls her wing tip over her face. "I wanted to talk with you without scaring you. I'm sorry I was dishonest. I know you hate liars, and I understand if you can't forgive me."

I push her wing back to reveal her angular face again. I've always loved the sharpness of Iggy's features. "There's nothing to forgive. I've loved you as Iggy since I was small, and I love you as Boudicca. What would you like me to call you?"

Visible relief washes over her face. "Boudicca is my real name. Xander gave it to me when they created me. Like a doting parent, they named all of us, even the ones in the menagerie. But you can keep calling me Iggy if you want to as a nickname. I don't mind."

Boudicca sits on the stone ground, her back against a wall. Taking my hand, she draws me into her lap. I set the book beside us and rest my head on her shoulder with a sigh. The peace I always feel in her arms settles around me. We've literally spent years together, and this combination of new and old has my head swimming with questions.

I want to touch her face and hair, to run my hands over the spikes on her shoulders and the long horns sprouting from her head. My hand hovers over her cheek, and I hesitate. Would she like that too? Is it too forward?

She came to me tonight, and before Elias interrupted, Boudicca was trying to tell me something. There had to be a purpose behind her visit. "Why did you come to my home?"

"To come clean and tell you who I really am. Would you be more comfortable if I looked human again?"

"No. I just want you. Human, gargoyle, whichever form you're comfortable with. You're a person no matter how you appear."

"A person?" Boudicca's eyes lock with mine searchingly as she places her hands on either side of my face.

"You've always been that to me." I tip my head to one side, tenderly kissing her wrist close to the crimson ribbon. Her skin is warm under my lips, and a pleasant sweetness fills my nostrils. Maple?

Her trembling fingers comb my hair. Blue-streaked gray eyes stare down into mine with such longing that I wet my lips. I want her to kiss me, to feel her against my mouth. My hands fall to her shoulders then trace the outside curve of her breasts, relishing the sensation. Closer, there's an exchange of breath. A little part of me is thrilled to know she breathes, just like me. I glide my nose along hers. Slowly, I trail my fingers up the graceful column of her neck to the three thorny spikes on her jawline. I stroke each one, enjoying the smooth texture and familiar feel.

"I always loved it when you touched me there. It's nice to know what it feels like without my stone shell in the way." Boudicca turns her head slightly to the side and kisses my cheek. "I love you, Viola."

I gasp, my chest growing so tight it might just explode.

"I was fond of you from the first time you crawled into my lap, and over the years, I grew to love you. When I crossed the Paris boundary, I proved that I have free will. It has nothing to do with any pendant sorcery." She places one hand on her heart and the other on mine. "I've felt the compulsion of magic. What we have is entirely different and new. Even Xander said they were wrong to make such a definitive statement about what would happen. This is magic of the heart. Your stories made me feel things I never would've experienced while perched on a rooftop. You've awakened me. I'm more than a magically created being now—I'm an individual."

Worry still whispers through me as I twirl a lock of her long mane pensively around my finger. "But what if part of

Xander's original prediction was right, and you die because of my presence?"

"It's not. But even if it was, given the choice, I would choose you. I would always choose you, no matter the consequences." Her lips land on mine, soft and tentative.

Boudicca doesn't taste like stone this time. She tastes like the night sky in all its glory—like flying and freedom. She tastes the way it feels when I'm leaping from one rooftop to the next, and I never, ever want to let that feeling go. I kiss her deeper, wrapping my arms around her neck as I melt against her firm torso. Her spikes lie in smooth lines against her powerful shoulders. Xander's vision of the future held change, but life is full of changes. In my heart, I know my gargoyle and I are meant for each other. We always were.

"I love you. I want to stay with you always," I whisper against her lips.

Boudicca pulls back just enough to study my face then nods. "Always."

I bury my face in her coiled mane, holding back sobs of relief. The heat of her hands soothes me as they sweep in long strokes over my back. It's easy to want to stay in this moment forever, but I know we have to face the world at some point.

"We should go back home, where it's safe," she murmurs as she drops a light kiss on my shoulder.

"I don't want to go home. I want to stay with you." I wince a little at my petulant tone.

"Our home, my brilliant librarian. Xander once offered you an apprenticeship. Will you take them up on it?"

Excitement fills me. Not only is Boudicca mine to love freely, but the whole world of magic has opened its arms. My life is about to become astounding. I grin up at my gargoyle, and I guess that says it all because Boudicca gathers me up, puts Lemaitre's book back in her satchel, and launches us into the sky.

36

VIOLA

My lips press to Boudicca's in sweet relief as the stars breeze by us in the velvety night. Eagerly, my fingers explore her curled lower horn before sweeping up her spiraled straight ones. Her long, pointed ears flick, and she nibbles my low lip. Her strong arms surround my torso, holding me securely to her as the city lights of Paris glitter beneath us like a diamond tiered necklace. I pull back to look at her, and my hair tumbles free to tickle us both.

She pushes it behind my ear with aching tenderness. "You're not afraid of me—that I'm not human?" Boudicca murmurs close to my cheek. Her giant wings beat a steady rhythm against the night sky before she coasts on the breeze.

"Why would I be afraid of you? You know all my secrets. I climbed all over you for decades. I know every inch of your body." I pause, flushing at the implication.

"You did," Boudicca teases. "It didn't make me feel anything inappropriate—well, not until recently."

"Does this feel inappropriate?" I trace her breast with my hand, delighting in the full curve and the responsive way her nipple strains against the gossamer fabric. I push my face into Boudicca's chest, breathing her intoxicating scent. Her hands tighten against my back, making me laugh and nuzzle closer.

"No," she whispers. "I just never dreamed..."

"That I'd love you no matter what? I've looked for magic all my life, and now I'm crazy for an enchanting woman. I don't care what your outward appearance is as long as you're comfortable in your own skin." I smirk. "Besides, now I don't have to choose. I admit I had some budding romantic feelings for Iggy the moment I knew gargoyles were alive."

"You did?" Boudicca grins. Her thigh slides between mine, and she spins us midair. "How shocking."

My robe whips open in the wind, leaving only my thin nightgown between us. "Best of both worlds." I giggle in exhilaration.

A daring gleam flashes across Boudicca's eyes, followed instantly by her lifting me onto her shoulder so that my bottom presses against her flexing muscles. "Trust me." The devil dances in her throaty voice.

I squeal. Flailing, I force down the panic of being seated on her like this while flying. Her forearm tightens across my legs, holding me firmly in place. The moonlit view is breathtaking, and my fear quickly melts into wonder. I've spent years leaping from one building to another in the city. There's always been that brief sense of flight, but it was never like this.

The wind rushes past, tugging my nightgown up to wrap around my waist, and Boudicca laughs. Her eyes grow wide then dark at my lack of undergarments.

"I was on my way to bed," I say like that's not the most obvious conclusion.

Her nostrils flare, and her body trembles on the air current. "Do you know how divine your scent is? That night we shared on the rooftop burned you into my senses."

She inhales deeply and then twists in the air, sliding me around her broad shoulders to straddle her face. My mouth drops open to protest as the wind tugs at my clothes. She isn't really going to do this while in flight?

"Grab my horns." Her feral growl tears through me.

Yep. She is. With a thrill of excitement tickling down my spine, I do as commanded, tugging on her horns to pull her mouth deeper into my slick vulva. Boudicca's hands cup my ass, lifting me against her lips. The tips of her claws prick my skin. I swoon against the soft feel of her mouth against me and the hard press of her shoulders The first lap of her tongue makes me dizzy as the air rushes past my naked thighs.

Her coiled mane lashes against my skin like a silken whip. I groan, the pleasure and exhilaration combining into a heady rush. Boudicca banks in the air, catching a current upward, and we fly through misty clouds silvered in moonlight. Ribbons of glittery magic stream around us, and it's so beautiful I gasp in wonder.

Boudicca's thick tail waves behind us like a rudder separating a heavenly sea of stars. Everything about her body is enticing, and I wish she were naked against me now, skin to skin. I shove at the lightweight dress she wears but the top is caught under the padded satchel strap. Her low chuckle vibrates against my center as she withdraws. Her breath whispers in a seductive dance along my flesh, tantalizing me further with each spoken word.

"My tale spinner, you're far more impatient than I ever thought you'd be. Let me love you. I promise your pleasure is mine."

Then her mouth is on me, tongue flicking against my clit in a rhythm that will drive me mad. My toes curl as my body combusts with desire. The flat of her tongue presses hard through my folds, teasing and tantalizing until I'm begging, but the wind steals away my words.

Boudicca spins in an act of aerial acrobatics that grinds me against her. My cries fill the night, and her encouraging moans hum against my skin. This is the feeling I've been seeking all my life, this unity of two hearts beating together, one soul blended. Boudicca is the person I've been waiting for.

The hot thrash of her tongue leaves me gasping and lightheaded. I almost forget we're flying until her wings fold around my body, and we plummet. She doesn't stop sucking my clit as gravity pulls us toward the earth. I crest in a rush, panting against the shield of her wings as my body throbs, until the leathery membranes snap open, and we race toward the moon again.

Boudicca slides me from her shoulders and cradles me in her arms as my racing heart calms and my body pulses with pleasure. Moments gallop by as I catch my breath. Then my hand slides down Boudicca's thigh, parting her dress. The smooth, hard feel of her skin is a divine wonder I wish to worship.

Sultry eyes darkened with desire watch me with interest. Our lips meet, soft and warm. I love the delicious tang of my passion on her tongue. The sweet scent of her surrounds me, unlike the stone she once smelled of. I press my lips to her throat, kissing along the column of her neck. Her low sighs rumble against my lips.

I move my hand to cup her mons, feeling the hairlessness of her body. I want to explore every inch of Boudicca until she's crying out with the same passion I just felt. I slide a finger along her slit, parting her flesh to find her gloriously wet.

Boudicca burrows her face into my neck with a purr as I stroke her. I'm not sure what I expected of gargoyle anatomy, but I'm pleased to discover it's similar to mine. A giggle escapes me.

"What is it?" she murmurs against my skin.

"I didn't know what to expect of your... features."

Boudicca tosses her head back with a throaty laugh. "Apparently, Xander finds the female form 'artistically pleasing' and was very thorough when carving my body. Not that I've ever been touched in this way in my own form."

"Oh, do they?" I glide two fingers along the swollen bud of her clit, enjoying the full roundness and Boudicca's throaty moans. "Well, I'm thrilled to find out your *details* are exquisite."

"Please, don't stop." Her wings arch against the sky, and her back bows at my touch.

I savor Boudicca's every gasped breath as we glide and dive through the air. Her body quivers. It shouldn't matter that I'm the first one to pleasure her like this, but I'm delighted. I slide two fingers within her, curling them gently until her moans shake the stars, and Boudicca fists her hands to not rake her claws on my skin.

"You're so damned stunning," I say, watching her tip over into a sea of pleasure.

Conveying my adoration of her heart and soul with every stroke, I sear Boudicca with another passionate kiss, swallowing her muffled cries. She tenses, folding her wings around us, and we freefall as she contracts around my fingers, pulsing and throbbing in the glorious wet heat of our arousal.

"I love you," she whispers against my lips then nuzzles against me.

My heart soars at her admission, and I kiss her nose. Then I pull back, sliding my fingers from her. The cocoon of her wings still surrounds us, only letting in a sliver of moonlight that glazes her features. "I love you too." I realize we're still falling. "Maybe don't kill us with a sudden stop."

Laughing, Boudica snaps her wings open, cupping them to catch the air. We lift then dip, jostling my equilibrium. "I'll get you to a bed." She kisses my cheek, then we glide into the night.

37

BOUDICCA

For the first time in my life, I'm cuddled in a bed. Not a settee in the bōc-hord. Not stealing moments in Xander's study. Viola sleeps in the curl of my wing, her cheek pressed against my breast. I watch her rest. I love the sweet, contented smile on her lips and the way her hands flex on me as she wiggles closer. She mumbled "Iggy" twice, and it made me so happy my heart practically bounced from my chest both times.

I shift a little, and the wooden frame of the bed creaks under my weight. I'm certain I'll have to ask Xander for something a little sturdier.

"Hey." Viola grasps one of my long spiraling horns and turns my head toward her. Her forget-me-not-blue eyes shine in the moonlight from the nearby window. "I just realized something."

I thought she was sound asleep. "What?"

"You can leave Paris without turning to stone. You also have wings. We can *go* places."

Freedom. I never dreamed I could leave the city, but she's right. We can go anywhere we want. "I'll take you anywhere you wish to go."

The bed takes that moment to groan in protest, then it crashes crookedly to the floor, dumping us in a pile against the headboard. Viola laughs as shouting comes from the other side of the tower. All my spikes straighten in alarm. I brought us through the east balcony because I didn't want questions from my siblings. No one knows I'm home.

"We may have to find other sleeping arrangements," I mutter. "Brace yourself for company."

The door bursts open, and Cass plows through, her bow drawn and a golden arrow nocked. With a squeal of shock, Viola pulls my wing down to shield herself. Not ideal.

"Sister." I nod, trying to pull myself from the wreckage of the bed while Viola clings to me.

Cass flicks one doe-like ear in amusement and lowers her bow. "Little sister, if you were going to mate with your tale spinner, you could've chosen a less fragile place."

Ariella strolls in, her head tilted to one side. "Did you find out if she tasted good?"

Viola turns pink from the tips of her ears to the curved lace of her nightgown. "We weren't *mating*. We were sleeping."

But we were doing that in the sky. I'd never admit that to Cass.

Baraq charges into the room on all fours, claws extended and muscles bunching. He skids to a halt, digging deep furrows into the wooden floor, as I stand. Confused, he looks at me then at Viola then back at me before he crouches upright. "I thought we were being attacked."

Cass's lip curls up. "Apparently, they were 'sleeping.'"

Ariella flexes her claws into air quotes, and the two women dissolve into a fit of giggles. I'm never going to hear the end of this.

Baraq wrinkles his nose. "In a bed?"

"Yes, people do that." Viola huffs. "Since you're here, please help me drag the mattress onto the floor and then skedaddle so we can continue sleeping."

"Skedaddle?" Baraq raises a whiskery eyebrow.

"Beds often break when you're 'sleeping.'" Cass holds in another laugh.

Groaning, I grasp a corner of the mattress and shove. "Viola plans to apprentice to Xander. We'll speak to them in the morning about room arrangements."

Baraq grabs the other corner of the mattress and hauls it off the broken bed frame. "Does this mean you won't be sleeping on the roof anymore? I'll miss you."

Viola smothers a giggle. "We'll arrange something suitable later. For tonight, I need Boudicca next to me."

Both of Cass's eyebrows shoot skyward.

"We can discuss it later." I grunt as we get the mattress off the wreckage and onto the floor. Then I pointedly look at my siblings and glance at the door.

Cassiopeia rests a hand on Baraq's shoulder and guides him from the room. "Come. We should let them rest after all their sleeping."

I roll my eyes at Cass's innuendo. She's the worst, always teasing. "Don't mind her," I say as the door shuts. But Viola is that adorable shade of pink again—or maybe still—and she's crying. "I'm sorry. My family can be a bit much."

She sniffles then tackles me, burying her wet face in my chest. "No, they're happy tears. I love your family. Every little bit."

38

VIOLA

Xander drums their fingers on the battered old desk as Boudicca and I sit stiffly on the couch. Dark smudges circle their eyes this morning, and their oversized dressing gown is more rumpled than usual. Red crystals spill from a pouch as they reorganize the piles of things that have been on the desk for ages, as if cleaning is preferable to this conversation.

Finally, I inhale deeply and squeeze Boudicca's hand. "I'd like to accept your offer to be your apprentice and negotiate the terms."

Xander splutters then removes their glasses and rubs the bridge of their nose. "Terms?"

"Yes." I jerk my head downward succinctly. "I'm not a very good cook, but I can keep things tidy and have excellent organizational and bookkeeping skills. Once I fetch my slippers, I can get around the city quite efficiently, making me an excellent candidate to deliver messages and run errands for you. Because I'm human, I can interact with individuals that your family cannot—well, not without being cloaked in an illusion, anyway."

Xander blinks.

"In exchange, you'll feed and house me and teach me any magic you deem appropriate for my level of skill, increasing the challenge as I progress. I'll do all the rudimentary grunt work for your studies that you loathe to free up time for your chosen activities. My research skills are top-notch. If needed, I can provide several references from scholars I worked with at the library."

Xander opens their mouth and cants their head before shutting it again. They smooth their ribbon-braided beard a few times before raising one beringed hand.

"In addition, I would like to continue my relationship with Boudicca, and together, we'll record the firsthand experience of her awakening, something no other gargoyle in history has accomplished. Oh, and I'll need to continue my weekly tutoring and group reading sessions at the Mazarine. And you'll return my pendant. Agreed?"

I inhale deeply then hold my breath with a nervous little tremor. This has got to work. Without my job at the library and the backing of my family, Xander's offer is my last hope.

"You're including me?" Boudicca whispers beside me. Her heart pounds so fiercely her wrist pulses against mine as we clasp hands.

Xander coughs. "I let it slide last night, but I don't need you destroying the furniture I've lovingly curated for my home. I heard from your sister—"

"We were just sleeping!" Boudicca says.

Xander clears their throat. "I'll have the room you stayed in last night remodeled this week to ready it for your use. As for the rest of your terms, I find them agreeable."

Excitement rushes over me, and I cuddle closer to Boudicca. "Thank you, Maker. It's a high honor."

"While in the tower, you'll address me as simply Xander. When we're in the ungifted public, you're my assistant. When we're attending magical events, I'll give you robes to wear, and you'll be my apprentice. You'll then refer to me as Maker Xander, as one day you'll be Maker Viola. As you probably guessed, you may not tell your family about the magical world. I'll have to review all the Covenant rules with you and get you sworn in at the next high council here in Paris. Durant

Lemaitre currently heads that, so we'll have him over for tea and introduce you."

I wriggle with joy. "I get to meet the author of the book I'm studying?"

"My dear, you're brilliant, and any mage would be thrilled to have such a talented pupil. Lemaitre will likely try to talk you into being his apprentice, but he has more than enough on his hands running the council. You deserve an education that would make your grandmother proud."

Xander gives me an indulgent smile that warms my heart. I already feel like part of this family. Boudicca puts her arm around my shoulders, holding me tight, and I beam up at her. This is going to work out. Impishly, I brush a soft kiss against her lips, and the ribbons of magic around us become radiant. Her eyes follow the lines, and I grin. I always thought it was dust I saw. It turns out it's the gleam of the mystical right in front of me.

Boudicca clears her throat. "We still have the issue with the shades. Last night, I saw with my own eyes that Elias is the one conjuring them. He's trying to get the pendants to create an army of stone soldiers."

Xander tugs their braided beard. "Well, that's never going to happen. I believe you, Boudicca, but I'm still not convinced it's entirely him summoning all the shades, especially those monstrous ones. He doesn't have that level of power. I guess we need to discourage him enough that he heads back to whatever hole he crawled out of."

"What should I tell my family?" I fidget.

"I have the perfect plan for that, and it may kill two birds with one stone." Xander's mouth curls into a devious smile. "We have an appointment at the library this morning."

I FOLLOW Xander as they practically float up the library steps with their long purple coat tails flapping in some unfelt breeze. Pushing open the library door with a wooden cane topped with a carved crystal bird, they exclaim a bright "Aha!"

Seriously, how do regular people not notice there's magic in the world when folks as flamboyant as Xander walk around blatantly magical, dressed like their wardrobe whirlwind attacked them? Then again, it's Paris.

Boudicca gives me a little nudge, and I pass through the vestibule in Xander's wake. A few elderly scholars look up at me but seem to completely ignore the bejeweled spectacle marching toward the office past the front desk. I narrow my eyes. Is Xander somehow masking their appearance? That could be useful. It's definitely something I'd like to know how to do.

Rap-ta-tap. The crystal bird whacks against the heavy oak door of the master librarian's office, and I flinch, but it doesn't shatter.

"Hello! Frederick, are you in?" Xander strides past the archway, not bothering to wait for a reply.

I linger in the doorway. The familiar form of the owlish master librarian isn't in the office, but instead, the velvet-coated hulking body of Lord Kensington squeezes behind the desk. Frowning, I look around. Everything that belonged to the old scholar is gone, even his little carved nameplate.

Kensington stands, rising to a height far taller than me and almost equal to Boudicca. Xander moves to meet him as he comes around the desk. Their wavy auburn hair stirs in a sudden breeze, and the loose papers on the desk tumble across the room.

"Where's Master Frederick?" I ask, standing next to Xander.

"He's out in the stacks somewhere. I'm sure I can help

you." Kensington's mouth curls in a way that makes my blood boil.

"I'm certain that you can't. Boudicca, would you please fetch the master librarian?" Xander pauses, and a faint breeze races around the room. "He's on the second floor near the third alcove."

I freeze my expression so I don't gawk. I definitely need to learn that trick.

Xander runs one finger over their mustache, smoothing it. "Lord Kensington, it's come to my attention that you wish to turn this library into a bit of an elitist club, and you see, that just won't do. The Mazarine Library has been open to the public for over two hundred years, and while there are restricted collections within it, the bulk of the materials should remain public."

I bite my lip. Is he referring to the bōc-hord? Is Kensington aware of it? At that moment, Master Frederick arrives, panting and red-faced with Boudicca beside him.

"Well, there's the little issue of the back taxes." Kensington sits on the front of the desk. "As I'm certain Viola told you. The government has no interest in whether this building is public or private. It really is unfortunate her little charity ball didn't bring in enough funds."

I quell a snarl that will do no good in this situation.

"Monsieur Xander Albright? I got the message you wished to speak to me." Master Frederick peers at Xander through his thick lenses. "Goodness, I haven't seen you in two decades. You haven't changed a bit."

"You're far too kind." Xander smiles. "I have a proposal for you to keep the library public."

"I've already made the deal with Frederick. The library will be by membership." Kensington sits a little straighter, still defacing the desk with his noble ass.

Xander rubs at their eye patch, lifting it slightly as their green eye bores into the Lord. "Mmm, that's a shame. Was the deed to the building already signed over?"

"Well, no. The notary was sick, and then the judge was detained in Gentilly," Kensington drawls.

"Excellent. So I can give Frederick this bank note as patronage to this fine establishment, and that should cover running the day to day for a while." Necklaces jangle as Xander pulls an envelope from inside their red-brocade vest and hands it with a small flourish to the baffled librarian.

Master Frederick slides his thumb along the lip of the envelope, breaking the wax. His rheumy eyes light up as he reads the contents.

"It would take a significant amount to not only bring the building out of debt but run its day-to-day functions as well." Kensington eyes the paper nervously, one hand raised as if to snatch it away.

"It does, but I feel contributing to the community pays for itself. I'm afraid I'll be stealing your best worker to handle my private collection." Xander winks at Master Frederick, who still stands, hands quivering, with the note shaking between them.

I don't want to know where or how Xander has that kind of money. I'm just thankful they helped without me begging. I look up at Boudicca, and her soft expression sends me soaring —even in her human form.

"Let's head to the Archambeau manor and get this over with," I say, sliding my hand into Boudicca's.

39

VIOLA

Boudicca rolls her shoulders, an uncomfortable expression on her human face. My parents sit across from us in the parlor on the pristine white couches. I've never sat in this room before. I'm not sure anyone has. Family portraits ring the room in heavy gold frames.

I study the one of my grandmother. She's done up in a frilly dress and an outrageously pink hat—not anything I'd ever wear, but her eyes are exactly the same as mine. It's like looking in a mirror. I hope I can create magical items as magnificent as hers.

"I was very distressed to find Elias in your room and you missing. We've been searching for you for two whole days, Viola. The panic you caused was immeasurable," Mother says with a trembling voice as she wobbles in her seat. The maid by her side increases her fanning to a comical level, sending my mother's artfully arranged curls up to tangle in her eyelashes.

"He attacked me in my room. I escaped off the balcony, and not knowing where to go, I stayed in my dear friend Boudicca's home."

Dear friend. It's mostly the truth. Except that I had a magic book and a gargoyle with which to defend myself. I try to look as shaken as a young maiden should be.

"Well, we certainly can't have you marrying the sort of ruffian that would assault his betrothed." Agitated, Mother purses her lips. "Consider the engagement off. Your father will take care of the undesirable loose ends for us."

More like Elias embarrassed my family enough to outweigh the financial gain.

Father stares at Boudicca, who sits up a little straighter. "How do you know my daughter?"

"The library, monsieur. My employer, Xander Albright, is quite involved there." Boudicca goes unnaturally still, and I pat her arm and give her a soft smile. She glances at me then relaxes back against the stiff couch.

"Albright? Goodness, I haven't heard that name in ages," Father says. "Those of eccentric wealth do tend to either keep to themselves or go a little wild in their twilight years, don't they?"

I tilt my head curiously at Boudicca. Xander appears to be younger than my father—certainly no older than their midforties.

"They're an excellent, generous employer, monsieur, but they prefer privacy. In the light of your daughter's recent engagement dissolution, Monsieur Xander Albright would like to extend an offer of employment to Viola, managing their personal library and assisting with research endeavors."

"I see. And is this something you'd like to do, Viola?" Father's eyes dart between Boudicca and me.

Sweat trickles down my back, and I suddenly feel hot. Are we sitting too close for propriety? I loathe the whole dance of social structure, and Boudicca is about to ask to court me anyway. If my parents don't react well to this at least I'll have a soft place to land at the Tower of Wind.

"It is. Xander is a pleasure to work with, and their library is both extensive and utterly disorganized. It should keep me busy for years and provide a healthy stipend for managing my own affairs. They've offered me a suite in their home."

Mother makes a strangled gurgling noise, and I wait to see if she'll swoon. Fortunately, she doesn't.

"It would be very prestigious for our family to have

contact with Xander Albright. Something none of your associates have." I watch my father carefully.

"True." He pats Mother's hand, and she straightens with a pensive harrumph.

"Monsieur Archambeau, considering Viola's dissolved engagement, I would like to ask your permission to court her. Your daughter and I have grown fond of each other, and we wish to continue to explore our suitability." Boudicca manages her rehearsed speech with a perfectly pleasant expression—which we also practiced. Fearful of my parents trying to barter me off again, she spent the entire morning speaking into a mirror to plead her suit.

"Viola?" My father's gaze pins me.

"Please say yes, Papa."

Mother starts to object, but my father's eyes go soft. I hadn't called him that since I was small, and I was certain it would hit his weak spot. Father lays a hand on my mother's arm, quieting her.

"I agree, then. Take what you need, but there will always be a room here for you." My father stands. "It's good to see you happy, Vi. It's all we really wanted."

"Thank you." My heart sings as my new magical life, with all its possibilities, shines before me.

Epilogue

VIOLA

I splay my hand over the open book. "Grandmother, please. I need to complete this last chapter."

The ethereal form of my grandmother soundlessly whisks herself closer before resting her ghostly elbows on my desk. Silver glittery magic sprinkles everywhere, getting into my ink well and all over my research documentation.

She pouts. "You haven't visited me in over a month."

I close the book and push it to the side. Part of me deeply regrets asking Xander if they could extend the boundary of Grandmother's ghostly confinement. They were able to attach her spirit energy to a book from her library. Thus, she can now travel wherever the book resides.

"You know I've been getting ready for the vacation I'm taking with Boudicca. We've barely had a break since Xander offered me employment." I glance at the shelves lining the long wall of my chamber and contemplate walking that book back to the Archambeau manor. At least this part of my room is separate from the bedchamber. A visit from her there could get awkward fast.

"Are you sure it's safe?" Grandmother asks.

I shrug. "We haven't seen any shades since Elias went back to Austria with his reputation in tatters—thanks to Parisian gossipmongers."

"The whole business still seems suspicious. I never should've saddled you with the responsibility of that pendant. I thought the ring would conceal it." Grandmother glides across the room to look out the window. She enjoys being able to see the world again.

"I'll be fine. Besides, Xander assigned this brave fellow to watch over me." My tiny gargoyle wyvern stirs at my feet then raises his pointy obsidian head with a shrill chirp.

I pat him before reopening my book, which details all the known intelligent species in the world. There are a dozen volumes in this set, all stacked up before me. I'm almost finished with the second book and ready to dive into volume three.

"I'll leave you to your studies, then." Grandmother fades off into mist.

Only a few moments later, a tap at the balcony door tears my attention from my work again. This time I don't mind the interruption. I leap to my feet, almost tripping over the tiny gargoyle as he charges out from under my desk with a ferocious wail.

"It's all right, Grimoire. You know who that is." I scritch the little fellow's ears.

Grimmy wriggles, blinking his bright-blue eyes and puffing rings of smoke as he charges excitedly toward the glass door. A rustle on the balcony has my lips tugging upward, and a tapping of claws on the glass brings a full-blown smile to my face.

Xander set me up in a suite, fully furnished with gargoyle-proof heavy-duty furniture and chairs meant to accommodate a winged species. *Species.* I love that word. In the world of magic, there are so many new things to learn, and Xander says I'm the most voracious pupil they've ever had.

I crack the door open, letting Grimmy out on the balcony to do a cheerful little dance around Boudicca's clawed feet. "What's the secret password?"

"I love you." Boudicca pushes the door open and sweeps me into her arms before drowning me in one passionate kiss after another. Both of us are breathless in moments, and my head swims with the heated feel of her deliciously hard body pressed to mine.

My hands tangle upward into her long silky locks, and I tug on her shorter curled horns. "I love you too. Another quiet night?"

Her hum vibrates against my neck as she places hundreds of tiny kisses there, peppering my skin until I'm giddy. "Mmm, yes. What about you? It's well after four. I expected you to be asleep."

"Full disclosure: I was waiting on you." I kiss her nose.

Boudicca lifts me higher, settling my legs around her waist. Her thick tail thumps in contentment against the wood floor. "Is that true, Grimoire?"

A series of pips and shrieks fills the air as my wyvern rats me out. Boudicca rolls her eyes. "Vi, my love, it was never Xander's intention for you to put in workdays that last from sunrise to after midnight."

"I know, I know, but there's so much for me to learn." I give her a wicked grin. "However, I do feel we should continue our *personal* research."

"Oh, should we?" Boudicca nips my lower lip, drawing a quiet groan from me. "And how would you propose we do that?"

"Definitely not by teasing me until I'm begging for you and then leaving me to sleep alone." I give her *the look*.

Boudicca winks. "Well, that very important research might need to wait, because tomorrow, I'm taking you on a trip."

"I have my things together. We could leave now." I'm unbelievably excited about the prospect. Boudicca plans to take me through the bōc-hord to a completely different dimension. She and Xander spent the last week exploring it to be certain the place was safe.

"We've both been up all night, my love. Let's get a few

hours of rest before setting out on our next adventure." Boudicca takes my hand and draws me into our bedchamber.

My robe slides off my shoulders to the floor. Boudicca's breath hitches, and her eyes grow dark. It's a dirty little game, but I'm certain she likes it. Grimmy immediately steals the garment, dragging it off to his fluffy-pillow hoard under my desk.

"Is this your way of telling me you're not tired?" Boudicca murmurs against my lips as we make our way to the bedchamber and tumble to the bed. The frame on this one is heavy-duty metal, and it's large enough for her wings.

I hook a leg over her sculpted hip, bringing her closer to me. With a quiet sigh, Boudicca slides her nose against mine. Our lips meet again, and she parts mine to slowly explore my mouth. I snuggle closer, enjoying the warm exploration of our kiss and the ways all our soft parts interlock. Boudicca's body curls against mine like we were made for each other. And maybe we were.

She nuzzles my hair, placing a kiss on the crown of my head. "I'm glad we were just different enough to fit together perfectly."

I HOPE you've enjoyed *The Librarian's Gargoyle*. Coming summer 2025 is book two, *The Apothecary's Gargoyle*, featuring the romance between Mirabelle and Ariella.

Reviews mean the world to authors and really help sapphic readers, like you, discover more great books. If you enjoyed this tale please take a moment to leave a review where you purchased the novel and give it a shout out on social media. It would mean a lot to me.

Also By

Stone Awakenings
The Librarian's Gargoyle
The Apothecary's Gargoyle - Summer 2025

Novellas
Selkie's Promise

Anthology
The Pull of the Tide

For other non-sapphic novels romantasy
novels please visit my website
www.Evelynshine.com

About the Author

Evelyn Shine (she/her) is a queer author of fantasy romance books for readers who enjoy steamy myths and swoony fairy tales infused with adventure. No matter what tale she's spinning, they all share a common thread of love, heart, and action. When she isn't writing, Evelyn enjoys traveling, playing with her crazy Australian cattle dog, riding her Vespa through the countryside, and spending time with her indulgent partner.

For more information visit https://beacons.ai/evelynshine

Acknowledgements

This story started its life as a short anthology piece that I shelved for well over a year after deciding it wasn't a good fit for that collection. My partner, Erin Branch, was the one to say, "Hey, rewrite that gargoyle piece as a sapphic novel. It's really sweet, and I bet it'd be popular. There isn't enough sapphic fantasy in the world."

My best friend, Christopher, agreed and they both urged me to contact Madison Brake to get a cover rolling. Thus began my first full-length sapphic novel and the start of what I hope to be an amazing series.

Thank you to all my beta readers, particularly Jamie, who speed read the final draft before it went to the editor. I really appreciated your thoughts and comments.

Last year I discovered the Golden Crown Literary Society, an inclusive, welcoming non-profit organization of sapphic authors, and I attended the July 2024 conference. I want to thank all of them for being so supportive and uplifting. If you're a sapphic author that hasn't joined this group, I urge you to check them out.

Thank you to Karen Dimmick of Arcanecovers.com. She did an amazing job with the typography and wrap design. The pointed font she found, reminiscent of the architecture of bygone eras, is amazing.

A cover is the first thing a reader sees of a book, and I adore beautifully illustrated covers. I want to thank Madison Brake of MadisonBrake.com for her gorgeous art. She really brought Viola and Boudicca to life, and I love the art nouveau-meets-Maxfield Parrish feel of the lovers flying over Paris.

I want to thank Christopher for being supportive of my art all my life. He's been there when my brain—which is a chaos-filled rave of squirrels—swaps from one hyperfocus to another. He's listened to me bitch about characters, edits, how hard breaking into the book world is, and has worried about my lack of sleep and eating habits for years. I want to thank him for loving my crazy artist self and enduring my creative efforts with a patient smile. I still owe him the full author read through of this story around a boozy campfire.

Finally, I want to thank my love and fellow author, Erin Branch. We started as critique partners and I never would have made it this far without her love and support. She's been there through the rewrites, the self-doubt, the complaining about social media, all while we wrote our first sapphic novels and launched a new annual anthology. This year has been such a wild ride, including U-Hauling to her to be together. I waited my entire life to meet Erin and couldn't imagine my world without her. Here's to the first of many books.

Cheers!
Ev